HOOD

◆ ◆ ◆

American Rebirth Series – Book One

EVAN PICKERING

First Edition

Copyright © 2016 by Evan Pickering

All rights reserved.

ISBN-13:
978-1523667222

ISBN-10:
1523667222

This is a work of fiction. Names, characters, businesses, places, events and incidents are either the products of the author's imagination or used in a fictitious manner. Any resemblance to actual persons, living or dead, or actual events is purely coincidental.

For my Brothers,

And Mom and Dad.

Special thanks to my editor Karen Kendall, Kathleen Pickering, Dan Pickering, Josh Schubart, Allison Cohen, Eastin Deverna, Kandice Lacci, Will Trapani, Stan and Liz Longenecker. You all helped make this book what it is.

"Our world faces a crisis as yet unperceived by those possessing power to make great decisions for good or evil. The unleashed power of the atom has changed everything save our modes of thinking and we thus drift toward unparalleled catastrophe."

-Albert Einstein

Chapter 1 – Campfire

Shenandoah Mountains, Fringes of Kaiser Territory, Formerly Virginia

The iron sights of Hood's AK-47 lined up perfectly between each other, trained on the dark-haired man in the muted blue of predawn light. Something was wrong. This man wasn't some lost wastelander. Any loner with sense would've given their camp a wide birth. There was an undeniable purposefulness to this man's approach—he was looking for them. Hood's heart sped in his chest as his breath quickened. *The Kaiser knows we're here. How many more are coming?* The image of a host of the Kaiser's soldiers waiting in the dark mountain woods set his mind ablaze. *Focus.* Hood took a deep breath of crisp woodland air to level himself. The man hustled to the next tree and crouched down behind it, leaning over to peer around the mossy bark towards the campfire up the hill. No one else followed behind him. *Maybe he's just a scout.*

The man's chest rose and fell quickly as he closed his eyes, pistol in hand. He switched hands on his pistol, wiped his palms on his pants. *He doesn't want this. He's just like you.* The thought surged into his mind unabated. Hood tried to cast it out, focused on keeping his aim true. *Just turn around and go back,* Hood pleaded. He had a perfect shot from his flanking position up in the tree, but his finger stayed still on the trigger.

You have to shoot him.

Hood chewed on the salty pull string of his well-worn hoodie, breathing in deeply and holding the air in his lungs as he squeezed the trigger on his rifle nearly to the firing point, keeping the sights steady.

The man stood up straight against the tall oak, steeling himself. He turned and dashed towards the camp. Hood kept the sights stable on him as he moved. A loud crack split the air from his rifle, a casing flying out of the chamber and down onto the forest floor below. The man cried out, then collapsed into a heap. He writhed on the ground, clutching at his shoulder. Hood let the air out of his lungs, running his hand through his short messy hair. *You had to do it.*

The air split with another gunshot, and the man lay still. Hood knew it was coming, but hoped it wouldn't. Whiskey didn't take chances. Hood should have just killed the man himself rather than leaving him to suffer before Whiskey finished it. *You can't let it all weigh you down*—they were Ian's words in Hood's head. It was a resounding memory, but it meant something much different when Ian said it years ago—brotherly words of advice on love. He wished more than anything Ian sat beside him in the tree. Somehow, it would make all of this easier. *I know you're still alive out there. I can feel it.*

Whiskey's broad, tall frame appeared from behind a nearby tree. He moved slowly with quiet steps towards the dead man with a lowered pistol at his side. He wore his usual stoic expression—it was surrounded by short cut black hair and a scruffy beard with a gray patch on his chin. A police issue black flak jacket rested over his dirtied, tan long-sleeved shirt. He always wore it with the sleeves rolled up. He should just cut the damn things off.

The distant cracking of more gunshots followed. Two, three, four, five-six-seven. Then silence.

That didn't go cleanly.

Hood whistled a melodic bird call. A similar one returned—so Billy had taken out whoever else was attacking. Whiskey was crouched down low, waiting for anyone else to come. The seconds dragged on, Hood straining to hear any sound in the dark woods. The forest sat still, save for the leaves of the trees rustling lightly with the wind. *They must've just been scouts.* Hood laid the worn black metal body of his rifle across his knees and bowed his head. *This is the way things are. You have to accept that.*

"Why didn't you make the kill?" Whiskey asked, his voice familiar, slightly southern.

"I missed." Hood slung his rifle over his back and dislodged himself from his foothold in the tree, swinging down from one branch to another.

"Like hell you did. You can't change the way the world is, kid. You're wasting your talent. And our ammo."

"It just doesn't feel right." Hood landed on the forest floor, bouncing up to a standing position. He looked over at the dead man lying in the grass.

"I ain't sayin' it's easy, but it's them or us. You know that." Whiskey stared off into the woods in the direction of Billy's post. "I'm gonna check on him. Head back to camp and get something to eat."

Hood couldn't move, staring at the dead man in the wet grass. A memory of the old world flooded his mind:

The sun was going down in the country, Hood, Ian and their sister Taylor taking turns shooting their uncle's compound bow at a fake-deer target pincushioned with arrows.

"Do you think you could kill someone if you had to?" Ian said, releasing his shot to the sound of a satisfying *thunk.* The orange sunlight illuminated his short blond hair.

"Who is it you'd have to kill?" Hood said, taking the bow and nocking an arrow.

"You don't know. You just know its either you or him."

"So it's a guy, then?" Taylor asked, shielding the setting sun from her eyes. Her phone *dinged* a text message tone in her pocket,

9

unattended.

"Does it matter?" Ian said.

"Of course it matters. What if it was a girl you guys had to shoot?"

"I kinda feel bad just shooting this thing." Hood aimed carefully, releasing the bowstring. The arrow snaked through the air and *thunked* an inch from the bull painted on the midsection of the fake deer.

"For feeling bad, you're pretty good at it," Taylor said.

"The way I see it, you don't know if the guy is good or bad. But we know we're good," Ian said.

"Just playing devil's avocado here, but if we shoot the other guy, are we still the good ones?" Taylor said with a smirk.

Ian laughed. "We can figure that out while we're still alive."

Hood gnawed his lip. He missed that life so much that the memories had become more bitter than sweet. Part of him wanted to forget. He would do anything to have Ian, Mom and Dad with them in this brutal new world. It would make it all bearable. Family against the chaos. He thanked whatever god would listen every day that he had Taylor. He only wished he could tell her they were alright. She'd be worried back in Clearwater, holding down the fort until they returned with the supplies they purloined from the Sheriff.

Only a few years ago Hood had been in college, skipping classes about the history of war and the rare revolutionaries like Gandhi who stood against it. War and death were distant concepts. Now civilization was a memory, and war was a part of life.

A squirrel ran down a nearby tree, darting through the grass and away from Hood before scrambling up the bark of a tall maple. Hood's shoes tread softly on the wet grass as he moved toward the man's body. He held the worn grip of his rifle, but kept it at his side. The corpse lay sprawled face-down, blood seeping into the dirt. The dead man was much taller than he'd looked from a distance. He was recently shaven, and his backpack sagged over the back of his head. Hood knelt down, opening it. A book, of all things, sat inside. He pulled it out, inspecting the blank black cover before flipping through the pages. It was hand-written. He tucked the book into the back of his pants, and removed the man's backpack.

What kind of person were you? At the very least, the type to keep a journal.

The guy wouldn't be doing any more writing. Hood grit his teeth.

He kept the rifle in hand, headed back towards the campsite. From the other direction in the woods, he could hear the murmuring voices of Whiskey and Billy.

Hood walked up the sloping grass to their camp in the wooded foothills, the fire flickering outside the small, red oak cabin. He tossed the backpack onto the ground near the concrete slab the cabin rested upon. Doug and Tommy sat in folding chairs around the campfire, passing a flask between them, rifles at their sides.

"Kaiser's men?" Doug inquired.

"Yeah, a few of them. You two take watch. I'm sure Billy could use a break too." The two of them rose to their feet with some effort, Doug stretching wildly.

"Damn, shift starts early, huh?" Tommy smirked. The two of them turned and headed northwest, in the direction Hood had come from. Tommy shoved the flask into Doug's midsection.

Whiskey and Billy emerged from the trees into the firelight. Billy was dripping blood from his left hand, which he held tight in his right.

"Oh shit, Billy Red's got some red on him!" Doug shouted as they passed by. "One of the bastards tagged you, huh?"

"Shut the fuck up!" Billy shouted, grimacing.

Hood moved to meet them halfway. Billy stared nervously at Hood with sharp blue eyes. He pulled his hand away, revealing the bloody hole in his left palm as his hand quivered uncontrollably. Hood flipped it around to the other side, saw the exit wound.

"You're lucky. It went clear through. Get the iron ready," Hood said.

"Oh fuck me, this is going to hurt." Billy bared his teeth as he stared at his bloody hand.

Hood clapped him on the shoulder. "Just don't think about it. And you might want to start drinking now.

Before Hood had finished speaking Billy had snatched the bottle out of Lucky's hands as he sat beside the fire. The two of them immediately started to argue, Lucky ranting about how searing wounds shut did more harm than good. Billy was having none of it. Not like Lucky was a doctor or anything, he just didn't want to give up his booze. Really, none of them were. It was a sore area of need, one they couldn't easily remedy. They didn't find many doctors wandering the mid-Atlantic countryside these days.

Whiskey put an old iron rod into the fire, shaking his head. Joey and Wedge plodded out of the cabin with a squeak of the screen door, unmistakably hungover. Ever since they had found a case of vodka on the last raid, this had been a regular occurrence.

Hood walked back towards the cabin, but Whiskey held an arm out, stopping him.

"You all right, kid?"

"Yeah, I'm fine." Hood ran his thumb over the sights of the rifle hanging at his side.

"The number of people we've killed is never gonna get smaller." Whiskey held his gaze. He had a fatherly look on his face, whether he knew it or not. "Just remember who we do this for."

Whiskey would make a good dad one day. If that was ever a possibility, the way things were now. Another guy might have found it uncomfortable, but Hood was glad Whiskey and Taylor were a couple. Under the circumstances, it only brought Hood and Whiskey closer. It's not like they had a hell of a lot in common other than they both fought to keep Taylor safe. Along with all the other people of Clearwater.

"I'm fine. I'm okay."

Whiskey's stern gaze lingered on him for a moment before he turned and walked to the fire to check the iron. Hood opened the screen door of the cabin and went inside. Whiskey was used to the darker side of humanity. He had been a cop for a long time before the collapse of civilization. The idea of someone trying to kill you wasn't foreign to him.

The poorly made, wood-framed couch and empty spaces on the floor were covered in bedding. Hood ambled slowly to the kitchenette, grabbed some salted jerky from a jar and chewed on it. He picked up the pan on the stove, scooped a few cold beans from the bottom and ate them while staring at a dark knot in the red woodgrain of the wall.

If a bear or a wolf came out of the woods he'd shoot it to stay alive. If a tree was going to collapse on his house he'd cut it down. If a pack of the Kaiser's men snuck towards their camp, he had to gun them down.

If they were all merciless killers it would be easier. Hood knew by now many of them were regular people just fighting to survive. Being a part of the Kaiser's army was the only chance for survival for countless refugees.

Maybe to them, Hood and Whiskey and the Clearwater crew were that bear in the woods.

Hood lay down on the couch, staring up at the defunct ceiling fan and the stained wood boards it was mounted to. The dead man's journal jabbed him in the back. He pulled it out of his pants, running his hands over the soft faux leather cover before opening it. The orange light from the campfire came in through the window. He could clearly read the man's surprisingly good handwriting. He opened the book to the first entry.

Maybe some other civilization will find this book some day and marvel at our great tragedy. I don't know why else I would bother to write this. I guess it's some kind of catharsis. It's been two years since the nukes and the chemical weapons destroyed our country. One day you're grocery shopping, the power cuts off. Everyone shrugs nervously and goes home and waits for it to come back on and it never does.

The weaponized virus or whatever the hell it was that made people into wild animals—that was what really ruined everything. Someone had the clever idea to call it the red death. It's catchy, I'll give them that. Most of the infected are gone now. Now the survivors just have to stop killing each other. Not like humanity's ever been able to do that.

I'm writing this because Bob is dead, and I have no idea what to do anymore. I have no one to talk to that I really trust. The Kaiser's officers are ruthless, and most of the other people are too afraid to go against them. Everyone stays in their lane, even if that lane is fucked.

One such ruthless asshole of the Kaiser's they call the Sheriff sends us out to take out U.N. remnants. I don't even know why they want them dead. They're so pathetically weak, just trying to survive like the rest of us. We fight rangers of the Sons of Liberty more often than not. They're the real threat to the Kaiser's dream of a new country. That's the idiotic party line the officers keep spouting. Honestly, I wish I could fight for the Sons instead. Supposedly the Crusader united the entire New England region under the banner of the Sons shortly after the fall. Though who knows, the Crusader might be as much of a self-righteous psychopath as the Kaiser is. People who've been here longer than I have said the Kaiser seized control over the mid-Atlantic region in only three months. Three goddamn months. The whole world has gone to shit.

I have to keep Danny and Kim alive. With Bob dead, I'm the only one left looking out for his kids. I never wanted to have to do that. That's why I never had any goddamned kids of my own. But they're good kids. They don't deserve this shitty world.

Hood let the journal rest under his nose, his hands starting to sweat. *You killed a good man today. You killed him because he happened to be on one side and you happened to be on the other. You did it because you had to. But it doesn't change the fact he's dead. Now those kids are alone.* The chemically treated paper had a sweet, nostalgic smell, one that reminded him of lying on his childhood bed reading fantasy novels as he wished he were on some grand adventure. He heard Whiskey's voice in his head. *Don't do this to yourself, kid. You've gotta let it go.* His hands acted on their own as he skipped ahead to the latest entry.

Just got our marching orders. I'm to go with Don and George to sneak into the camp of this country-ass gang that's been raiding supplies from everyone. The Sheriff says it's a skeleton crew, and we can take them by surprise. I don't like it. It doesn't make that much sense, and it seems an awful lot like a suicide mission. But I don't have much of a choice. I should've kept my goddamned mouth shut. He probably knows I haven't been too happy with this bullshit they're making us do lately. I wish there was a way I could get Danny and Kim out of this disaster. Part of me wants to just run off. But lord knows what they'd do with those kids. God, you miserable prick, just give me a way out of this.

Hood exhaled slowly, closing the book. Every fight Hood won was someone else's loss. *Whiskey said it was us or them. The whole world thinks it's 'us or them,' though.*

Hood could justify killing an evil man, if he had to. But this man? He felt a closeness to him in reading his raw thoughts. He could've easily been one of their crew.

Hood wanted no part of this war. All he wanted was peace and quiet with his family, and maybe to find a girl who lived like the world wasn't in ruins. That's a greedy thought in a world like this, though. He'd be happy with peace alone. Not that it would happen. He dreamed that Ian and Mom and Dad would just show up at Clearwater one day. But back in reality, all he could do was protect his sister and pray his family was still alive out there.

Billy's screams and curses reverberated through the walls of the cabin, interrupting his musings. Hood was glad he'd never had to sear any wounds closed with the iron.

The screen door creaked open and the main door swung in with a crash.

Billy's blue eyes were wide behind unkempt brown hair. He held his left hand in his right like it was a sick bunny.

"I NEED SOME BOOZE!" He shouted, hurling bedding and clothes every which way with his right hand, desperately digging for someone's stash.

Hood laughed, knowing full well Billy didn't want to hear a damn thing he had to say. He sat up slowly to make his way out of the cabin.

Lucky was standing over the campfire trying to ignite the end of his hand-rolled cigarette. The orange glow lit up his round, olive face and the flames reflected in his dark eyes.

Whiskey leaned back into the folding chair, crossing his arms and gazing absently at the dancing fire.

"You guys aren't going to give him any?" Hood said, nodding towards Billy in the cabin.

Whiskey *hmmphed*. "He already drank half of mine. Crybaby. I ain't giving him no more."

The fire crackled and popped as one log broke into two and fell into the embers below. Hood sat down on a tree stump and basked in the heat from the fire. It was a subtle comfort, but it was something. The three of them stared at the flickering flames, the occasional pop and crack accompanying the birds starting to chirp in the distance. The smell of burning pine brought Hood back to the old world again; he and Taylor and Ian as teenagers sitting around a bonfire at their cousin's house in Maine, roasting marshmallows on metal shish-kabob sticks and talking about their future in a world that still had one.

Billy emerged from the cabin with another creak of the screen door. He walked over to a folding chair and plopped down, an entire bottle of vodka in one hand. He unscrewed the cap with his teeth and spat it into the dirt, taking a deep swig.

"Man, this is boring," Lucky said, leaning back and puffing smoke into the air.

"Here, let me shoot you. It'll keep you distracted." Billy pulled out his pistol and pointed it at Lucky, who flipped him off.

"Why ain't we found any stand-up comedians from back in the day?" Lucky said, spitting out some tobacco that had made its way out of the butt of the cig.

"Well damn Lucky, isn't that why you're here? I mean, you

couldn't shoot a waster that was listening to the barrel of your gun to hear the ocean," Hood said, aiming a finger gun and biting his lip in mock consternation.

"Hey, fuck you, I got bad depth perception, all right?"

Whiskey snorted. "Bad depth perception? That's a new one. I always thought it was on account of you being about as jittery as a cat in a washing machine."

"Y'all are just jealous of my devilish charm and good looks," Lucky said through the cigarette, each breath punctuated with puffs of smoke. "You're lookin' at a superior male specimen, fellas."

"Male specimen, my ass," Whiskey grumbled.

Billy came up for air with a sigh, in between swigs from the bottle he clutched to his chest. "Seriously though, anyone know any new stories? I could stand to be distracted."

"I'm not sure we haven't heard every true story and twice as many made up ones at this point," Whiskey said, unscrewing the top of his flask and taking a drink. Hood smacked him in the knee and beckoned it over with two fingers. Whiskey handed the flask off to him. Hood tipped it back, holding his breath to keep the taste but not the burn.

"Yeah, actually, I got one," Hood said wiping his lips on his knuckles. He looked down at the stainless steel flask, a smile growing from the fond memory. "It's from high school, actually. You aren't gonna believe it's true."

Hood looked up at the three of them. Billy and Lucky stared back, attending to their bottle and cigarette respectively, while Whiskey kept staring into the fire. Hood handed the flask back to him, breaking his reverie.

"Well shit, don't keep us in suspense," Billy said, resting the bottle on his knee.

"Bet a bottle it's another one about his adopted brother Isaac or whoever," Lucky pointed at Billy.

Hood picked up a pebble and threw it at Lucky over the fire. Lucky snatched it out of the air, and jumped to his feet in a crane

17

stance.

"You see that Mr. Miyagi shit? Like a ninja, son!"

"Congrats you caught a rock, sit down and let him tell the damn story," Billy grumbled.

"Nah that's cool, Lucky wants to practice his Tai Chi," Hood said.

"Stop being an asshole," Billy gestured at Lucky with his bottle.

"Don't get all butthurt. Go on, tell your fuckin' story," Lucky sat down, pulling the cigarette out of his mouth.

Hood rubbed his palm with his thumb, launching into the saga. "So yeah. Way back in high school Ian was all about this girl Deirdre Connelly. Ian's the kinda kid who was single-minded in his focus. She was a pretty girl, but spoken for all through high school until senior year she and her dude broke up. She skipped class one day, apparently getting pretty high and sexting Ian with her address, saying her parents weren't home. Problem is, his teacher saw him on his phone and took it away, giving it to the front office for my mom to pick up. . ."

Lucky had perked up at the mention of a pretty girl and sexting, taking a strong pull from the cigarette as he watched intently. Hood chuckled to himself remembering it. The memories almost didn't feel real, like it was a different world.

"Anyway, so Ian obviously isn't going to let this stop him. He sneaks out at lunch, meets up with this chick he knows who's a makeup artist at the mall. They come up with a plan, and they go full Mrs. Doubtfire, turning Ian into my mom. I mean full-blown: dress, stockings, heels, wig, makeup, everything. I swear, it was pretty goddamned convincing. He strolls right into the front office claiming to be Mrs. Huntington, there to pick up her son's phone. He had the voice pretty good too. Unbeknownst to him, I had just got caught drinking cheap vodka in the bathroom and they decide that while 'my mom' was there, they should take me to her for discipline. So I'm in the front office and I see him all done up. Immediately I lose it, I'm howling, dying, I can't help it. Afraid his cover is going to be blown, he launches into a rant about me being more responsible and taking away my phone and X-box and grounding me and how mad my father is going to be when he finds out, and the whole time I'm in tears. Someone finally musters the nerve to question Ian's facade. Ian tries desperately to whisk me and his phone away but is caught when the Dean calls my mom's cell. Ian was so pissed I thought he was going to kill me, but I didn't care, it felt like the best day of my life. The dean rambled to us about integrity and the whole time I couldn't stop laughing and Ian wanted to stab me."

Hood drew the story to a close, staring off into the fire.

"Well?" Lucky said, staring at Hood. "Did Ian bang that chick?"

Hood shook his head. "You're an idiot."

"Don't leave it like that, douche! Tell me what happened!"

"Yes, you moron. They hooked up on and off all through senior year. It was a huge dramatic pain in the ass. Not exactly a limited-time-offer."

Whiskey shook his head, wearing a slight grin. "That's some funny shit. How come you never told that one?"

"I guess I normally don't think about high school much. But I just remembered it." Hood leaned back, the fire so warm it felt like it was burning his face. Maybe it was partly the liquor.

"High school huh. I bet you were one of those swoopy-haired kids who listened to that weepy ass music all the time," Lucky said, staring down Hood for his reaction. Hood didn't dignify it with a response, giving Lucky the finger.

"Who the fuck's Mrs. Doubtfire?" Billy said, blinking slowly.

Whiskey snorted, rubbing his forehead. "Goddamned kids."

The fire had died down suddenly. The glowing red chunks of wood lay broken atop each other, glowing suddenly brighter as a gust of wind blew smoke and ash towards Hood. The leaves on the trees swished softly. Lucky tossed the cigarette butt into the fire. Billy was swaying in his seat.

"Should I get more logs?" Lucky asked no one in particular.

"No. We're going to pack up and head home. The Sheriff will know we're here for sure when his men don't come back. He'll tell the Kaiser by tomorrow or the day after. I want to be gone by then. They're not too happy with us raiding that stockpile, so we should take the supplies back to town and lay low," Whiskey said. A look of exhaustion hung in his eyes as he stared at the embers.

Hood was sure he knew what he was thinking: That sooner or later they were going to piss off the Kaiser enough that he wouldn't be able to ignore them anymore. But they had little choice. Hood knew just as well as Whiskey how much the town needed food, water, gasoline, and every little thing in between. They had a long way to go before they could learn to farm enough food to support themselves, let alone find a way to sustain every other need.

"Well, shit. You ain't gotta tell me twice. I'm sick'a this busted-ass cabin," Billy slurred, standing up and moving towards the house in one motion. His foot caught in the legs of the folding chair and he slumped into the grass with supreme drunken inelegance. The airborne bottle of vodka thunked into the grass in front of him. Lucky exploded off his seat, howling in laughter, berating Billy loudly between breaths.

"Damn dude, you all right?" Hood said, trying to suppress his own snickering.

"Changed m' mind, I'm jus' gonna lay here awhile," Billy said, the side of his face pressed against the grassy earth.

Hood looked over at Whiskey, grinning. Whiskey shook his head in annoyance, but couldn't suppress a smirk. He stood up, hands pushing himself up from his knees.

"Well Lucky, that leaves you to get the trucks out of the hiding spot. Come on, we got to get movin'." Whiskey stretched his right arm behind his head.

Lucky complained loudly about Billy's drunken stupor as he stomped off down the hill. Whiskey made the rounds and gathered the crew from out on watch. Everyone started packing up the supplies and loading them into the trucks Lucky parked by the cabin.

All Hood could think about was the dead man and the kids he

wouldn't be able to look after. He hadn't had many choices. Very few people did anymore.

Hood believed completely that Ian and his parents were still alive; what would they do to protect each other if they lived under the Kaiser's rule?

Morning light had broken through the trees and onto the dirt road by the time Hood and Whiskey headed off with a truck laden with supplies. It shed clarity on an unpleasant thought.

One day when I look down the sights it might not be a stranger I see walking through the woods, gun in hand.

Chapter 2 – One Man Gone

Hood slammed the door of the truck. The bright sun blared down on an old house that remained largely intact. He'd seen this exact sight before: an unhinged red front door and pile of rotten wood shingles that lay in a heap next to the walkway. They'd already been to this house, months ago.

He scanned the area, looking over each shoulder. The narrow lake shimmering in the sunlight nearby looked much more sylvan now than in the nighttime.

"Whiskey?"

"Mmm-hmm?" He replied, the crunch of his footsteps on gravel unceasing as he strode towards the old farmhouse. It still held the air of the majestic country home it must've been some years ago.

"Why are we looking in the same place again?" Hood's tone did nothing to hide his annoyance.

"Just keep an eye on the truck," Whiskey said, entering the house with his police-issue shotgun half-raised.

Hood breathed in deeply, leaning his head back and letting out a grumbling sigh. He looked out over the still lake, a few lost pine cones bobbing about like ships at sea. He turned around, observing the vast overgrowth of grass and weeds on what must have once been fields. The old barn, covered in flaky brown paint, was listing so heavily to one side it looked as if Hood yelled at it, it would collapse.

In the distance, over the top of the treeline, he could see the rise of the Shenandoah Mountains. At least, he was pretty sure that's what it was.

He hoisted his rifle onto his shoulder, letting it rest there lazily. At least it was a gorgeous day, even if they were in yet another ghost town.

He wondered what his old home in D.C. looked like. The parts of the city that still stood had been on the brink of chaos when Hood and Taylor left two years ago. They'd waited for days hoping their parents would show up, but fled when the survivors grew desperate. Radiation sickness had decimated many of the people who had survived the blast.

How different would Hood's life be if his entire family had been together during the fall. They probably never would have met Whiskey and become a part of Clearwater. He hadn't seen Ian in over a year even before the fall. Their brotherhood had become a long distance text conversation and occasional Skype call. Ian had been busy starting his family and Hood couldn't figure out what the hell he was doing with his life. They both had treated separation like a temporary nuisance, the distance in the modern world seeming so small. *God, I miss you bro. What I wouldn't do just to get to sit down and talk with you again about nothing.*

It was hard transition going from global, instantaneous communication to a life where your survival depended on being cut off from the world. A bird of prey was floating slowly on the strong winds high up in the blue sky. *Nothing to see here, buddy.*

Wearing a blank expression, Whiskey walked out the front door of the house, heading straight for the truck.

"So I'm gonna go out on a limb and say... it's still an empty house," Hood quipped.

"Come on, I want to check in town a ways," Whiskey said, hopping inside and starting the engine with a deep rumble. Hood shook his head and climbed into the passenger side. *I should have brought a god damned book or something. What I wouldn't do for a PSP or a 3DS, with even just a few games and infinite battery life.*

Hood's brain rattled off into the land of the ridiculous, spurred on by boredom. "You ever wonder how long pubes would grow if no one ever shaved? Maybe you could make like a groin-beard, or make braids or something nice." Hood cast an absurd look Whiskey's way.

Whiskey looked incredulous.

"Man, not even a smile?" Hood turned his head, chuckling, and stared with tired eyes out the windshield. The weather-worn, one-lane, two-way road lay baking in the sun. It looked barely wide enough to accommodate two different directions of traffic. *Ian would've thought that was hilarious. Or maybe not. At least he would've fired back with something.*

"It's like you're drunk when you're sober," Whiskey grumbled.

Hood shrugged. "You never thought about shit like that?"

"No."

They both stared ahead again at the sun-baked road. Whiskey scratched his bearded jawline.

"How did the hobbit ruin the boxing match?"

Whiskey glanced over at him, annoyed.

"What, you not into Tolkien?"

"Not particularly."

Hood shook his head, looking out the passenger side at the overgrown fields passing by.

"I bet you used to give out bags of pennies for Halloween."

A slight grin crept over Whiskey's face. *Victory.* "Tootsie rolls. I like Tootsie rolls."

"You're a man of boundless curiosity, you know that? The body of a thirty-something, but the spirit of an eighty year old losing at bingo."

Whiskey laughed quietly to himself. "You know what Sue Morris said to me on my last patrol before we left town? 'Be careful to keep the lord with you. It's the devil's curiosity to find a way into our hearts.'"

24

Hood scoffed. "Her husband doesn't do much to ward off the devil. All he does on guard duty is sit in a chair, farting in his sleep."

Whiskey propped his arm on the door and rested his chin in his hand, gnawing at the first knuckle of his pointer finger. He knew they needed more people to defend the town in case they ever were attacked outright.

Hood furrowed his brow. The roadside was empty save for overgrowth and a gas station that looked as though it had been stripped down long before the nukes had changed their world.

"My old partner, Alan," Whiskey said. "He retired four years ago. That farmhouse was his grandfather's, and he told me he wanted to move there." He finally addressed the latent question in the air.

"Well, considering we've been here before, and this time we have a truckload of invaluable food and gasoline, I'd consider this visit a waste of time," Hood said, looking through the back window into the loaded bed of the truck.

"We could use his help. We've got too many guys who won't be worth a damn if wasters find our town with blood on their minds."

"You can just say the dude is your friend and you want to find him," Hood shifted in his seat, moving back to sit up straighter, giving himself more leg room.

Whiskey rubbed his chin. "Yeah, I suppose there's that too," he murmured after some hesitation.

The one-stoplight town was the kind you might not be able to find on a map unless you knew where it was. The only buildings of note in the intersection were a long-cleaned-out old grocery, a faded white house—once a local diner—with peeling paint, and an old wooden church. The road curved past the church and over a river with a low, flat wooden bridge across it. Whiskey turned off the truck and Hood hopped out of the passenger side, his shoes grinding dirt into the pavement.

If there had once been people living in this town, they certainly weren't here anymore.

"Look there," Whiskey said quietly, pointing to a watery, muddy trail that lead from the rushing river to the church doors.

No animal did that. Hood's pulse quickened.

The two of them hustled over to it, guns in hand. Clearly someone had dragged himself out of the river. Puddles still remained, and wet footprints. Hood's eyes met Whiskey's. He didn't need to say anything.

They moved swiftly and quietly along the wet tracks to the church. The outside smelled of a musty, aged wood that stirred up vague memories of his grandfather's garage. Was it cedar? Whiskey gave him a glance, then grabbed the cast-iron door-handle.

Hood held up the rifle to sight.

Whiskey pulled the door open and the hinges groaned.

Beams of sunlight lit up the empty pews, and leaves covered the floor. Many of the windows had been shattered. The muddy trail led down the center aisle and then to the left of the altar, where it became lost to sight. Blood trailed along the faded white stone floor.

He motioned to Whiskey: forward and to the left. The two of them entered, their footsteps echoing throughout the room despite their best efforts, followed by a gust of wind that sent leaves and dust swirling in front of the altar.

"You win. I can't run no more." A man's voice echoed through the church. A pistol clattered to the ground, sliding to a halt in the empty space in front of the altar.

"Jammed. Ain't that my luck," the hoarse voice said with heavy resignation.

Hood and Whiskey turned the corner, guns raised. A wiry dark-skinned man sat on the floor, his head resting against the prayer pedestal with its rows of candles. He was drenched, his jeans and long-sleeved shirt dark and heavy with water.

After a second, Hood lowered his rifle.

"We're not here looking for you," Hood said.

The man stared at him, squinting. "Are you gonna kill me?" He asked.

"No," Hood said immediately.

Whiskey cast him a disapproving glance. "Provided you don't do anythin' stupid," he added, shotgun still raised.

The man raised his hands weakly. "Who are you? I thought for sure you were the Kaiser's men," The guy broke into a wry smile, avoiding Whiskey's question. "You boys look like angels to me."

"Don't go getting all excited," Whiskey grunted at the man. "We ain't nobody's saviors."

The man shook his head slowly, eyes closed but still smiling. "I disagree."

"You were running from the Kaiser?" Hood asked.

"His militants, at least. I was one of their prisoners," the man said at length, still breathing slowly.

"No you weren't," Whiskey said, sizing the man up.

"Sharp, this guy. No, I wasn't. But I felt like it by the end. I joined 'em early. They were part of this whole separatist group, all military and doomsday survivalists at first. The Kaiser was just some wanderer. He showed up soon after the fall, covered in blood like it was no big deal. The leader at the time, an angry fella named Gary took exception to the Kaiser's attitude and he tried to kill him. I swear the Kaiser slit ol' Gary's throat before he even got close. Never seen someone move like that. He declared that he didn't want to fight, said he just wanted a place to be. He felt genuine, and many folks didn't like Gary—he was a wild, power hungry man. Soon enough everyone came to like the Kaiser and wanted him to lead. After he took over, we started raiding, and slaving, and everything got out of control. He had some grand plan but it all seemed sideways to me. My crew tried to fight back, tried to stop the whole thing. They been hunting us down ever since. I'm the last one left." The man didn't bother to hide his exhaustion.

"What were you doin' in here? Praying?" Whiskey scoffed, still holding up his shotgun.

The man shook his head. "Nah. Tabernacle usually has wine in it. Somebody beat me to it though," He pointed at an ornate gilded container, lying empty on the floor.

27

"Do you know where survivors from D.C. might have gone?" Hood asked the man.

"Hell if I know. West, maybe."

"You know of a man called Alan Dale?" Whiskey lowered the shotgun to focus on the man's face, though he still held the weapon at a hip-fire position.

"Why, he done you some wrong? Is that why you boys are out here?" The man looked back and forth from Hood to Whiskey, reading their expressions.

"Just answer the question."

"No, I don't know of him. But I tend to remember the ladies a bit easier. . ." He seemed content to leer off into some fantasy.

Hood reached into his pack and pulled out a half-drunk bottle of water and a sleeve of crackers. He tossed them onto the man's lap. He looked up at Hood in shock for a moment, then drank greedily and started shoving crackers in his mouth.

Whiskey grimaced and rubbed his forehead.

Hood walked over to the jammed pistol on the floor and picked it up. He removed the magazine and tried to rack the slide. A casing was lodged in the ejection port. Hood handed the gun to Whiskey, who knocked the casing free with the heel of his hand and then successfully racked the slide. The dented round clicked as it fell onto the stone floor.

"How much have you seen out there?" Hood asked the man.

He wiped his mouth of cracker crumbs. "You boys haven't had much contact with the outside world, huh?"

"Not much. We try to keep it that way," Hood said.

The man chuckled. "Smart thinkin'. It's all gone. I seen a man's arm fall clean off from the radiation, but the biological shit that tore through the cities was the real nightmare. If you was lucky it killed you, and didn't turn you into an animal while you was still alive."

Hood and Whiskey exchanged a glance. Whiskey's face seemed to express some doubt. Maybe he didn't want to believe it was true. But it lined up with what Hood had read in the dead man's journal.

"You two got any alcohol?"

"No," Whiskey snapped.

"It's for my leg. I need to clean it."

Hood looked at Whiskey, nodding towards the man. Whiskey breathed deeply in annoyance, reached into his cargo jacket and produced a flask, handing it to the man.

He poured it onto a sizable gouge in his thigh, then took a swig, grimacing. He handed it back, then tore off his sleeve and tied it around the wound, baring his teeth as he worked.

Whiskey nodded at the man's pistol in his hand. "Keep the dirt out of the magazine, and keep the barrel clean next time."

The man looked up at Whiskey inquisitively. "You sure you ain't angels?"

"No. I'm keeping it. Consider it payment." Whiskey put away the pistol. "For your life."

"I'm dead without it," The man said simply.

"Or you can die right now," Whiskey replied, holding the man's gaze. The man clearly deliberated saying something, but decided against it.

"Thanks for the food," The man said eventually as he stood up, favoring his wounded right leg.

"Where are you gonna go?" Hood asked. The cool gust of wind through the broken window felt relaxing and unsettling all at once.

"West. Someplace in Colorado. I've heard rumors it's better out there."

"Colorado, huh." Whiskey looked ready to see the man gone.

"Col-o-ra-do," he repeated, limping past them down the aisle.

Hood looked around the desolate church, ransacked of everything but prayer books and Bibles in the pews. Whiskey followed the man closely behind, shotgun still raised. The man pushed his way out the front door. Whiskey followed him. Hood turned and walked out, his footsteps echoing lightly.

The sun still shone strong. Their truck sat still and undisturbed. The man whistled at it.

"Damn, you boys don't mess around. Where'd you get all that cargo?"

Whiskey glowered at him.

"Never mind. Shit. You sure you don't need someone to help you with all that?"

"I thought you've got Colorado," Whiskey replied, scrutinizing the man from under his intimidating eyebrows. They could damn near scowl on their own.

"Right, well, yeah. Right."

"You gonna limp all the way there?" Whiskey didn't hide his doubt well.

"No, I'll catch a ride. I'll get some beater up and running," The man said. "Was a mechanic, once upon a time."

"Good luck," Hood said plainly.

"Name's Donte. I'm thinking I won't see you two again. You sure I can't get that shooter back?" The man asked Whiskey directly.

He shook his head slowly in response.

"All right." The man turned, his gaze lingering on the two of them before hobbling over the small bridge heading west. Hood and Whiskey watched him as he walked out of sight.

"Something's not right about him." Whiskey turned back to the truck, putting the man's pistol in the center of the seats.

"Why do you say that?" Hood walked around to the passenger side, putting the rifle down against the seat and climbing in.

"I just have that feeling," Whiskey said. The truck started with a whine and a rumble.

"It's because he's black. You're racist."

"Don't be an ass."

"It's okay to admit it. Lots of people are racist," Hood quipped, unable to hide his grin.

"It's because of his story about the Kaiser," Whiskey snapped. "Why am I even answerin' this crap?"

"So are you like, self-loathing, since you're part Hispanic?"

"I'm going to fuckin' kill you." Whiskey grunted at him.

Hood laughed, leaning his head against the back window. "Take everything more seriously, please. It's fantastic."

There was a momentary lull in the cabin. The suspension squeaked as the truck bobbed back and forth.

"We should've killed him." Whiskey's face remained stoic as he stared out the windshield, one hand on the steering wheel. Hood turned to look out the passenger-side window, the sunlit overgrown trees speeding by. He rubbed his bristly chin with his thumb and forefinger. He was glad they'd let the guy live, but he hated the fact that Whiskey was probably right.

Hood was ready to be home. The place he called home now, anyway.

Chapter 3 – Homecoming

The quaint streets of Clearwater rested peacefully in late afternoon sun. Hood breathed in the familiar smell of honeysuckles and wild growth on the air. He could feel the muscles in his back relax. With the window down, he rested his hand on the passenger door, his fingers drumming on the metal of their own accord.

Trader George stood out on his front porch, repairing the leg of a wooden chair. Probably something he'd soon be selling out of his garage-turned-trading post. He rose up from a kneeling position, nodding at Whiskey as they passed by. Whiskey held out his hand in acknowledgment.

"It's good to be back," Hood said.

A young girl was chasing her teary-faced younger brother around on a black bicycle on their front lawn. *Micah and Katie. Ted Anderson's kids.*

"Yeah." Whiskey said, turning the corner to head down their street.

Whiskey wore his typical stoic expression.

Hood reached over and slapped him on the shoulder.

"Hey. We're still alive, we took a nice haul from the Sheriff, and it's a beautiful day. Save your worrying for when there's a problem worth worrying about."

"I wouldn't mind gettin' a few steps ahead of our problems."

Hood shrugged, smiling. "Y'know, the seeds will never grow if

32

you never empty the bucket."

Whiskey screwed up his face, looking over at Hood. "The hell is that supposed to mean?"

"I don't know, I just made it up. Sounds profound though, right?" Hood leaned back in the seat of the truck, stretching his arms behind his head, holding his elbows.

"You're a strange kid." Whiskey pulled the truck into the driveway of their home.

The gravel of the driveway crunched under Hood's feet as he stepped out of the truck and closed the door with a thud. Calling it home still felt a little strange, but in truth, after two years, it *was* home now. Hood had certainly never envisioned living in an old Victorian house out in the country. But he also hadn't envisioned much of anything about the life he now lead.

The faded white paint was chipping off the siding of the house onto the grass around it, and the roof sagged under its own weight, but it was a warm, comfortable place plenty big enough for Hood, Whiskey and Taylor to each have their own space.

The heavy wood front door swung open and *thunked* against the mudroom closet as it always did. Hood pulled his rifle off his shoulder and propped it against the wall.

"Hello!?" Taylor's voice echoed from upstairs.

Whiskey placed his shotgun on a shelf in the mudroom.

Hood smiled, shaking his head at him. Hood mouthed, "No respect."

Whiskey smiled, putting a finger over his mouth. The two of them stood at the bottom of the stairs that led to the second floor.

"Hello??" Taylor repeated, walking to the top of the steps and looking down at the two of them. Her green eyes lit up, a wide smile forming familiar dimples on either side of her heart-shaped face.

"Take your time, sis. It's only your family," Hood said with a grin. She ran down the stairs, her dark hair flying behind her as she leaped into his arms. She squeezed the hell out of him. He lifted her off the ground for a second.

"Oh man! You been packing it on. I do hope there's some food left in the pantry," Hood said, his head resting on top of hers.

She broke out of his hug and punched him in the arm. It stung like hell.

"Ah, come on, it was a joke!" Hood laughed, rubbing the sore spot.

"Asshole! I was so freakin' worried about you guys! How did it go?" She looked over at Whiskey.

"Yeah, we're good. It went well," Hood said, "We're just glad to be home."

"So... I take it you haven't found any sign of Mom, Dad or Ian."

Hood shook his head. "I'm sorry."

She smiled resolutely. "We'll find them."

Maybe it's better this way. Hood could live with believing they were out there somewhere, surviving and worrying about him and Taylor the way they were worrying about them. That they weren't dead.

Taylor moved slowly to Whiskey, getting on her tiptoes to kiss him. He held her in his arms, and they said nothing to each other. Hood admired their love. It wasn't ostentatious or needy, it simply was. They meant the world to each other, and they meant the world to him. If there was one good thing that had come of the collapse of everything he knew, it was the relationship between them. His parents would've loved Whiskey. He could picture his dad, especially, taking a liking to him. They shared the same no-nonsense demeanor.

Hood's feet carried him unconsciously up the creaky steps to his room. Fading orange sunlight came in through the windows at a sharp angle, casting long rectangles on the threadbare tan carpet. A thin layer of dust lay upon the old wooden desk and dresser. Simply entering his room, he felt lighter, the tension of survival melting away. His head hung heavy, though, and the pillow on his bed called to him. *We live like this because we have to. You're not just fighting for yourself out there, you're fighting for everyone else.* He tossed his backpack onto the desk. He stared at it for a moment, and considered taking the dead man's journal out again. *But everyone is fighting for*

34

someone. He took a deep breath and exhaled slowly. *Give it a rest.*

He unzipped his black hoodie and took off his .38 and chest holster, tossing them all on top of his bag. He flopped face-first onto his bed, the familiar stale smell of the bedding relaxing him completely. He felt the pull of sleep as his mind went quiet.

He climbed the hill up to the defunct lighthouse. Ocean sprayed up all around the nearby cliffs. The door was open, and the spiral staircase inside had thin trails of blood trickling down the steps. Immediately he started to climb the stairs, holding onto the rope railing hooked into the wall. His heart went wild, his chest tight like it was belted in place. The farther he climbed upward, the more blood poured down. There was so much of it his feet slipped and more than once he fell forward, the blood soaking into his clothes. You know whose blood this is, the voice in his head said. His mind launched into a state of panic. At the top, there was a hatch in the ceiling. Blood dripped out of the corners of it. Hood pushed open the hatch and climbed up to the Lantern room. Tied up against the great lamp were Mom, Dad, Ian and Taylor. Blood poured from their slit throats, and beside them stood . . . Himself.

His doppelganger was tall, skinny, with messy brown hair and green eyes, wearing jeans and a black hoodie. He held a bloody knife in his hand.

Why did you do this? The other Hood seemed to say to him. Why would you do this to them?

He moved closer to Hood, taking his right hand, and drove the knife deep into it.

Hood startled awake, his hand a balled fist. It throbbed in pain, the muscles cramping.

His skin was damp with sweat and his mouth had drained of all moisture. He felt more tired than when he'd gone to sleep.

There was a knock at his door. "Hey Rob, you awake?" came Taylor's melodious voice.

"Yeah, come in. Why's it so damn hot in here?"

"Ah, sorry, I got cold, so I started up the fireplace." She came in the door, moving to his bed and handing him a glass of mostly-clear water.

"Mind reader. How did you know?" Hood asked, guzzling it down despite the slight metallic taste.

"When Whiskey showed me the supplies and I saw how much booze you guys got, I figured you'd need it." She sat down on the bed, smiling.

"I didn't even drink that much." Hood put the glass down on the neglected antique nightstand beside his bed. Taylor looked like she didn't believe him. The house was quiet aside from the muted sound of cicadas in the darkness outside. "Where's Whiskey?"

"The other guys haven't returned with the rest of the supplies. He thinks one of the trucks broke down. Y'know the blue one, that's always freakin' breaking down? So he went back out to find 'em."

Hood chuckled. "Yeah, that sounds about right."

Taylor stared at the floor, but didn't really seem to see it. "This place gets so damn empty when you guys are gone. I can only spend so much time on watch, or on trying to teach the townspeople how to be anything other than useless with a gun in their hands. I wish I could go with you guys."

Hood shook his head. "Hey, I know you can take care of yourself. But Whiskey feels differently about it. He worries."

"*Whiskey.*" Taylor mocked, in a fake deep voice. "Just call him John. You idiots and your damn nicknames."

Hood grinned. "I like them. There's something bromantic about it. And if you hate 'em so much, take it up with Lucky. He came up with 'em."

"Oh, great. Did he give himself his own nickname?"

Hood laughed, rubbing the back of his head. "Nah, we just call him that because he's such a spaz he has to be the luckiest motherfucker just to have made it this far."

Taylor laughed, nodding in agreement. Her laugh was just like Mom's. It was the only similarity they shared. Ma always said Taylor was like her grandmother. The room fell silent. Hood swung his legs

36

out of bed, stood up and stretched, touching the ceiling with his fingertips.

"Do you think we'll ever find Ian or Mom and Dad?" She asked, out of the blue.

"I don't know, Tay. I wish I could say I was sure."

"I keep wondering if Mom and Dad went back home. Do you think we should go back again?" She asked, looking down at her hands in her lap.

"We stayed there as long as we could. But D.C. is no kinda place anymore. They'd have no reason to go back," Hood said, staring at his backpack.

"What if they returned to look for us?"

It would be an incredibly dumb, stubborn thing to do. It also was exactly the kind of thing their parents might be exactly dumb and stubborn enough to try. They had to know that Hood and Taylor would've left home behind, but it was the one place they all had in common. The one place they all might find each other.

"Maybe if we head back up north soon, we could check it out. It would have to be fast, and quiet. I'm not sure Whiskey would be willing to take the risk."

"Don't worry, I'll convince him," Taylor said, picking up the glass from the floor.

"Ew, gross," Hood said, screwing up his face.

"Not like that, you sicko! I hate you." She punched him in the shoulder again.

Hood laughed at her as she walked out the door. She popped her head back in for a moment.

"It's good to have you home again, Robbie."

Nobody but her had called him that in a long time. "It's good to be home, sis." Hood said, plopping back down into his bed.

Daybreak came fast. Hood spent much of his time lurching in and out of sleep. Frustrated, he pried himself out of bed and plodded down into the kitchen, where he stuffed his face with handfuls of honeyed granola before washing it down with some more murky water. He was grateful he couldn't remember any of his other dreams, still unsettled from the nightmare. He saw the lifeless faces of his family so vividly, and his own face staring back at him, so impassioned, accusatory. *Why did you do this?* He shivered, wanting to shake the thoughts out of his head. Even though he knew dreams weren't real, there was an unpredictable unconsciousness to them that made them hard to ignore.

He grabbed his gear and headed off into town. Sitting around and doing nothing gave him anxiety. The fear of being caught unawares was strong in the new world. It was still too early in the day for any signs of life. The deep blue haze of early morning hung over Clearwater, along with the lazy branches of the trees that encompassed it. The houses were still quiet, though knowing the townspeople were safely asleep inside gave Hood a feeling of comfort. Obscurity was the hamlet's greatest defense. Unless you knew where it was, it was pretty hard to find by accident, nestled deep in the woods.

The church stood empty and in disrepair, as churches usually do without a pastor or a congregation. Hood walked down the aisle, past the altar into the rectory, and then up the stairs that led all the way to a hatch into the bell tower. There was no real bell, just a defunct loudspeaker and slatted walls they had long since removed.

Of course, no one was on watch. The chair sat empty save for the binoculars and the Remington hunting rifle. *Glad to see the townsfolk are taking their civic duty seriously.*

Maybe the people relied too much on Hood and Whiskey and the crew. Reality was, though, that many of the townsfolk probably wouldn't survive very long without them.

Where the hell is Whiskey with the rest of them? They should just leave the damn truck behind if it really did break down again. It's getting to be more of a liability than it's worth.

The sun rose, and slowly the murmurs of everyday life filled the town below. Many of them worked hard to farm the open tracts of land they had cleared, but without much farming knowledge and trees taking up much of the room and the soil's nutrients, they didn't have a lot to work with.

Hood pressed the binoculars to his eyes, looking out as far as he could. He could see almost all of the small town, but not very far beyond. In the distant west horizon, he could make out the faint outline of the Shenandoah mountains.

Something glinted in the bottom of his field of vision. He focused on it. Atop the trees, sunlight seemed to be reflecting back at him. . .

Get down, his mind screamed.

He dropped to the ground as the shot splintered the wood behind him. Suddenly, horribly, it all made sense. *The Kaiser wanted us to raid the Sheriff's stockpile It was bait. The few men who showed up at the cabin were only sent there to spook us into going home.*

The Sheriff's men followed us. The crew didn't have truck trouble. They've been attacked. The goddamned Kaiser wanted us to come home. He wanted to track us back here.

Hood picked up the foghorn from on the floor and fired it twice, plugging his ear with his other hand. He hustled down the stairs, through the aisle and out of the church.

Already he heard the sound of gunfire not far in the distance. Lucky stumbled down the street, clutching his side, wet with blood. Hood sprinted towards him, and Lucky collapsed into his arms.

"You gotta tell everyone to run," Lucky said, choking on his words.

"Where's the crew?" Hood struggled to hold him upright, but he was slick with his own blood.

"They're not gonna make it. There's so goddamn many of the bastards. It's just you, Hood. You gotta get them all out of here." He coughed violently over Hood's shoulder. Hood felt the blood on his neck.

"Lucky! Lucky, stay with me. You can make it through this."

"Let me lie down. I just need to rest." Lucky slid off of Hood, down to his knees, and then lowered himself to the ground. There already was a large pool of blood at their feet.

"Get them out of here," he repeated quietly.

Hood's eyes were wide and his body cold with shock.

You can't. You're not gonna. . .

He backed away, staring at Lucky's motionless body.

Not now. You can't freak out now. Stay focused. They need you. Taylor needs you.

Hood snapped into motion, running down the street, honking the foghorn. Townsfolk had already started to come out of their houses, hearing the gunfire.

"EVERYONE GET OUT OF HERE! TAKE YOUR FAMILIES AND HEAD INTO THE WOODS. WE'RE UNDER ATTACK!" Hood shouted.

He pulled out his .38 from its holster and cocked back the hammer. He ran straight home, screaming as loud as he could and firing the air-horn until it was empty. He tossed it aside, disgusted.

How could we let this happen? How did we not see this coming?

Hood's mind raced. They'd been too complacent. They hadn't known how big a threat they had become to the Kaiser and his mongrel Sheriff. They had taken too much from them not to face reprisal.

The road home was quiet, and he knew what that meant. The distant gunfire had stopped. Hood felt sick to his stomach. *Lucky is dead. They're all dead. Maybe some of them got away. You can't think about that now.* The dark, consuming emptiness of loss had gripped him. Hope all he like, he knew what happened to people outnumbered and taken unawares. His legs burned from sprinting and he gasped for air, but he kept running.

He dashed through the covered bridge over the stream in town, his mind racing with fear. *Where is Taylor? She must be at home still.* The old style homes packed together in the woods, surrounded by horse fencing with great expanses of shrubbery all stood quiet. *At least some of the townspeople will get out. I pray they will get out. Don't stop running, whatever you do.* Hood turned the corner at the intersection. Ted and Karen Anderson with their kids Micah and Katie stood in front of the old brick library with its sagging roof and faded hanging sign that read Clearwater Town Library - Knowledge and Peace. They were a tall, lithe family all gripped with fear. Ted saw Hood and hurried towards him, his wife and kids following behind. He held an old revolver in hand, and looked scared to have to use it, his eyes darting around.

"What's happened? Where is everyone?" Ted shouted, wide-eyed.

Hood slowed to a stop, breathing heavily. "Just run. Take your family and run."

"Come with us!" Karen implored, staring nervously back towards town.

"I can't. I'm going back to find Taylor." Hood leaned down and propped himself up by his knees, his head throbbing from dehydration.

The kids cried to their parents for an explanation. Karen gave them a soothing shush as she held their heads. Ted's dark glare into Hood's eyes said what his voice would not. *You did this. You all brought his wrath down on us.* Hood did not blame him if he thought that. *When horrible things happen, we all search for a reason. We refuse to accept that maybe it was inevitable.*

"You can't fight it. Just run into the country. Stay off the roads. When you can't run, hide. And stay hidden. You can do this." Hood stood up straight, looking at every one of them. The kids wore the fear of the unknown in their eyes. The parents wore the fear of something worse.

"Come on," Ted said to his family, ushering them away.

"Go. Get out of here!" Hood turned and broke into a run again down the street towards home, not bothering to watch them leave. *Hate me if you want. Just stay together and survive.* Hood cut behind the old grocer with its faded, empty parking lot into the woods. *Maybe this was our fault. Maybe we pushed too hard, took too much. How can this be happening? Please, someone tell me this isn't real.* The path through the tall grass and the trees no longer gave any feelings of nostalgia or

41

calm, instead pure, unfiltered fear that seized him. *She's smart. She can take care of herself. You just have to find her.* Hood wound up and over the short hills until it spat him out onto the old road to what had become their home. He turned to face the tall colonial, and he felt his entire body shiver with intensity.

Outside the front door of his house a man was dragging Taylor off of the property. She fought back, punching and kicking wildly, but the man grabbed both her arms, trying to subdue her. Hood heard Taylor screaming out Whiskey's name, then his own. The man's voice boomed in an imploring shout:

"Listen to me, I'm trying to save you!"

He recognized the voice. It didn't fully register in his mind as Hood strode forward, taking aim of the man. He lowered the pistol, stunned, as the man's face came into view.

It was Ian.

He looked older, much older than he should've looked in only a few years' time. He stood tall with a calm determination, and his blonde hair was cut short now. But it was him. *You're alive. What are you doing here?*

A faint rustling came from behind him. A rough arm wrapped itself around Hood's neck and a hand mashed a wet cloth over his face. It smelled of chemicals. Hood leaned forward, trying to leverage the man off his back. But his vision blurred and he felt weak. As he hit the ground, he saw the old Sheriff's crooked smile looking down at him with the blue sky and tree branches above.

"This moment is even sweeter than I dreamed it'd be." The Sheriff stood up, the sun framing his head.

Hood called out for Ian as the world faded away.

Chapter 4 – Desolation

A murky haze slowly lifted from Hood's mind as consciousness came back to him. He vaguely remembered dreaming, but what about, he couldn't say. Hunched in a chair, he tugged at his hands which were locked behind his back, the cuffs digging into his wrists. *Taylor and Ian. What happened?* His shoulders throbbed, and his hands buzzed with a stinging numbness from lack of circulation. He blinked slowly, still seeing only darkness. The smell of used motor oil and sawdust permeated the air. He tried to move his legs, but they were bound fast to the legs of the chair by rope.

"You're a damn fool," Hood whispered to himself.

He tried to replay it all in his mind. It kept snapping back to the image of Ian holding Taylor by her forearms, trying to subdue her.

Are you working for the Kaiser? Why? Hood thought about the dead man's journal. *Do you even have a choice?*

He knew the town was going to get massacred. He was getting Taylor the hell out of there. *If Ian knew I was there, he'd have mowed the Sheriff down, even if they were working together.* Hood tried to shake his mind free of the confusion. He hung his head, his chin on his chest, before swiveling it around to stretch his sore neck. He had more important things to think about. He was alive. He didn't know why, but he wasn't about to look a gift horse in the mouth. Maybe they wanted him as a slave. There had to be a reason he was here. He had to find out what it was.

Lucky's dead. They're all dead. The town is gone.
The dark thoughts in his head ran free.
You failed them, you acted like everything was fine and no one was ever going to come try to kill you all. You just wanted to pretend the world wasn't fucked. Now you're going to die, too. Hood bit his bottom lip, wanting to turn the pain in his head into something he can feel. *Maybe Ian does know I'm here. He might come and find me. He was trying to keep Taylor out of harms' way.*

With a click, light filled the room, so bright Hood had to turn his face and jam his eyes shut.

"You're getting full of yourself," came the hoarse voice of the old Sheriff. "Thinking you could get away with stealing from us."

The idea that the Sheriff had Hood's life in his hands was a dark seed in his mind. He needed to buy some time, find out why he was here, why he was still alive.

"Yeah, you're probably right," Hood answered at length. The yellow floodlight nailed to the wall still shone in his eyes, but they'd adjusted enough to be able to see that they were in a portable, arch-shaped metal warehouse.

"Of course I'm right." the old man said, pacing in front of him. "Sneaking through my land, thinking you and your gang could just run back home unmolested. You and your self-righteousness. I swear, I can smell your naivete on the wind."

Hood licked his lips and kept silent. The old man leaned in close. His breath smelled like old cigarettes. His bald, middle-aged face was worn and weary around blue eyes. It was disappointment, the look of a vulture flying over picked bones. He seemed to lament that his search for Hood was over.

"You know what it is that did you in?" The Sheriff asked with a weak smile. "It's pride. The same pride that God saw in us when he smote us down."

Hood smirked, his head leaned forward to keep the light out of his eyes. "Granted, I've never read the good book cover to cover, but I'm pretty sure you don't qualify as the godly type."

44

The Sheriff swung his pistol at Hood's face. The handle connected with his eyebrow, and his head snapped back from the blow. There was a throbbing numbness at first, followed shortly by searing pain.

The worn barrel of the Sheriff's pistol hovered in front of Hood's right eye. Inside the barrel was darkness. A tight frown quivered on the Sheriff's face. "You don't talk to me about godliness. You're just a mongrel, slinking around this hell on earth."

Hood breathed in slowly, closing his eyes. Despite being provoked, the Sheriff still hadn't shot him. *Small victories. Gotta keep him talking.* Why was he being held here?

"What's that saying again? Morality ends where a gun begins?" Hood asked, looking up quizzically. "Shit, I can never remember who said what."

The old man laughed aloud, with a self-satisfaction that left him looking around for someone to share it with.

"Don't conjure up the words of the dead like they mean something. You believe you are different. But you are too young to understand the truth."

Hood squinted up at him, then away at the rusted table-saw across the room. It was covered in coagulated blood. He remained still, averting his gaze from the gruesome sight.

Is the old bastard going to torture me? What for? Is he just a sick fuck who loves to torture people?

Fear filled his stomach, but Hood shook it off.

Focus on what you can control.

The wind howled against the thin metal siding of the portable. Then it was silent again. The old Sheriff resumed pacing, taking time to stop and stare him down.

 "This was so easy. After all this time, all this hunting you down. We just had to bait a trap and follow you home. I wish I could take the credit. The Kaiser is one crafty bastard. You don't get to be where he is without being one, I guess."

The old man sat down in a nearby folding chair, elbows on his knees, chin in one hand. "You are pretty, for a boy. Maybe the

45

Kaiser's a damn sodomite." The Sheriff chuckled, amused. "Frankly, I don't know why he wants you."

That makes two of us, old man. The Kaiser. What an idiotic thing to call yourself.

He'd certainly turned the title into something to fear, though.

"What happened to Taylor? I saw Ian taking her," Hood said, trying to ignore the throbbing pain in his brow as he searched the Sheriff's eyes for recognition of the names.

"Ian?" The Sheriff snorted derisively. "That's nothing for you to concern yourself with, clueless boy. Your ass is being taken up to the Church of the Epiphany in D.C. Hell if I know why. Maybe the Kaiser wants to sacrifice you to the devil. Maybe he's just gonna make an example out of you to show what happens to those who stand against him. That is, if I don't kill you first for being a smug little shit." His cold gaze locked on Hood.

"Well, make up your mind soon, because I have to piss," Hood said. "Haven't pissed my pants since I was three and I'm not about to start again now."

The Sheriff laughed, and stood up quickly.

"You know it's better to die here than be given over to him. God knows what living hell he would put you through." The Sheriff produced rolling paper and some tobacco, deftly rolling and licking it. "You've been a knife in his side for a long time."

"Not that long," Hood said, and grinned. "Maybe we can go with an option C that involves not dying or being tortured?"

The old man sported a grim smile, taking pleasure in Hood's plight. "It's a bit too late for that, wouldn't you say? The Kaiser might have to be disappointed. I don't know if I want to take the risk of dragging your ass to him alive." He paused to inspect his hand-rolled handiwork before lighting it with a burst of match-flame and a puff of smoke.

"I say it's better for you to die, get off this sinking ship and go to the devil or oblivion," he said, letting out a smoky sigh before turning his gaze back to Hood, still hunched over in his chair. "I just

46

want to enjoy this for a little bit more."

Hood stared down at the dirty knees of his jeans. He looked up and saw movement in the dark near the entrance to the portable. It was a familiar silhouette. He moved his finger to his mouth. *Oh sweet Jesus, Allah, Buddah, Mary Poppins, whoever got him here, thank you. I'm not going to die here. Not today.* Hood avoided looking directly at him, trying not to draw attention.

"Talk to me," said the Sheriff. "You know your fate. Consider me your holy man before the electric chair."

Hood scoffed. "I'd like to request a new priest." He paused. "And a last supper." The shadowy figure slid inside the portable without a sound.

"What do you miss most of all in this ruined world?" The Sheriff asked, entranced with the depravity of watching someone at the doorstep of death.

Hood thought for a second, looking down at his dirty sneakers and their frayed laces.

"My family." He gave a melancholy smile. "And I guess the internet would be a close second."

The old man chuckled, standing up from his chair. "Yes. There's some honesty. Have you ever heard of the idea that we've all been here before, and we'll all be here again?"

Hood nodded. "Yeah, I've been to a philosophy class, once upon a time."

"It's something to think about. I'd hate to think this whole miserable shit of an existence would have to happen over and over. But maybe it's comforting, too." The old man rested his hand, still holding the cigarette, against his brow, the red ember fading.

He gestured at Hood with his cigarette. "It should be for you. There's not so much to be worried about, then." He took a drag, running his hand over his shaven head while he held the cigarette in his mouth. "What would you say to that idea, ye who struggled so hard against the destruction of mankind?" The old man said with a gratified smirk, pistol hanging in his other hand.

47

Hood lifted his drooping head. He wondered if he looked as tired as he felt.

"I'd say, 'See you again someday, Sheriff.'"

The shot echoed throughout the portable. The empty casing rattled to a stop on the floor, followed by the faint caws of distant birds.

The old Sheriff collapsed to the floor, limp and lifeless. Blood was splattered across the wall and now pooled at Hood's feet. Whiskey rose from a crouched position in the shadows, his broad frame moving slowly into the light.

"You're alive, you beautiful bastard. My God, I could kiss you." Hood couldn't help grinning. "I've never been so glad to see your ugly face."

Whiskey said nothing, his movements heavy, as if he carried some invisible weight around his shoulders. He took the keys from the Sheriff's pocket, unlocked Hood's cuffs and cut the ropes binding his legs. Hood stood up, stretching his aching shoulders before reaching as high as he could into the air. He felt euphoric just to be able to move again.

"They're all dead," Whiskey uttered in a low tone. "We're the only ones left."

Hood stood frozen in shock.

They trusted you. They believed in you. They died for you. What are you going to do with that? He bowed his head, running his hand over his mouth.

"Taylor's still alive," he said slowly. "I saw her. They took her captive."

Whiskey's head whipped around. "She's alive? What, are they sellin' her to slavers?" He moved towards Hood, the jaw muscles on the side of his face flexing, his eyes demanding a response.

Hood rubbed his raw wrists. "It was Ian who took Taylor. He's working for the Kaiser. Though I'm sure he has no choice in the matter." Just saying the words was a strange mix of relief and fear. *I should be glad I saw her with Ian. He won't let anything bad happen to her. But how did he get mixed up with the Kaiser militants?*

Words seemed to fail the both of them for a moment.

"Well, that's some family you got there," Whiskey grunted.

"He was trying to save her! I heard him say as much," Hood shouted.

"You're defending him? You said it yourself. He works for the goddamned *Kaiser*." He nearly spat the name, baring his teeth slightly with his eyebrows set hard over his blue eyes.

"It's because of Ian that she's still *alive*. You can bet your life on that!" Hood bit off the words, pointing at Whiskey. "And at least maybe. . ." Hood paused, unsure if he even wanted to say it. "At least maybe he can protect her from anyone doing. . . anything to her."

Whiskey moved closer to stare Hood down, the creases in his forehead pronounced. Someone exploiting or hurting Taylor was an idea Whiskey didn't look like he wanted to entertain. "Let me explain something to you. We have to save her. Every hour it takes us to get to her, her life expectancy goes down. I don't give a damn if he's your long lost clone. I don't care what he thinks he's doing. If anyone gets in the way of us getting her back, they are not long for this world."

Hood shook his head, his brow set as he stared back at Whiskey. "You don't think I feel the same way? She's my fucking sister, Whiskey. But Ian is my brother. He's not some maniac. You and I know damn well not every person under the Kaiser is doing it of their own will. I'm telling you, we're on the same side."

Whiskey did little to hide his doubt. "Yeah, well. It sure don't seem that way." He turned away, resuming his search for anything of value.

Hood shook his head. "I got the Sheriff talking." He looked at the old man's contorted body. "That murderous bastard thought himself a godly man. He won't be stringing up any more innocent people in the name of god anymore. He told me the Kaiser wanted to bring me to the Church of the Epiphany in D.C.. Stands to reason if that's where they are headed, that's where Ian will be bringing Taylor."

49

Whiskey's demeanor softened, the weight of not knowing where to go lifting from his broad shoulders. "No kidding. How'd you get him to tell you that!?"

"I just kept talking to him. He sure as hell wanted to talk. Just a lonely bitter old man, I guess," Hood's eyes again were drawn to the crumpled body.

Whiskey clapped Hood on the shoulder. "Hell of a job, kid. I don't give a damn what this Kaiser thinks he's doin'. We're gonna get her back."

Hood grinned. "Took the words outta my mouth, kid." He said it in a mock-Whiskey voice. *You can fight. That's what you can do for those who died. Fight to save your sister, fight for anyone worth fighting for.* That's what they would do.

"Come on. We've got to take what we can and get moving," Whiskey had returned to his stoic demeanor as he turned to continue inspecting the contents of the portable, though clearly he carried himself with a renewed determination.

Hood exhaled deeply through his nose, thinking about the crew. There would be no more nights when the whole crew would pile into Hood and Whiskey and Taylor's house to drink and party and gamble until they'd watch the sun rise over the trees on the roof. The image of Lucky in his last moments, collapsing in the road was stuck in his mind. Lucky would never again drunkenly try to breakdance or hide in the bushes to scare Whiskey on patrol. Billy would never again sing inebriated guitar ballads about Kate Anderson's ass or about Lucky's made up sex stories or the day they stumble upon a wandering band of women to correct 'the ratio' of Clearwater. *They're all gone.* Hood's eyes welled, and he gnashed his teeth, trying to fight it back. *It doesn't make sense. How can people who were once so alive just disappear? Gone for good.*

Stop it. You can't think about them now. There will be a time and a place to mourn those you've lost, but it is not now.

Hood walked over to the old man's fading cigarette on the ground. He snuffed out the remaining embers with his foot.

"Sorry, Sheriff," Hood said quietly, squatting next to the body. "Maybe try not to be such a murderous bastard next time."

Hood picked up the old man's Glock. The black finish was worn down to metal on all the edges. He pulled back the slide and caught the bullet that came out of the chamber. The same bullet that could've ended up as shrapnel in his brain, under different circumstances.

"You deliverin' a eulogy?" Whiskey said impatiently. "We gotta get what we can and get out." He picked up the keys to the truck on the nearby table, holding them up and shaking them for Hood to see, a thanks-a-lot gesture. "The old man kept fuel out here somewhere."

Hood couldn't look away from the body. The slack-muscled look of the dead still unsettled Hood. The smell of urine was hard to ignore. The old man's face was stuck in mid- sentence, mouth open and a bloody chasm in the back of his head. Hood wanted to bring him back to life and kill the old man himself for what he did to the people he loved. But that anger quickly faded. *Is it his fault? Or is he just a depraved old man who's lost his mind? It's the Kaiser who did this. He built an empire of violence and control. But maybe that's just an inevitability. Remove law and government and someone will take over.*

"I know this bastard deserved it twice over," Hood scratched the stubble on his cheek. "But I still feel kinda bad for him."

"It's about time you get over that nonsense." Whiskey said, his words calm but the demand clear. "There's no room for that anymore."

Hood still crouched over the Sheriff's body. "Don't worry. I won't hesitate to waste any evil fucks trying to stop us."

He stared at the lifeless body, trying to accept it. A person one second, nothing the next. *You forfeited your right to live, you sick bastard. You and everyone else like you.*

"What, you wanna ask him out on a date? Or are you gonna do somethin'?"

Hood looked over at Whiskey, who was waiting for him to acknowledge the need to get moving. His jaw was set but his bushy

51

black eyebrows sat calm over his eyes. Hood tossed the Sheriff's pistol to Whiskey, who snatched it out of midair, glanced at it, and tossed it back. Hood didn't want to even carry it, vaguely afraid that it had absorbed all the horrible things the Sheriff had done over the years.

Hood walked over to the workbench and picked up his AK, along with two magazines taped together upside down for quick reloading. He unwound the leather strap that was wrapped loosely around the stock. His .38 with chest holster sat on the table too. He took off his hoodie and put the pistol back in its rightful place. He tucked the Sheriff's pistol into his backpack, throwing it over his shoulder.

"Looks like you're headed back home to D.C.," Whiskey said, picking live rounds out of a toolbox.

"Yeah, looks like it." D.C. was a wasteland now. It was home only in the nostalgia of his mind.

Hood walked outside the portable, arm resting on the AK slung across his chest. The sun had almost entirely disappeared behind the old dark shack and tall grain fields. A crow pecked at the corpse of one of the few wasters the Sheriff had kept around, skewered by one of Whiskey's crossbow bolts. The crow lifted his head as Hood got close and flew away in a flutter. The nerves of dancing so close to death came out in a shiver as Hood breathed deep.

The sunset sat on the horizon over the distant tree line the same way it had that day. He and Taylor had waited in D.C. for days after it was clear civilization was falling part. They held on to hope that Mom, Dad or Ian would come home. But once the D.C. survivors started to turn on each other, they'd fled into the country.

He could still remember the orange glow of the sunset lighting the plastic red gas can on the oil-stained concrete, as he sat deflated against an empty pump station, lost, directionless, with no idea what to tell Taylor when he got back to the car. Next thing he saw was Whiskey standing there, lowering his rifle. For some reason Whiskey had decided he was not a threat. Hood never asked him exactly why.

He could've shot him, or just walked away without ever saying a word to Hood. Now Whiskey was the closest thing to family Hood had left. It was an uneasy alliance between them at first—Hood was skeptical of Whiskey's intentions when he first took them in, and Whiskey never said much about it in his usual manner. But slowly Hood and Taylor had grown to love their new life in Clearwater. Hood had gained a sense of purpose like he had never had before. Through the camaraderie of fighting for Clearwater, Hood and Whiskey had developed a bond. But they were in unfamiliar territory now. Clearwater was gone.

Hunger rumbled in Hood's belly. He exhaled deeply as he looked out over the fallow field. Hood leaned his forearm on his rifle, the strap digging into his shoulder.

Hold on, sis. We're coming for you.

Chapter 5 – Strangers

The truck bounced on the cracked old road. The crates of food and supplies and tanks of gas all clattered loudly as the truck shook. They had more than enough supplies than the two of them would need. It was almost a hindrance, having so much valuable cargo. But they weren't about to leave it behind. So in the back it all sat, making too much noise and reminding Hood of everything they had just lost. His eyes still itched. The images from the destroyed town still hung fresh in his mind. It was surreal to go back and see everything they had built so quiet, so devoid of life. Instead of kids running in the streets and townspeople working in their fields, Clearwater was the smell of ash in the wind, burned down houses and bodies, so many bodies. Bodies that days ago were people who sweat and made jokes and held each other. It seemed that some of the townspeople got away, but it was hard to be sure. They didn't have time to mourn, to bury, even to search the whole town over. They had to save Taylor, and time was not their ally. They had no idea how long the Kaiser would stay in the ruins of D.C..

Whiskey's shotgun sat in between him and Hood in the cab of the truck. Hood left his AK between his knees, barrel pointed up, safety on.

"It's hard to believe it's all gone." Hood's arm hung out the window, the barely visible scrub on the side of the road passing by in the dark. "We didn't even get to bury them."

"We're not talkin' about it," Whiskey kept his eyes forward, urging the truck along faster than his normal cautious pace.

"You just want to forget that it all happened?"

"That's not what I said."

Hood clenched his fist, digging his nails into his palm before resting his thumb on the barrel of his rifle. He wanted to put it all out of his mind, stay focused on what they had to do. But the drive was long and there was little else to think about. Even the house the three of them called home, burned to the ground.

"The Kaiser has his whole damn empire. How are we going to do this?" Hood asked, leaning back into his headrest and staring at the plastic gray interior ceiling.

Whiskey rubbed his beard. "Very, very carefully."

Hood looked over at Whiskey, who still stared straight ahead. Hood shook his head with a disbelieving grin at the absurdity of it all. Whiskey looked trapped in his own thoughts.

"This is fucking crazy." Hood focused on the arc of the headlights cutting a path into the darkness, illuminating the leaf-covered road. "But it could be worse."

Whiskey snorted. "How do you figure?"

"It could have been Lucky who rescued me." Laughter started to well up in Hood. It was all wrong. He didn't want to laugh, he wanted to cry, he wanted to burn away the memories of the crew that were stuck in the forefront of his mind, memories he wanted to hold on to, memories that brought the pain of knowing so many people he loved had died so suddenly. "In which case he'd be sitting there right now, swearing up and down about how he once saw a smokin' hot babe dragging a dog with no legs around on a leash."

Whiskey's laugh was deep and unexpected, still focused on the road. "How could you even say something like that?"

Because that is who he was. Hood closed his eyes. *They all deserved to live long lives, and they're dead. The Kaiser kept me alive, like I deserved it and they didn't. I wanted to run away from reality, wanted to pretend I didn't have to kill, wanted to pretend we could take and take and take and no retribution would come.*

Whiskey itched his elbow, hand on the wheel. He wore a faint, melancholy smile and his eyes looked far away. "Every goddamned story he somehow works a smokin' hot babe into. He could be talking about his grandpa's funeral and he'd start with how this smokin' hot babe served him coffee, or instead of a pastor there was a smokin' hot babe givin' the sermon."

"So dis' one chick, she takes me home to her parents' house, and I swear, she wants me to read her a bedtime story while we're doin' it, so I'm like, OKAY." Hood mocked, gesturing excessively with his hands and pretending to smoke a cigarette.

Whiskey bellowed, holding his wrist in front of his mouth. "I don't know what's worse, If he made that story up, or if he didn't."

"That fucking kid," Hood was unable to stop himself from smiling. What the hell would Lucky say to him now? He knew exactly what he'd say: *Yeah, real great, Rob. Keep mopin' and feelin' bad. You're a real piece of shit for survivin' in this fucked up world. Or maybe, you should find that punk ass Kaiser and make him a fuckin' cheese grater for me. Maybe you should find some sweet thing and ride her into the sunset. I know you're one of those one woman dudes. You're one of those penny loafer dads. That's cool. But I'll be fucked if I got lit up just to see you sit around and feel bad.*

The laughter died down and the only sound to fill the cab was the hum of the engine. Hood bowed his head, his hands resting just below his knees. *How many people has the Kaiser done this to?*

"We have to kill him," Hood stated. "Or this will never stop."

Whiskey clicked his tongue.

"There will always be people like the Kaiser. We got only one thing to do. Get Taylor back."

"Yeah, of course," Hood said. His jaw was set so hard his teeth started to ache. He worked his mouth, trying to relax.

"We'll be lucky if we don't die just trying to save her. It's only us, here. We're not saviors or revolutionaries, kid."

I don't want to be either. I just want to live in peace with the people I love. The people I have left.

Hood reached up and grabbed the roof handle by the door. The truck had begun to shake again as it rumbled down the broken road. Whiskey rolled down the window and spat. The cold night air whistled into the cab. It smelled like dirt and ash. In the dark the emptiness around the road seemed to go on forever. *I lost everyone I knew in my old life. But in my mind they could still possibly be alive out there. I didn't have to see their bodies.*

A loud bang reverberated through the truck, and the front right side sagged considerably. Whiskey cursed, slowing the truck to a stop.

"We better hope there's no one around." Whiskey turned off the headlights, and they were swallowed whole by black.

"And pray this thing has a spare." Whiskey finished, getting out of the truck and walking towards the bed. The weak cabin lights turned on with the door open, but it didn't offer much outside of the truck.

Hood got out, eyes searching for danger, though it was futile. He couldn't see a damned thing. There was no moonlight, and they were out in the open. He looked down at the dark shape of the weathered, deflated front right tire. "Do we have any flashlights with us?" He said.

"Looking. Can't see shit."

Hood leaned back in to the truck and checked the glove compartment. An empty pack of cigarettes and some papers fell out. Title and registration. Underneath was a picture. It was the Sheriff, some years ago, arm around a young boy who shared his features. A son, a nephew maybe, in front of this very truck in a nicely paved driveway. It had a shiny dark green paint job and the sun reflected off of it. Hood tapped his teeth together lightly. The look on the Sheriff's face was one Hood hadn't seen in the depraved old man he met. It was calm, a momentary contentment.

Whiskey rapped on the back window of the cab.

"What are you doing?" He grunted through the window.

Hood put the picture back in the glove box. "Nothing in here."

"Well, we have a jack and a spare. Doesn't look to be in great shape though." Whiskey jumped off the bed of the truck. "Not going to do us much good if we can't see anything."

Hood stepped out of the cab. The cold wind roared past him. It had the smell of rain.

"We better figure this out fast." Hood said. "I think a storm is coming."

"I could turn the headlights back on." Whiskey said, shaking his head. "But it won't give us much light and we'll be shining like the sun."

"Yeah, well, I don't--" Hood stopped, turning his head to the road in front of the car.

Hearing a sound, he held his finger up to Whiskey.

It was faint, something scraping the dirt. Footfalls.

Hood crouched behind the truck door and pulled his Taurus .38 special out of its holster. Whiskey drew his Glock 9mm and crouched down behind the truck itself.

The footsteps grew closer. But they were off, somehow. Slow, a careless shuffle.

"Get the headlights," Hood whispered.

Whiskey crawled into the cab and flicked on the lights. With the craggy road illuminated, they saw a man in worn slacks and a dusty button up shirt and jacket slowly moving towards them. He had a short, thick beard and looked only at the ground as he approached.

"This is a trap," Whiskey growled. "Shoot him."

"Show me your hands!" Hood shouted, standing up, still next to the car. The man lifted one hand to shield his eyes from the light.

"Take me to them." His voice cracked, and he kept shuffling forward.

"Just shoot him!" Whiskey shouted. He slid out of the cab and looked frantically at the hill to the left of the car that was shrouded in darkness.

"Stop!" Hood shouted. "Get down on the ground!"

The man smiled a faint smile, no longer shielding his eyes from the light. His eyes were bright red and he looked blistered and sick. Probably irradiated. His arms were down and he continued to move towards Hood.

"Take me to them," the man said. "I just want to see them one more time."

"Just fucking stop!" Hood shouted, his blood racing. His eyes itched from the dust, though he didn't dare close them. He could feel the sweat from his palms on the knurled grip of his pistol. He took aim at the man and started to squeeze the trigger, but kept it from firing. *He's not a killer. He doesn't even look like he knows where he is.*

The man shuffled closer. He looked to be in his fifties, his receding hairline wild and unkempt. The wind brought the smell of sweat and dirt and blood.

"Please," the man said, tears appearing on his face, cleaning paths through the dirt and sweat.

Two gunshots cracked the air. Whiskey had opened fire. The man fell down to the dirt. Whiskey ran around the truck, gun still in hand. He looked down at the body, then at Hood.

"What the hell is wrong with you? If that guy was bait for a trap we'd be *dead*," Whiskey shouted at Hood. "I told you we don't got any more room for hesitation, kid."

They looked at each other momentarily before searching the darkness for motion. The wind blew and the door of the truck creaked as it closed slightly. Hood put his gun away.

"It wasn't a trap," Hood said.

"But it sure as hell could have been."

"Just someone at the end of his rope. I'm not just going to shoot everyone I see from now on, Whiskey."

Whiskey shook his head. "They ain't gonna have a fuckin' sign on 'em that says 'bad guy.'" He put away his pistol forcefully. He glared at Hood, then back at the dead man. "Here's to guessing wrong." He pulled his flask from his pocket and drank. He screwed the cap back on, and knelt next to the body.

The dead man's face was hard to distinguish in the shadows cast by the ambient light of the headlights. Whiskey closed the man's eyes and stood up, scanning the area. Hood recognized the worn, unexpressive look on Whiskey's face. It wasn't blame, or self-doubt. He did what he had to in order to survive. It was the countenance of exhaustion, of being sick of having to live like this.

The soft patter of pebbles and dirt sliding down the hill to the left of the truck drew their attention. They looked at each other, and Hood darted quickly ahead up to the hill, pistol in hand. He checked back with Whiskey, who had his gun pointed over the hood of the truck. He nodded. Hood took a deep breath, and ran up and over the hill, sliding down the other side with gun raised. His eyes hadn't adjusted, so he crouched down close to the ground and waited. He thought he saw a shape move in front of him along the ridge.

"Get on the ground if you don't want to die!" Hood boomed. His heart raced, and the itchy feeling of being watched crept up his neck and over him, raising every hair. The wind blew hard, whipping dust and dirt and still smelling of rain. His grip tightened on the handle of his pistol.

"I'm on the ground." It was a woman's voice.

Hood was startled, and lowered his gun for a moment before raising it once more.

"Do you have a weapon?" he asked.

Silence.

He thought maybe Whiskey was right about the trap after all. This was awfully elaborate, though.

"No," she replied.

Hood hesitated. "Come into the light."

He backed up over the hill, keeping his pistol trained on her.

She followed him with her hands up.

He stood in the headlights and faced the road, watching as she became illuminated. She walked casually and stood a bit closer to him than he expected.

She was pretty. Beautiful, even. Brown hair that hung just above her shoulders framed her delicate face. She didn't make eye contact but Hood got the feeling she didn't miss a detail. She wasn't overly skinny, like most starving wastelanders. She had tight, womanly curves that weren't hidden under her black jeans and grey zip-up leather jacket. Hood thought he was dreaming. There was no way this was real.

"Hi," she said simply. "Please don't shoot me."

"Uh." Hood scratched his head, gun still in hand. "What are you doing here?"

"Surviving," she said simply. "I'm a bit more resourceful than the other clueless wanderers out there." She nodded at the dead man on the ground.

She wore weathered, plain boots, gloves, and a red handkerchief tied around her neck for protecting her face, presumably, and a beanie. It was strange how calm she seemed. They had run into desperate or dangerous wanderers and dying vagrants out in the plains before. She was nothing like any of them. He seriously doubted she'd just wander here by herself. There had to be much more to her story than that.

Whiskey leaned against the truck, staring at her. No one seemed to know what to say.

"I'm Kerry. Nice to meet you." She extended her hand to Hood. Pure blue eyes looked calmly into him.

"I'm Rob, and this is John—er, Whiskey. You can call me Hood though," he said, reaching out to shake her hand. It felt strange, uncomfortable even. He hadn't shaken a stranger's hand in a long time. Her hand felt different, smaller. He glanced at it in the light as she pulled it back. She was missing most of her pinky finger.

"What are you doing out here alone?" Whiskey said, moving forward from the truck.

"Following that guy." She pointed at the dead man casually.

"Why were you following him?" Whiskey said. Hood itched at the scruff on his jaw, unable to sort out his thoughts.

"Safest way to travel," she said, putting down her backpack. "I always follow people. If something bad is going to happen, it will usually happen to them first."

"That's not what I meant," Whiskey said.

"Where are you coming from?" Hood interjected.

"Ah, that's a long story." She took off her beanie, her shoulder length hair coming out, some of it rising from the static electricity. She smoothed it down with on hand. "This is obviously not the best time." She paused. "Where are you guys headed? Do you think I might be able to catch a ride?"

Hood and Whiskey looked at each other. Whiskey's brow furrowed and he stared purposefully at Hood.

"You don't know who we are, where we're going. You're not worried about any of that?" Hood asked, feeling strange for stating the blatantly obvious.

"Well, I figure you didn't shoot me on sight, and it's pretty clear you guys aren't slavers."

Whiskey laughed. "Wandering the wilderness, alone, not a care in the world, asking two guys who just shot someone for a ride." He shook his head. "Now *this* has to be a trap."

She shrugged. "It's complicated how I ended up here." She paused. "And I saw what happened. I would've done the same in your shoes. You can't trust wanderers out here."

"That's exactly my point," Whiskey growled.

Hood put his gun away. "Do you have a flashlight?"

"I got a lighter." She patted the pocket of her jeans.

Whiskey gave Hood a disapproving look.

It's not like we couldn't use the help, he wanted to say aloud.

"We could make a torch," Hood said instead. He stared at Whiskey with a wry smile. *Remember who we are, Whiskey. Not everyone is our enemy.*

Whiskey frowned, stepping forward to face her. "Turn around, spread your feet and put your hands on your head," he barked. She complied. He patted her down aggressively.

"Don't get any ideas," she quipped. The nervousness in her voice belied her joke.

"The only goddamn idea I have is to shoot you. Give me your backpack." Whiskey grabbed the backpack, produced a pair of handcuffs from a Velcro pouch of his flak jacket and cuffed her hands behind her back. He walked to the back of the truck. Hood followed to get the jack and spare. Whiskey was staring at Kerry and hadn't put away his gun.

"Is this necessary?" Kerry asked. "I think I'm being pretty reasonable here!"

Whiskey ignored her.

She reached her hands down and stepped over the cuffs to get her hands in front of her body when he wasn't looking. Hood shook his head at her, sure his expression was beyond incredulous. She looked back at him and shrugged, as if to say 'I don't know what to do either.' *This girl is either very dangerous or has been very sheltered.*

Whiskey got an old yardstick from the back of the truck and wrapped a cloth around the end, dousing the cloth in gas.

Whiskey stuck the makeshift torch in the ground beside the blown-out tire. Kerry reached into her pocket with her hands cuffed together, and produced a zippo. She handed it to Whiskey, who looked considerably annoyed she had moved her cuffed hands to the front. Flames jumped up as he lit the torch. Whiskey got to setting up the jack. Hood got the cross wrench and started loosening the lug nuts. Whiskey paused to toss the lighter back to Kerry.

"Where are you guys headed?" Kerry said as she caught the zippo with both hands, before pulling a strand of hair out of her mouth.

"Don't ask questions. Don't even talk." Whiskey said, voicing his irritation from under the truck. He pulled himself out from underneath the truck and started cranking the old portable spring jack. The suspension of the truck creaked.

Hood stood up, cross wrench in hand, wiping his brow with his forearm.

"We're going north. That's about all I'll say." Hood exhaled, looking at her. "Where are you headed?"

She wore a blank expression. "I don't know anymore," she said, solemn. She looked away to watch Whiskey as he worked.

Hood waited to see if she would say anything else. She glanced back at him momentarily and managed a faint smile. Hood crouched down to remove the now-loose lug nuts by hand and take off the wheel. No one spoke and the wind continued to blow sporadically. Hood glanced over at Kerry as she knelt next to the dead man's body, checking him with her cuffed hands for anything of value. She moved away from the body empty-handed, crouching next to the truck and staring at the dead man's unshaven face. It began to rain.

Hood couldn't shake the thought that she seemed all too comfortable in handcuffs.

Chapter 6 – Dissent

Hood watched the rain water drip from Whiskey's short hair. He stared intently through the windshield as the old wiper blades struggled to clear off the torrents. Between the two of them, Kerry was asleep, her head leaned back against the seat and her cuffed hands lying in her lap.

Whiskey flicked a glance over at her, then to Hood, who raised his eyebrows inquisitively. She lay asleep, lithe and lazy, wobbling slightly with the truck as it shook. Whiskey's forearm worked as he squeezed the steering wheel, his attention on the road. Hood waved his hand in front of her face, no reaction. He shrugged.

"This doesn't seem strange to you?" Whiskey whispered.

"I'm not going to complain about it," Hood said simply.

Whiskey shook his head, keeping his voice low. "She's sleepin'."

"So?"

Whiskey turned his attention from the road for a moment to cast a serious look at Hood.

I know. If it were me in her shoes I don't think I'd be sleeping. But who says that's a bad thing?

Hood lifted up his left leg onto the dashboard, drumming on his knee with his fingertips. The predawn light painted the world an inky blue. Slowly the rain let up until the wiper blades squeaked loudly against the dry windshield, prompting Whiskey to flick them off. The road was smoother but the truck still rocked back and forth from time to time. The surrounding area was nothing but defunct farm fields and huge swaths of trees. The air smelled like wet grass.

"She's exhausted, probably." Hood's voice was just above a whisper.

Whiskey chortled. "I know why you're okay with this."

"Pff. Ever occur to you I just want to help her out?" Hood retorted quietly.

"Yeah, you want to help her out of something, all right."

Hood laughed, struggling to keep his voice down. The cab of the truck grew quiet again save for the hum of the engine and the squeaking of the suspension. Kerry remained comatose, her soft rhythmic breathing of someone deep in slumber. Hood couldn't deny his attraction to the girl. It was a dangerous way to feel about a stranger. He wanted to believe she was just a good person trying to survive. And that was precisely the problem.

"We're not a taxi service and we ain't headed into something pretty." Whiskey switched hands on the steering wheel, leaning his left arm on the driver side door.

"Maybe we could use her help."

"You want to drag her into this shit?"

"What, now you're looking out for her?"

Whiskey said nothing. He glanced over at her in suspicion of her sleep.

A wry smile crept over Hood's face."You look fat and your hair is gross," he said to her.

She didn't move, continuing to sway gently with the movements of the truck.

"See?" Hood said to Whiskey. "One hundred percent asleep."

"What was that?" Kerry murmured with her eyes still closed, turning halfway to rest the side of her head on the seat.

"Nothing."

"Liar," she said. She shifted to get more comfortable. "Shouldn't talk about someone while they're asleep."

The sky grew brighter and the cab stayed quiet. The line of inquiry clearly didn't pique Kerry's interest because she quickly slid back to sleep. The terrain outside was still wide open, dotted with scrub grass and a distant abandoned house and silo.

"I don't trust her," Whiskey said, eyes on her as if he wanted her to wake up and hear him say it. He turned his gaze back to the road, digging around behind the seat with his free hand, switching hands on the wheel to check both sides. He produced a carpenter's pencil, making a scribbling motion. Hood opened the glove compartment, digging for paper. He pulled out the first sheet he felt and passed it to Whiskey. He wrote on the center of the steering wheel, eyes darting back and forth from the paper to the road. Eventually he passed the paper to Hood.

It read:

If we find out she works for someone I will kill her

The writing was soft and scrawled and he could see where the indents of the steering wheel were. He knew Whiskey was right in one sense; she could be a huge liability. But she also could be someone just trying to survive, like they were. Maybe both. Either way, Hood wasn't going to let Whiskey kill her.

Hood crumpled up the paper and tossed it out the window. "That's not who we are."

Whiskey ran his free hand up the back of his head, and sighed.

"We don't have the luxury of conscience anymore, kid."

"We're no different than the Kaiser if we start down this road," Hood said. He gnawed his bottom lip as he stared out the passenger side window. A green SUV with shattered windows and a wheel-less, empty U-haul sat inert on the side of the road, long since abandoned by some unlucky souls.

"We don't have a goddamned chance to save Taylor if we don't go down this road. After everything that's happened, I ain't gonna sit here and argue with you about how high of a goddamn pedestal we need to sit on--"

"Whiskey... WHISKEY, THE ROAD!" Hood gripped the door-handle, shouting as they careened towards a downed telephone pole in the road. He stomped his feet against the floor reflexively, trying to hit a nonexistent brake pedal and brace himself.

Whiskey jammed on the real brakes, swerving to the left lane. Kerry was thrown forward out of her seat and braced herself on the dashboard. The truck screeched to a halt. The telephone pole was ripped from its wires, and lay half in the road.

Whiskey whipped his head around and pulled out his pistol, looking for any sign of wasters. Hood grabbed his rifle from its place at his feet. The seconds dragged on with Hood's thumping heart as they waited for signs of life. None came.

Whiskey breathed out through his nose, wearing the pent-up adrenaline on his face.

Kerry rested her forehead on the dash for a moment before sitting up.

"God *damn man,* what the fuck?" Kerry shouted at Whiskey. Hood smelled the stench of burning rubber coming in through the vents. Whiskey kept his eyes on the road and said nothing, starting to creep the car forward into the other lane to get around the fallen pole. A time-weathered sedan peppered with bullet holes had lodged itself into the base of it, telephone wires snapped and sagging with the dark wooden mast as it hung low.

"Jesus, what, did you fall asleep at the wheel? How did you not see that?" she continued, glaring at Whiskey.

"Take it easy, it's just a damn telephone pole," Whiskey grumbled.

"The fucking thing nearly speared us." she said, dropping her hands onto her denim-clad thighs before replacing one on her forehead and exhaling deeply. "Just focus on the road. Whatever happens, I am *not* going to die in a crash."

Silence returned in the cab of the truck save for the rumble of the engine. Kerry seemed legitimately shook up by the near miss. Hood thought her reaction was a good sign. It felt like a genuine display of emotion. *You want to believe she's like you. That's she's just a regular person trying to survive. Because she's beautiful and you want her.* Hood lowered the butt of his rifle back down to the floor. There was nothing here. *This road, this land has been long abandoned, just empty space the Kaiser could claim as his on a map. Don't get caught up in all this. Whatever she is, you can't focus on it now. Everything we do is for saving Taylor. Whiskey is right, if she gets in the way of that. . .*

"So you two on your own, or. . .?" Kerry broke the silence in the cab.

"Yeah," Hood replied.

She turned and looked out the back window, rapping on it softly with her knuckles. "That's a lot of supplies for just two people. You sure it's just you two?"

"Yes." Hood repeated.

Her skeptical gaze lingered on him for a moment.

"So you're just--"

"Stop asking questions." Whiskey snapped. "Better yet, stop talking altogether."

"You can't fool me. Act like a tough guy all you want, I know you're good people," She said, her voice relaxed, a smooth timbre to it.

Whiskey snorted in response.

"The fact that I'm sitting here unscathed is proof of that."

The cabin got quiet. *She has us there. But why was she so cavalier about it all? Maybe it was a defense mechanism, acting like it was all no big deal.*

"And you. . ." she said, scrutinizing Hood.

He purposefully didn't look her way. *To hell with her analysis.* "I don't think I've met a guy as nice as you in a long, long time."

He turned to scan her gaze for intent.

She shrugged slightly, in a 'what-can-I-say?' gesture. It was such a strange observation, and he wasn't sure it was a compliment the way things were now. How could she assume that? He hadn't heard anyone say that about him since he was young.

"In fact, It puzzles me how you are not dead," she concluded.

69

Whiskey was staring a hole right through him over her shoulder.

"Some people are just lucky," Hood said, keeping a blank expression on his face.

"So you say," she said. "I don't think it's luck."

She sat back in her seat, hands on her legs again. She looked back at the bed full of supplies. "Considering you guys have a bit of surplus for two people, do you think I could have some food? I haven't eaten much these past few days."

"Don't be looking to make yourself comfortable," Whiskey said.

"Is he always like this?" She said to Hood.

Hood blinked, unsure of how to handle her excessive familiarity.

"Why do they call you Whiskey anyway? Guys love making up bad nicknames and never explaining them."

Whiskey didn't dignify her with a response. This was possibly the most annoyed Hood had ever seen him. Whiskey might just shoot her for the peace and quiet. Why was she talking so much? They certainly weren't asking her anything. Maybe that was the ploy. Deflect the attention away from herself.

"Why are you here?" The words came out more forcefully than Hood intended.

"What?" She said, raising her eyebrow. "What do you mean? I asked if I could get a lift with you guys."

"Yeah, Why? What do you want? Where are you coming from?" Hood said, calmer this time.

She shook her head. "I'm not coming from anything good."

"You have to tell us."

She bit her bottom lip, picking at a small tear in the knee of her jeans with her pointer finger. Her nails were surprisingly well kept, but dirty.

"My family—my dad, my two brothers and I, joined up with these survivors. We had left home to find food and they offered us some in exchange for my brothers and my dad agreeing to help them fight. When they left on a raid, they came back without my dad or my brothers, and they. . . I had to escape. I managed to get away. Since then I've been heading towards Richmond. I know a guy there."

"Who is it? Why don't you still want to go there?" Hood asked, looking over at Whiskey to see if he wanted to start his own line of questioning. His expression was that of extreme skepticism.

"He's my ex, if you must know. I'm not even sure he's alive. Or if it's even a good idea." She let out a labored breath. "When I saw how you guys at least showed some remorse after you shot that desperate guy, I decided I'd take my chances. It's a long walk to Richmond. After all, you weren't looting his corpse. It was a risk, but it was that or be alone."

Hood stared at her. "Why didn't you just tell us that?"

She gathered her hair and pulled it over to one side of her head. "I don't know." Her gaze looked empty as she stared out the window, sinking into thought. Hood continued to watch her, demanding a better response. She shrugged, turning away from him. "It's painful to talk about how bad things are."

"Yeah," Hood looked down at his rifle. "There's a lot of that going on now."

"I won't let it hold me down. I'm still alive for some reason."

Hood smiled. "Yeah, to piss Whiskey off."

Her laugh had a melodic quality to it.

"My true calling." She smirked and looked over at Whiskey.

"Nothing? You just Driving Miss Daisy over there?" She said, waving at him.

"It's a sad story," Whiskey said, his emphasis on the word 'story'.

"You don't trust me." Kerry shook her head, a look of acceptance on her face. "I get it."

Hood didn't know what to say to her. His thoughts were wrapped up in trying to decipher her story. *If she was lying, why?*

"If you can't loosen up though, you might as well have died when the bombs went off." She crossed her arms. "Just 'cause it's the apocalypse everyone hates fun," she grumbled.

Hood laughed, reminded of his old life before the fall. Images of hanging out with friends in parking lots, laughing, talking trash and

71

drinking all their problems away.

"That's the most ridiculous shit I've ever heard." he said.

"See? That's more like it," she said, smiling at him. "Feels good."

Damn that's a pretty smile. Hood rubbed the back of his head and watched the road curve along the rusted old guard rail. The sun was rising, and the sky was blue. Whiskey drummed the steering wheel lightly with the carpenter pencil. Kerry sat staring straight ahead, content with her pot-stirring for now. *What are you all about?* It was hard to make sense of how she could end up here, with them.

And what if people are looking for her?

Chapter 7 – Crossing

The three of them stood in front of the truck, staring blankly at the broken stone bridge ahead. Whiskey crossed his arms and spat. Hood scratched the back of his head and turned around to look at the truck. His mind itched with impatience, knowing the longer it took to get them to D.C., the more Taylor was at risk. He felt the same stress emanating from Whiskey. Hood felt at least some measure of comfort knowing Ian was there with her. Whiskey might not understand yet, but there is someone looking out for her within the Kaiser's empire.

Two days of driving, and it felt like they'd gone farther backwards then they had forwards. Some roads had been purposefully destroyed, others were cut off by endless rows of weather-beaten cars long abandoned in traffic jams. They were lucky the truck hadn't gotten stuck on any of their off-road detours. The only positive was that with each day Whiskey seemed to soften to Kerry a bit more. If she was here for any sinister purpose, she was doing a terrible job of it. She didn't seem to care where they went. She just seemed content to be there. And Whiskey wasn't blind to that.

"Well, shit," Kerry said flatly at the sight of the broken bridge. She and Whiskey did not mask their frustration at the idea of another detour. Hood wasn't even sure where they would go from here.

Whiskey sighed. "Might as well get something to eat," he said, turning to walk to the back of the truck. He stopped mid-stride, pulling a key out of his pocket and grabbing Kerry's cuffed wrists. She scanned his face, a look of relief and surprise. He didn't look at her, deftly peeling off the handcuffs and tucking them into a pocket of his flak jacket.

She rubbed her wrists, looking at Hood for confirmation that that had actually just happened. He shrugged, smiling.

"Why did you do that?" She called after Whiskey.

"You want 'em back on?" He replied.

"Hell no. God, it feels so good just being able to spread your arms!" She stretched her hands wide and reached up for the sky, standing on her toes. Hood watched her move, enjoying her stretch almost as much as she was.

"Whatever you're doin' here, you're not trying to kill us." Whiskey rummaged through the back of the truck. "So you might as well help us."

Kerry was beaming. "Can you believe this guy?"

"Win the crowd. Win your freedom." Hood said dramatically. *That's gonna go over her head.* But he wanted to try it anyway. He and Ian used to watch that movie religiously. Quoting it was like a second form of communication.

Kerry blinked. "What?"

"Nevermind. From Gladiator. It is to guys what The Notebook is to girls."

"I never saw either of them. I guess I won't ever."

"S'aright. Come on, lets get some food."

The sun shone down on the broken bridge, while the wind blew fast and cold across the river.

"How do you figure that happened?" Kerry said to Whiskey. She pulled her hair back and tied it up to keep it from the wind.

"I don't know," Whiskey said, both arms digging into a crate in the bed of the truck.

"What do you think we should do?"

"I don't know."

Hood walked up alongside her. She sported a devious grin, her

attention still on Whiskey rummaging through the bed of the truck.
"You hotshots gonna point your big guns at the bridge and demand
it put itself back together or else?"

"Oh my *God*, shut up! We will figure something out!" Whiskey
yelled, standing up straight.

"Relax, cowboy. I'm just making light of the situation," she said,
tapping her fingers on the side of the truck, a series of dull metallic
thuds. Whiskey reached into a box from the back of the truck and
tossed her a granola bar in shiny packaging.

"Here, eat."

"Aw, is someone finally warming up to me?"

"No, it just guarantees at least a few seconds of silence," Whiskey
said, tossing another one to Hood who snatched it out of the air.
Hood laughed, and Whiskey couldn't hide a slight smirk.

Hood devoured the entire bar in short order, chewing a mouthful
of sweet granola as he opened the passenger door and pulled a map
out of the glove compartment. Hood dropped into the passenger
seat, inspecting it. The cool river air swirling through the truck
wanted him to relax, but the broken bridge out the windshield was
another reminder of brutal reality that just getting the chance to save
Ian and Taylor was a longshot. Whiskey walked up to the open door,
leaning on the roof with his forearm.

"The big crossing at 95 has been under Kaiser control for a long
time. We know that," Hood said. He ran his knuckle across his
mouth in contemplation. "We have to go further west."

"It's way out of the way, and we don't know if those roads are
even passable." Whiskey frowned, gesturing to the country roads
stretching far inland to the west.

They both stared at the map in silence. The wind blew through the
cab. The door of the truck started to close on Whiskey but Hood kept
it open with his foot.

"Well," Hood paused. "We don't have a lot of options."

Whiskey shook his head.

"I don't like it." He looked around at the outside world for signs of life. "We're gonna be vulnerable as hell further out west. It's deeper into the Kaiser's territory and we have no idea what the area is like now."

"Well, I don't see what else we can do," Hood said, folding up the map. "We can't leave the truck behind."

Hood got out of the truck, Whiskey moving out of the doorway to let him pass. Whiskey stood there, frozen, looking over at the supplies in the back. "It'll take too long to walk there. We don't know how long the Kaiser plans on stayin' in D.C."

Hood looked out at the bridge, then back at the truck. He bit his bottom lip in consternation. "Then let's drive across the bridge."

Whiskey stared at him. "Huh?"

Hood pulled a cord of heavy rope and a briquette of charcoal from the back of the truck. He walked over to the old mortar-and-stone bridge, sizing up the damage. Only part of it was destroyed. It still managed to span the river in the simplest sense of the word. On the left side there was a stone wall with guardrail implanted atop it, but the right side had shattered and large chunks of the bridge sat jutting out of the river thirty feet below. Where before it was able to fit one lane of traffic on either side easily, now only a part of the left lane stood. Whiskey followed Hood to the bridge. Hood placed the end of the rope against the wall on the left hand side and then laid it across to the narrowest point of the collapsed side, marking the length with the charcoal. It was definitely shorter than the wheelbase of the truck.

Using the same end of rope, he had Whiskey hold it in place where the narrowest area of the gap started, and measured the length of the narrow space, marking it with the charcoal. It was significantly longer than the first measurement. This would be a challenge. Hood backed up and looked at the broken bridge. From where he stood it looked as if something had taken a big bite out of the right side, the way the stone crumbled into the river. *Someone probably tried to blow this thing to keep people away and did a terrible job.*

Kerry had been standing at the start of the bridge watching them work. Hood and Whiskey walked back towards her and the truck.

"So?" she asked, arms folded.

"So it's going to get interesting." Hood said simply. "Just from eyeballing it, it looks like there will be a few feet where one side of the truck will be entirely off the ground," he said, looking back at the bridge. He held up the end of the rope, gesturing towards her. "The measurements will tell us for sure."

"What do you mean, off the ground?" She said, taking a step in front of Hood as he started to walk.

"That's the interesting part," he said with a smile, and walked backed to the truck.

She just stood there, staring at the truck, then back at the bridge.

Whiskey leaned towards her as he walked by. "What, no snappy jokes?"

She glared at him for a moment as he kept walking, a smirk on his face.

She took a few steps towards the truck, the wind blowing the few unbound strands of hair into her eyelashes. She pulled them away.

"Who's going to drive it across?"

Hood was half in the cab of the truck, but leaned out to shout back. "You are!"

Kerry stood still and stared blankly at the truck before briskly walking over to the both of them.

"This thing has locking differentials on it right?" Hood glanced over at Whiskey for affirmation. He nodded.

"Yeah. Funny, I didn't take the Sheriff to be the type to go mudding."

"I think this was for his son," Hood said, looking down at the worn bed of the truck. "Found a picture of them in the glove compartment."

Whiskey remained stoic, presumably thinking the same thing as Hood: some people just lose it in the face of so much death. Whiskey turned his head, looking out over the rocky hill that sloped down to the river. Whiskey didn't talk to Hood much about his past, but

77

Hood got the feeling he had lost loved ones.

"What if I say no?" Kerry interjected, wearing an expression of defiance.

"Too bad," Hood said. "We need you to do it. We will have our hands full trying to keep this beast from falling into the river." Hood slapped the side of the truck with a metallic thud.

"Uh-uh. No way. I won't do it. This is insane!" The tone of her words fell somewhere between standing her ground and pleading for reason.

Hood and Whiskey exchanged a prolonged glance. Hood winked at him with the eye turned away from Kerry, and a smile flickered on his face. Whiskey closed the door of the truck, and they both turned to face her. *Whiskey will enjoy this.*

"You don't have a choice," Hood pulled his .38 out from under his hoodie and pointed it at her. Whiskey had his pistol in hand too. They were motionless.

"Whoa, hey. Wait. What's this?" She said, holding up her palms and stepping back.

"Just do as we tell you and everything will be fine," Whiskey said, stepping forward. "Don't make us use force."

"What? What the hell has gotten into you two?" She shouted, continuing to backpedal. They kept pace with slow steps.

"We won't hesitate to kill you right here." Whiskey took a step towards her. "You know too much."

"What!? I don't know shit about you guys!" Her chest rose and fell with panicked breaths.

"I'm sorry. We must destroy you—" Hood cracked and Whiskey slipped into laughter.

"Destroy her? What the hell was that?" He bellowed.

She laughed nervously with them, putting one hand on her hips and running the other over the top of her head. Hood was doubled over with his hands on his knees, pistol in his right hand.

"You should've seen your face," Whiskey said. "Such gold."

Hood was a bit surprised Whiskey had run with the joke

considering the situation, but it was good to hear him laugh. It had been awhile. At the least, it meant Whiskey was confident the situation was not outside their control.

"I thought you were going to cry," Hood said, holding the back of his neck. "Ah, so worth it."

"That's not funny!" She punched Hood in the arm. He grinned at her expense and walked to the back of the truck.

"Come on. Whatever happened to having fun with the apocalypse?" Hood said, putting the gun away. "Just drive the damn truck. I promise you'll be fine."

"How can you be sure of that?" She said.

"I can't, really." Hood said with a shrug. "But we don't have much choice. We gotta get this beast across." Hood slapped the body of the truck with a hollow thud. "Whiskey is going to stand guard to make sure we don't get gunned down with our pants down. And I'm gonna be the one keeping the truck from falling into the abyss."

Kerry looked down at her feet and bit her lip, kicking idly at the dusty ground. "I'm sorry. I'm not gonna do it."

Hood rubbed his head in annoyance. "Come on. You got this, EZ game. Time to go badass on us. You're gonna be like the Danica Patrick of broken-bridge-truck-drivers."

"I'll do anything else you need me to do. I don't care. Just not that." She wore a nervous expression, her eyebrows raised.

Hood walked back to the truck and pulled out another coil of rope. "Don't worry, the gasoline in the truck alone is worth more than your life. We won't risk losing that."

"That's not very reassuring!" she shouted.

"Kidding!" Hood shouted back. "Everything will be fine!"

She stood motionless in the road, looking profoundly uncomfortable. They needed her to drive, there wasn't much way around it. Hood had to convince her. He didn't think she'd dare try to drive away without them if they actually got the truck across. But if she did, they'd have no choice but to shoot her. He hoped she wasn't that reckless. Hood was good with moving targets.

♦ ♦ ♦

Kerry stared out the windshield of the truck at the broken bridge ahead of her. The sun was high in the sky and the wind rushed through the river valley. The empty road and tall grassy clearing past the bridge might as well have been miles away. The tall grass swept and swirled about in a graceful dance with the wind, and she wanted nothing more than to just be there on the other side, on that solid earth with the overgrowth. Her hands clutched the wheel tight. Her mouth was dry and her eyes felt bleary from lack of sleep.

"Pull the truck in close," Hood said from behind the guardrail atop the wall. Behind him was a straight drop to the riverbed, but he looked as though he didn't notice or wasn't worried. "Closer. Pull her all the way against the wall. Who cares about the paint job."

Kerry turned the wheel and then counter-turned to slide the truck closer. The front left panel of the car scratched and squealed as the stone bridge dug into its side.

"That's it, nice and tight," Hood said. "We want to get as much leverage on this baby as we can." He slapped the hood of the car with a metallic thud. To Kerry, the wall was one more thing trapping her inside the truck. She closed her eyes and exhaled. Sweat beaded on her forehead and made the steering wheel slick under her hands. Her worst nightmare had come to life.

She kept seeing the image from her childhood play over and over in her head. She sat in the back seat staring at her cell phone like any other twelve year old, her parents discussing the upcoming weekend in the front seats. They crept through the intersection, and from beyond the driver's side window came the front grill of a truck. Glass exploded as the car flipped over and over. She slammed her eyes shut, feeling herself spin in the air as she was slung out of her seatbelt into the ceiling. She opened her eyes, numbly looking at her own shattered hand covered in blood as she lay on the ceiling of the up-side down car. Her heart started to race at the memory.

She should have just kept hiding in the darkness the night she'd encountered these two. Then she wouldn't be caught between Whiskey threatening to kill her and having no choice but to play chicken with deep-seeded terror.

Hood leaned in through the window, then lifted up his aviators she was sure he was wearing just for cosmetic effect. It's not like he was wearing sunglasses when it was high noon.

"So you know what you got to do?"

"Yes." She sighed. His automatic rifle hung off his shoulder, pointing at her. "Can you not swing that thing around?" She took two fingers and turned the barrel away.

"Relax." He smiled, but slid the rifle to face down outside the truck. "This lil' murder monster is the only thing keeping us from being food for crows if some hungry wasters find us trying to get this beast across the bridge." He paused and lifted an eyebrow. "Well, maybe they'll kill Whiskey and me. But you, well, you know. Not good."

"That's not funny. Don't even fucking joke about that." She shook her head. Her mouth was so taut that her cheeks felt strained.

Hood just grinned. "Don't worry, you're in capable hands." He drummed on the door with both hands. "This is how *I* have fun with the apocalypse." He dropped his glasses back onto his nose.

As stressed as Kerry was, Hood did seem remarkably relaxed about the whole process. If this was fun for him, he was a sick bastard. But of course, it wasn't his life at stake. It was hers.

The truck squeaked as it slid higher up against the stone wall. Out the broken glass of the back window, Whiskey took the barrels of gas out of the back and placed them on the bridge with a grunt and a thud. They had smashed out the back window and cleaned out the sharp bits of glass, insisting it was part of the 'plan.' She could've sworn they were just doing random things and calling it a plan.

"There. Happy now, princess?" Whiskey shouted, breathing heavily.

"Don't even. . ." Kerry shouted back. "I don't think its crazy to get some of the weight out of this thing."

Whiskey pulled a bandanna out of his police-issue flak jacket and wiped his forehead. "Hate to break it to you kid, but two barrels of gas ain't gonna change a thing if the ropes don't hold."

She turned around to the driver's side window, unaware that Hood had already reached inside and looped the wrist-thick ropes through the driver's side window, then out the back window of the cab. He tied them tight around the guardrail twice. The ropes bound the truck to the guardrail and would slide along the railing as the truck moved forward, holding the truck upright when crossing the chasm. That was the plan, anyway.

"Welcome to Air Guardrail. This is your captain speaking." Hood spoke into an invisible walkie-talkie, standing on the bridge wall. "Here at Air Guardrail, we take the utmost precaution to ensure that our passengers don't fall into a chasm and explode."

"Stop acting like this isn't a big deal. This is a big deal," Kerry said. She wiped her palms on her jeans, but they kept sweating profusely.

"Relax, you'll be fine," Hood said. "I promise I'll hold your hand the whole way."

"Really?" She said, somewhat bewildered.

"No." He shook his head with an eccentric frown. "We good back there, Whiskey?"

"All set," he replied. He was crouched down on the opposite side of the bridge with an automatic rifle in hand, looking at the truck. "You've got about a foot until the front wheel is off the ground."

"All right, sister," Hood said. "Hit it."

She sat still. "That's it? There isn't anything more to do to prepare?" Her heart felt like it had jammed itself up into her throat, trying to leap out of her body and run away from this mess. *This is going to work. It's just a short distance. They value this truck too much to let it just fall in.* Her mind pleaded with reason, but all she could envision was the weight falling out from underneath her, the truck tumbling down, her head hitting the ceiling. . . Her body tingled in the anticipation of weightlessness.

82

Hood shook his head. He sat down on the rail so he could look at her.

"Showtime."

She put her foot on the gas pedal but couldn't make herself push down. The engine hummed quietly. She stared out the windshield at the broken expanse of nothing, where most of a bridge should be in front of her. Her heart was already beating out of control, just imagining the truck moving forward. Again and again she felt the terror as the truck rolled down through the chasm to the river below, so real as if it were actually happening.

"I can't do it." She closed her eyes. Why would they make her do this? It was a living nightmare, and she knew how her nightmares ended. Whatever they needed her to do, she could do. Just not this.

She'd taken a liking to Hood, and understood Whiskey's paranoia. He even seemed to hate her a little less now. Not that it mattered. She had to prove herself to them; she didn't have any other choice.

Hood stood up, climbed into the bed of the truck, opened the passenger door and swung in to sit next to her.

"Here. Let me help." He put his hand on her knee and jammed down on the gas pedal. An ear-piercing screech of stone wall against the paneling of the truck rang out as it lurched forward, noticeably listing to the front right side. She inhaled sharply, hands vice-gripped on the steering wheel.

Please, please just let me make it through this in one piece, she pleaded with whatever god would listen. She hated Hood for forcing her to do this, but at least he was trying to help her. Having him in the cab with her was reassuring, knowing he was risking his life with hers. If only he would stay there.

"Wheel is in the air!" Whiskey shouted. "Maybe take it easier next time."

"Yeah, I got that." Kerry glared at Hood.

"See?" He raised his hands with a smile. "Fine and dandy. Just keep your eyes ahead, on solid ground. Focus on where you're going, not where you are." He unceremoniously climbed over her out of the driver side window and back over to the wall of the bridge.

"How's the rope?" Whiskey shouted.

"A little frayed, but still fine." Hood replied. He nodded to Kerry.

You've been through worse, Kerry told herself. Just get through this.

Steeling herself, she slowly pushed down on the gas pedal. The screech was slower but still horrible, and the truck continued out over the expanse. Her heart raged in her chest, and her teeth ached from her clenched jaw. She was sick of feeling this way. She could either sit there and be paralyzed by her fear, or kick it in the teeth and push ahead. If she was going to die, she'd rather die angry than terrified.

"You're good," Hood said. "Keep it comin'."

She leaned on the gas again, with similar results. When the truck came to a stop, the groan of the guardrail gave her goose-bumps and a shot of adrenaline. Fueled by sudden panic, she started climbing out the window.

"Relax. You're okay. Metal flexes. Trust me," Hood said.

"That does not sound good," she said, not yet returning fully into the truck.

"You've got about a foot until both wheels are off the edge," Whiskey shouted.

"Hang in there. I won't let you fall," was all Hood said, staring at her from behind his sunglasses.

She wanted to trust him. He had done a lot for her up to this point. He had seemed a genuine person, one of the few she had met. Yet years of experience told her not to trust anyone—especially not a guy who was making her do a high-wire circus trick with a thousand-pound truck and no safety net. *You're just a new piece of ass to him. That same quality that can make you mean so much to a man can also make you mean so little.*

This was not going at all according to plan. Nothing ever did.

Slowly she re-entered the truck, exhaling through her mouth when confronted with the steering wheel and gas pedal again. She stepped on it quickly, before she could think too much about it.

The truck again screamed ahead, the engine rumbling loudly before the truck listed even more towards the chasm. She couldn't stop the panicked breaths or the tears welling in her eyes, but she blinked repeatedly and focused on the road ahead. *Think about where you're going, not where you are.*

"Both right side wheels are off the ground," Whiskey announced. He had his pistol in hand, and glanced around. "We should speed this up. We're making a lot of noise."

"Hold on there, killer," Hood said into the cab. "The rope is pretty frayed and up against the first strut. I have to put the next rope on. Hang tight."

"Yeah, no problem," she said sarcastically, thinking that any moment the whole damn thing would career into the abyss. She wiped the sweat from her brow on the forearm of her jacket and pulled her hair behind her ears. All she wanted to do was jam the gas pedal down. The truck made a symphony of creaks, groans and rattles as it listed slightly towards the chasm. Her pulse raged quicker, her tongue felt thick and numb and her jaw locked in place. She could feel the sweat bead on her face, and she longed for the solid ground around her yet so far away. *If I feel it fall, I just have to lunge for the wall, grab onto the railing. . .*

Hood ran the next rope through the truck and around the guardrail, past the support strut, tying it as tightly as he could. "You're doing great, Kerry. Hang in there."

She did not feel reassured. She dared to look out the passenger side window. It had angled down slightly, showing the rocky river below. She squeezed her eyes shut, trying to blot out the image. *Why would you look, you asshole?* She just wanted to lean on the gas pedal until the engine blew or the damn truck made it to the other side. Her body kept conjuring the weightless sensation, the out-of-body feeling of being thrown about inside a vehicle hurtling through the air. *Never again, never again. . .*

"Get down." Hood said.

"Huh?" was all she could manage.

"I'm cutting the first rope so we can keep moving. Get down so it doesn't snap and hit you."

She leaned over awkwardly close to the seat. Hood pulled out a hunting knife and sawed at the first rope. She could hear the faint plucking sound of the fibers being cut.

The rope snapped, the right side of the truck sinking a bit further down. It felt like it was inches from hurtling down into the river. The guardrail creaked, but the listing truck stayed in the air. Her hands shook uncontrollably, her vision narrowing to only what was straight ahead of her. She gripped the steering wheel as hard as she could manage, releasing pure unadulterated fear through locked muscles.

"Let's go," Hood said. "Come on, quickly."

She leaned up and pushed hard on the gas pedal. The engine roared and the car howled against the stone as it lurched again.

"Front wheel is close to the other side," Whiskey said. "Almost home."

A loud snap echoed across the open air and the truck listed even further.

"What's happening?" Kerry screamed.

"Shit, the guard rail is coming apart at the next strut. Gun it! *Go now!*" Hood shouted, slapping the roof of the truck. "GO!" he screamed

Whiskey cursed loudly.

Kerry stomped the pedal to the floor. The engine roared like an unchained beast. The screeching of metal against stone and the groaning rail combined into a horrible cacophony and she felt consumed by panic. The truck sagged and slid forward until a considerable bump shot the front of the truck up, but the back kicked out from against the wall and started to sink into the gaping chasm, ready to swallow her. The supplies slid loudly across the bed of the truck and thumped into the gate. She could feel the blood thumping behind her eyes as the windshield pointed up to the blue cloudy sky.

With the RPM's redlined, the engine screaming and the pedal down, the smell of burning gaskets crept into the cabin. *It's not gonna make it. It's falling in.* Her stomach tried to hurl itself out of her throat. She could feel the truck sliding backwards as the front of the truck leaned up.

With a loud chirp and a lurch, the truck's front wheels gripped onto the broken maw of bridge. Bouncing this way and that, the back wheels hit something solid. The truck lurched and bounded forward, rumbling up and over onto flat ground. The tires screeched and a loud crack shot through the air. She drove a full twenty yards just to make sure she was far away from the bridge before turning the engine off. She dropped her forehead onto the steering wheel and tears of fear and relief slid down her face. A hollow clicking sound from the engine compartment slowed to a halt. The first sound from the outside world she heard was Whiskey and Hood clapping through the open window.

She looked up at the side-view mirror to see the rope was still attached to the truck, which was dragging a bent section of guardrail beside it.

Hood jogged over to the truck. "You got so excited to be free you took the goddamn bridge with ya." He laughed. "I just hope the truck can still make it the rest of the way."

She climbed out the window clumsily and shoved Hood with both hands after regaining her footing.

"Asshole!" she shouted. "You almost got me fucking killed!!"

"You're fine, right? Teamwork makes the dream work," he said with a smile.

She wanted to slap his smile straight to hell. They'd put her life at risk for this. But she felt an intense satisfaction blooming up within her, knowing she had overcome something she feared so deeply. Whiskey reached out to shake her hand, grudging respect on his face. She looked at it and looked at him.

Whiskey held her gaze, his face calm. "Well done."

She reached out and shook his hand.

"I don't know what your angle is in all of this, but you helped us out a lot here. That wasn't easy to do," Whiskey said.

"Thanks. And you're *welcome*," she said with enough anger that it didn't sound completely genuine. "Will you stop trying to kill me now?"

"Hey, let's not get crazy," Whiskey said, the slightest smile cracking his face. Hood laughed.

Kerry managed a nervous grin. "You're insane." She ran her hand through her hair to the back of her head where she scratched compulsively. She leaned back against the truck. It was hot from all the friction and engine heat. The driver's side of the chassis she leaned on was ruined, broken and gouged beyond repair.

"Seriously," Hood said. "Thank you. You're welcome to stay with us. When you know what we're doing, I'm not sure you'll want to, but it's up to you."

She sized him up, wondering if this was for real. He had a relaxed stance, looking her in the eyes.

"Yeah?"

"Like I said, you've earned it. You risked your life to help us. Even if it did take a little persuasion."

Whiskey stood off to the side, looking displeased, but didn't say anything.

"I think that works for me," she said. "For now."

Was this all a test? It seemed unreal. This was a lot of trust he was putting in her. Too much trust. What were his motives? Things too good to be true always were.

"What if I want to leave?" She asked.

"Whatever you want," Hood said. "It's just an offer."

"By all means, take your leave," Whiskey said.

Hood shot a glance at Whiskey, and they seemed to be communicating angrily without saying a word.

"What…tell me what it is you guys are doing, really." Kerry found a kind of solace in leaning against the truck, as if it was on her side. It had been through hell with her. She crossed her arms, then uncrossed them to pull an errant hair out of her eyelashes.

Hood and Whiskey looked at each other. Whiskey's expression was one of premature anger–a don't-you-say-it look.

"We're going to D.C.," Hood said. "We're going to D.C. To rescue my brother and sister and whatever other survivors there are from our town."

Whiskey sighed, long and slow.

Her eyebrows raised compulsively. "Wow. That's. . . That's not what I expected."

"You should probably know. We're going to rescue them from the Kaiser. Now if you'll excuse us, we have some barrels of gasoline to reload into this truck."

Kerry watched as they turned simultaneously, walking to the truck together. Hood reached back to flick Whiskey in the ear but he swatted Hood's hand away and barked something. Hood laughed.

The Kaiser. Kerry felt as if the air had been let out of her. Oh no.

Hood rolled over in the cab of the truck. The felt surface of the seats itched his arm. The sky had become overcast, a bright gray. He looked out the windshield over the faded dashboard. It was foggy, and he could just make out Whiskey's figure walking down the road. He rubbed his face with his right hand, still feeling tired. He stretched as he kicked open the driver's side door of the truck. Both the old blankets Whiskey and Kerry had used as sleeping mats outside were disheveled and empty.

"Hey!" Hood shouted. He couldn't see anyone now in the fog. He felt a tickle of doubt--maybe that wasn't Whiskey at all. He pulled out his pistol and looked around in all directions. It was hard to see very far.

He reached back into the cab and pulled out his AK, putting the pistol back away. He flipped the safety, kept his finger on the trigger guard and walked down the road. There was little wind and the only sound was the crunch of dirt under his feet. He felt his pockets for the keys. Whiskey must have taken them. He clenched his jaw and kept walking. He kept the butt of the rifle against his shoulder and strode forward with quiet, soft steps.

The high grass and reeds were close to the road, and the north side was still fairly rocky terrain. The road was empty and the double yellow lines were all but worn away. He heard the guy before he saw him. He pointed the rifle to the north side and moved forward until the figure appeared out of the fog.

"Hands in the air," Hood said.

The man turned around. It was Whiskey.

"It's me, you jackass," he said. Hood put down the rifle and stood up straight.

"Why did you leave the truck?" Hood said.

"Kerry's gone," Whiskey said, frowning. "I came back from scoutin' the area and she was gone. I knew we shouldn't have trusted her."

Hood walked forward a few steps and let his rifle hang by its strap on his shoulder.

"Gone, huh. Is anything missing?"

Whiskey turned his head to stare Hood down.

"Yes, gone. No, everything is still in the truck. Your dick is going to get us killed," Whiskey said, putting away his pistol.

"Oh, cut the shit," Hood spat. "For all your threats, I didn't see you kicking her to the curb. She just didn't want to go on a suicide mission with us."

"I want you to use your goddamned brain. The Kaiser is looking for us. Wasters want us dead. And *you* told her where we're goin' and what we're doing."

Hood shook his head. "So from here on out, everyone we meet is our enemy?"

"Yes, for Chrissake!" Whiskey shouted, "We don't trust nobody. Got it?"

Hood stared at him. "I'm not gonna live like that."

90

"Then you ain't gonna live at *all!*" Whiskey growled at him.

Hood stared at him, shaking his head. Dirt ground beneath Whiskey's feet as he turned and walked back to the truck. Hood followed him. *I know how dire this is, Whiskey. I know what we're up against. But I refuse to let this nightmare turn me into everything I hate.*

"She probably is part of a drifter gang that's gonna' hunt us down." Whiskey's jaw flexed from grinding his teeth, and his brow furrowed. "Or worse, she works for the Kaiser."

"Or she was some leftover nobody from an abandoned town who didn't want to be with two guys who made her risk her life driving a truck across a bridge," Hood said. "Either way, there's nothing we can do now."

Whiskey looked like he was fighting the urge to argue. Hood decided not to push it any further. They walked back in silence across the bridge to the truck. The fog was thinning as the sun re-emerged.

Someone was sitting in the cab of the truck, Hood saw. He lifted his rifle.

"Do you have the keys?" Hood asked.

"No."

Whiskey pulled out his gun and they spread out to either side as they moved toward the truck. The person inside stayed still until sighting them. Then she climbed out of the truck.

It was Kerry.

Hood let his rifle hang by his shoulder again. He sighed and rubbed his forehead with thumb and forefinger.

"Where the hell were you?" he shouted.

"*Me?*" she replied. "Where were *you?*"

It was funny how much Whiskey distrusted her, considering how alike they were in their stubbornness.

Whiskey didn't put down his Glock. He walked straight up to her and grabbed her by the collar of her jacket.

"Whoa! Hey, what's going on?" She asked.

"Where the hell did you go?" He snapped at her.

"I was bored from sitting there doing nothing so I decided to take a walk." She tried to pull his hand off of her jacket. His hand may as well have been a vise. "Let me go, you maniac!"

"Bullshit," he yelled. "Who did you meet with?"

"What? What are you talking about?" She continued to struggle out of his grasp. "If you really want to know, I had to go to the bathroom."

"You were gone for a long time." Whiskey turned his head in skepticism.

"Like that is any of your business!" She shouted.

Hood stepped in, putting his hand on Whiskey's arm. "Hey, dude. Come on, let her go."

"You can't fool me with your innocent bullshit. Tell me where you went!" Whiskey said, ignoring Hood.

"Whoa, just take it easy!" Kerry implored. "I didn't think it was a big deal. I don't want to have to tell you every time I have to pee, like a child." She looked as though she would squirm out of her jacket if she could, her brown hair blowing all over her face.

"Let her *go*. Whiskey, she didn't do anything." Hood said, trying to separate the two of them. Whiskey didn't move.

"This ain't a jury of her peers. And all of this, her appearing out of nowhere to find us, looking for a ride, with her bullshit story, it's all too perfect," Whiskey said. "I don't believe it for a second."

Hood took a moment to study Kerry. He couldn't tell if her expression held confusion or fear. Or what that meant. What if Whiskey were right? He didn't want it to be true. But it might be. He'd never killed a woman. Much less a pretty one with a sense of humor.

Whiskey may be a tough bastard to deal with at times, but Hood knew Whiskey was one of the few people who would always act in Hood's best interest. Or at least, what he thought was his best interest. And Whiskey was his family now.

"*I drove this fucking thing over thin air,*" She screamed, pointing at the truck. "And you're waving a fucking gun in my face? Yes, I was going to leave because I don't exactly want to end up dead or as the Kaiser's slave, but I have nowhere else to go, so I guess I don't have a fucking choice but to pray like hell you two have some goddamned masterful plan in place!"

Her eyes were wild with anger as she stared intensely back at Whiskey. For whatever it was worth, Hood believed her. At least about this, anyway.

Hood bumped his shoulder into Whiskey's. "Let her go," he said quietly. "We need her help."

Whiskey slowly let go of her black denim jacket and put away his gun. She leaned back against the truck and wiped the sweat from her forehead with the back of her sleeve.

"For being the smartest person I know you're a god*damned* moron," Whiskey grunted at Hood and walked away.

Kerry pulled her jacket straight and then tucked her hair behind her ear.

"I'll go talk to him. Just don't fucking go anywhere," Hood said, holding his hand up to stress the point.

"Yeah, you do that," she said with venom. Hood expected her to spit in anger, but she didn't. He had clearly spent too much time around guys. She marched to the back of the truck and sat in the open bed, leaning back on her arms.

Hood slung the rifle over his shoulder as he walked towards Whiskey, who stared out into the empty road, arms crossed. Hood walked up next to him and kicked idly at a piece of asphalt that skittered back and forth down the road.

"Everything's just gone to hell," was all Whiskey said.

Hood nodded slowly. *Yeah, it has. But we're still here.* He rubbed the back of his head, which lead to a compulsive stretch and yawn. He needed much more sleep. They weren't going to get it anytime soon. *Time is ticking away and we still have a ways to go to get to D.C.. Taylor's in the belly of the beast and you can't get out of your own way. I know Ian will do everything he can to keep her safe. But can he really protect her?* Dirt kicked up by the wind flew into his eye and he blinked it away.

"Taylor. . ." Whiskey seemed hesitant to even give the thoughts air. "She's all alone, prisoner. . . We're all she's got left. We can't take risks."

"I know how bad things are. I know what we're up against. But we can do this. And Kerry might be able to help us save her. Don't you think you're being too paranoid?" Hood said finally. Whiskey uncrossed his arms.

"No."

The sound of the high grass swishing heralded a particularly strong gust of wind. The sun finally peered out from a hole in the clouds.

"Why is it so hard to believe she's just a regular person trying to survive?"

Whiskey worked his mouth in frustration. His short stubble had slowly become a beard. It felt like a year had passed since they left Clearwater to raid the Sheriff's cache.

"Because girls like that don't just get left alone."

Hood squinted at the horizon, considering this. It certainly was a hard thing to argue. Even if Hood believed her story, there was the question of how she'd been able to escape. Her story was just a story, whether it was true or not. But she had a genuineness about her that Hood wanted to trust. After all, her introduction to the group had been not unlike his own. But he couldn't afford to trust too easily. Hood looked back at the truck. She looked like she was rooting through her bag inside the cab.

"Listen, I get it. But what future do we have if everyone we ever meet is an enemy to us? You trusted me when you met me. Why?" Hood gazed out to the other side of the river. The clearing filled with tall grass gave way to a wall of trees, cut into only by the worn, graying road.

"Because I knew you were a good kid," Whiskey said definitively.

"How could you have known that?"

Whiskey opened his mouth to speak but stopped himself. He

94

shook his head ever so slightly, and turned to look upriver. "I could just feel it. . . And I can feel that this girl is hiding something from us."

Hood rubbed his eye still itching from the dirt before breathing in deeply, arching his back to stretch. "Yeah, she probably is."

The two of them sat in silence. A raccoon appeared from the tall grass and scurried over the road a ways ahead of them.

"I have to believe we can give her a chance. If not, I don't know why we're still alive and human. I won't let you kill her just because she *could* be working for someone. And I guess, in a selfish third place, you're right: I think I like her a little bit."

Whiskey sighed. "Well, if she's sold us out, we're screwed no matter what happens." He rubbed his short beard. "To hell with it. You've already made up your goddamned mind and I don't have it in me to argue anymore."

"I was a stranger, and I turned out to be a solid addition, I'd say!" Hood slapped Whiskey on the shoulder. "So was Taylor."

The two of them stood silent. Hood knew they both were thinking about her, about what they could be doing to her—whether she was even still alive. The fear built in the silence, and they needed to kill the fear. It did nothing but hold them hostage. *We're coming, Tay. If we have to ride a fucking radio flyer through hell to get there, we will.*

"Yeah, it all worked out goddamned great." Whiskey grumbled, turning to walk back to the truck.

Hood laughed, turning on his heel, adjusting the rifle strap with his thumb as it tried to slide off his shoulder. "Aww, someone's getting grumpy in his old age! Want me to build you a porch so you can yell at me to get off of it?"

Whiskey held up his middle finger over his shoulder.

"When you used to open up fortune cookies, did they all say 'out of touch old man thinks everyone is out to get him?'" Hood shouted.

"I bet you were one of those kids who used to wear skinny jeans and look sad all the time," Whiskey said loudly.

"Ohhh shiiit," Hood tossed at him, walking back towards the

truck. "Someone get the old man some new dentures, because he's spittin' fire!"

Chapter 8 – In The Dark

As he lay on a mat of blankets in the bed of the truck, with the band of the milky way bright in the night sky above him, Hood wanted to indulge the fantasy that he was on a vagabond road trip straight out of Kerouac. Forget about the war that his life had become. But there was no time for that; it was his turn to sleep while Whiskey drove, and sleep was a precious commodity. And it felt so damn good.

The bright full moon shimmered a path across the Atlantic. The sound of the rolling waves crashing on the beach had a rhythmic therapy to it. Ian's phone binged with a text message. Then another. The two of them sat in the sand side by side, both with their forearms resting on their knees. Ian took a swig from his beer.

"You gonna answer that?" Hood said.

"It can wait," Ian said calmly.

"Probably your girl."

"It can wait."

The salty air howled off the ocean, whipping Hood's unkempt hair in his face. He finished his beer, pushing the bottle into the sand next to the other empties beside him.

"I'm not cut out for this shit."

"It's a part of life, man. Don't let it all weigh you down," Ian punctuated it with another drink.

"It feels like she's gone. Like she died. Like a part of me died. Do other people get this torn up? I wish I could just not care about it at all."

"No you don't," Ian smiled at his bottle. "Then you'd be a miserable asshole like me."

Hood laughed. It felt good, it felt real. A momentary reprieve.

"Come on. Look around you. Look how awesome this is. We got this place for the weekend, lets just enjoy it. Forget about her. I'm sure there's some girls our age around here."

"I can't even think about that. I can't stop thinking about her," Hood said, picking up a handful of sand and letting it run through his fingers.

"You two still talking?" Ian said, finishing his own beer and twisting it into the sand.

"Yeah," Hood said, pulling his phone out of his jeans to check it.

"That's your problem," Ian said, snatching the phone out of his hands. He stood up and hurled it towards the ocean. It glimmered in the moonlight and plopped into the sea.

"WHAT THE FUCK, DUDE?" Hood yelled, jumping to his feet.

"Relax, I'll buy you a new one! Now you have to enjoy your weekend."

"Dude, all my contacts, what the hell, seriously?"

"Fuck your contacts. What are you, an ambassador?" Ian ran down to the shoreline. Hood laughed, charging after him.

"Fuck you!"

Ian held his arms wide in front of the moonlit ocean, the din of the crashing waves booming behind him. Hood grabbed him, spun him around and tossed him into the surging water. Ian popped his head up, laughing. Hood grinned uncontrollably. He hurled himself headfirst into the water, the cold sea exploding around him. Ian pulled off his shoes and threw them onto the beach. The waves rose up like abyssal monsters, and Hood dove through them each time.

"What, are you trying to find it?" Ian said loudly.

"Nah, fuck it, it's gone," Hood shouted back.

"Yes it is!" Ian grinned wide, standing up in the water and running his hand over his face. "There's the Rob I remember."

Hood floated on his back, out past the breaking waves, staring up at the glimmering night sky and the bright moon. Dotted along the shoreline sat dark summer homes and hotels. The water didn't feel so cold anymore.

When the two of them trudged back onto the beach, ocean pouring out of their sodden clothes, Taylor stood on the shore with folded up towels under her arms.

"How did you know?" Hood said, calling out to her with a smile.

"Come on," she said. "Like I don't know you."

"You shoulda come in!"

"I prefer it when the sun is up, thanks." She said, holding out towels for the both of them.

"You're an angel Tay," Ian said.

"You don't even know. I just ordered us a pizza. Now come back inside and we can drink and watch Mystery Science Theater."

Ian and Hood looked at each other, still sopping wet despite their best attempts to towel off..

"You two? You're all I need in this world," Ian said, smiling. "Fuck everything else."

Reality came and went with the shuddering of the truck. When he roused from his slumber, it was daytime again. The memory from his past life lingered, still fresh in his mind. *God I miss them. I could deal with this. I could deal with everything if they were just here with me.* He hoisted himself up off the blankets, arching his back to stretch it. He scooted backwards, leaning against the broken back window and letting his arm rest over the side of the truck. There was the simple problem of freeing them from the Kaiser once they found them. Not that it mattered. It's not like anything would stop him from trying.

The wind howled in his ears and the truck glided smoothly for once as they sped north on Richmond highway. His rifle lay next to him, a reminder of how ready he needed to be. As he looked back at the road, the once normal world slid by on either side of him, empty commercial and industrial complexes hidden behind thin layers of trees. The sky was gray, but wasn't dark with coming rain. He put up his hood to stop the whipping wind.

They sped by a black BMW parked on the shoulder, still shiny and with all windows intact, surely left there by someone who had run out of gas. Why anyone would have decided to drive north towards D.C. under the circumstances was beyond him.

Maybe Mr. black BMW was like us, trying to find someone.

If so, he pitied him. Or her. They faced long odds.

They drove by a golf course to his left, the grass tall and overgrown. It wasn't much of a course anymore, but there were tell-tale wide expanses of green with flags protruding from encroaching weeds. Something loomed in the distance, deep in the overgrown field of grass. Hood turned towards it, squinting. It was dark and slender, possibly a person. It didn't look like it was moving. He leaned over a box of supplies to look more closely.

The truck screeched to a halt, nearly throwing Hood into the cab as his head smacked against the frame of the truck. He checked for blood, but there was none. In the road in front of them stood a man in jeans and a button-up shirt, breathing hard, with both hands up.

"Please help me. She's about to give birth!" He said.

Whiskey turned and looked at Hood as the truck idled.

"We've got to help them!" Kerry said.

"No, we don't," Whiskey said, pulling out his glock and pointing it at the man. The man raised his hands in the air, backing away. "Please," he begged. "She's been in labor so long, something's wrong. I don't know what to do."

"Get the *fuck* out of the way if you don't wanna die!" Whiskey shouted out the window.

Kerry opened the door and got out of the truck.

"Kerry, wait!" Hood shouted.

"Let her go," Whiskey shouted at him. "Let her make her own choice."

Hood froze. *Whiskey won't think twice about leaving without her. But she's not really giving us much choice here. There's no time to play doctor.* The man thanked Kerry and they started down a dirt path beside the highway, one used for industrial equipment. Hood cursed and jumped out of the back of the truck with his AK.

"No!" Whiskey yelled angrily. He got out of the driver's side of the truck.

"I can't just let her go," Hood said.

"We don't have time for this shit. If she wants to play nurse, let her. How long will it be before the Kaiser decides Taylor isn't worth keeping hostage?"

"You don't have to remind me. She's *my* sister. But we could use Kerry's help. Let me bring her back, convince her this isn't our business. I don't want to leave her here. Just give me two minutes."

Whiskey shouted his name loudly, twice. Hood tore off in a run down the path.

The last thing Hood wanted to do was leave Whiskey alone with the truck. But he didn't want to leave Kerry behind either. At some point everyone's interests conflict.

The orange clay path was surrounded by tall pine trees on either side. Hood pulled the butt of his AK to his shoulder and looked around cautiously. There was no sign of either Kerry or the man.

He stalked silently from the path into the cover of the trees. His footsteps padded on sparse grass and a thick carpet of pine needles. The tall, straight tree trunks weren't wide enough to hide someone easily, and the woods appeared empty. He moved forward, staying parallel to the dirt path as it bent slowly. The path was only occupied by a backhoe, its huge shovel arm resting on the ground. That's where he'd expect people to hide—behind it. But no one was lying in wait, and there was no sign of Kerry or the troubled man.

Maybe this was a trap for her, not a trap for them. He leaned his shoulder against a pine tree, trying to make sense of the silence. He looked up at the bright gray sky, peering between the tall branches of the pines.

He pulled the AK back to his shoulder and moved forward towards the backhoe. Nothing could be heard but the soft pat of his shoes on the bed of pine needles. Not even the wind. The backhoe stood inert like a monolith. Last time someone had used it, they'd probably still had   salaries and work weeks. He walked around the giant machine, covered in grease and dirt, until he got to the shovel arm. On the other side of it Kerry stood in the clay path, her back facing him with her head down. The other man was gone.

"Hey, what happened?" Hood said, moving towards her.

"Why didn't you just stay in the truck?" Her voice wavered, as if she was crying.

A cold emptiness filled Hood's chest. *Whiskey was right the whole goddamned time.*

"I tried to leave that day after the bridge. I didn't want to do this to you guys. But I didn't have a choice. They have my family." Kerry said, turning to face him, tears sliding down over her guilt.

Hood spun around. A group of men crept out from the other tree line, all with guns pointed at him. Normal men, wearing jeans, shirts, varying lengths of beard and serious expressions. One middle-aged guy stepped forward, a revolver in his hand. He had a dark bushy mustache and slicked back hair. He wore a dirty black suit with a red T-shirt on underneath.

"I don't think I need to tell you to put down your weapons," the man said.

Hood dropped the AK in the dirt. He turned his gaze to Kerry. *I don't know who I hate more, you, or myself for being duped by your bullshit.*

She didn't look back at him, holding her elbows and looking at the ground.

"All of them." The man motioned with the revolver.

Hood reached into his hoodie, pulled out the .38 and dropped it on the ground. The man pointed at his leg with the gun. He pulled out a hunting knife he'd strapped to his leg and tossed the blade down into the dirt.

"There's a good sap. What's your name?" The mustached man asked.

"Fuck you," Hood spat.

The man shook his head and waved the pistol in disapproval. "That's not very smart. After all, I know who you are whether you tell me or not."

"I wanted to tell you," Kerry said, her voice barely above a whisper. "I didn't want this to happen."

The men moved closer to him.

Whiskey had been right. The whole goddamn time. About everything. He didn't know if the thought drove him more insane because he hadn't listened, or because Whiskey's psychotic paranoia was justified. *You let this happen. You haven't learned your lesson from Clearwater. The world is fucked, and you can't trust anyone. And now you're going to die.* Rage boiled in his blood, blurring his vision. He wanted to grind his teeth to dust. *You're a goddamned child. You left him to save Taylor on his own. Either these men work for the Kaiser, or they're slavers, or maybe their just wastelanders who love to torture and kill survivors. Either way you're fucked, because you just had to let your dick make your decisions. You're going to die here, alone.*

Kerry flickered bleary eyed glances at him, her head heavy with guilt. His own face felt blank, his hate channeling through his stare she was avoiding. One of the men tied his hands behind his back, and another threw a black hood over his head and duct taped it around his neck.

"Seems fitting for a man with your name," he heard the mustached man say.

♦ ♦ ♦

They threw him in the trunk of a car. The drive was relatively short and smooth so they must've taken him to somewhere close by. The rope around his wrists was old and dry. He tried to work them loose but only succeeded in creating a painful burning sensation. His legs were free but he could do little but kick at the walls of the trunk. The car smelled like a Christmas pine-scented air freshener. His first thought was that it was a taxi.

When the car pulled to a stop they opened the trunk and lifted him out by his arms, pushing him to walk. He heard the squeak of metal joints, and he was led down a steep staircase,   distant indiscernible shouts echoing outside. They walked him a few paces to a wall. It was dark and damp, wherever they were. Someone removed the ropes from his wrist, and he felt the thud of a gun barrel pressed against the back of his head.

"Back against the wall."

He turned slowly and backed up against the wall. The sound of rattling chains echoed as he felt two metal cuffs clamp down on either wrist. The gun barrel removed itself from the back of his head. Someone tore the duct tape off of his neck and pulled off the hood. It was dark and he could see very little. The light of day peered from the narrow staircase they climbed down. It was the only thing illuminating the dark cellar he was in. The floor was bloodstained concrete with a small metal drain in the middle of the room.

Footsteps echoed from the stairs. The mustached man in his faded suit appeared. He had a pistol in his hand and a lit cigarette in his mouth. Hood stood staring at him and said nothing. The man stared back, smoking his cigarette at an easy pace.

"Where's your friend?" The man finally said.

Hood didn't reply.

"You know, your comrade in arms?"

"Conflict of interests," Hood said. "He's gone."

The mustached man breathed smoke out of his mouth in almost a whistle. "You think I believe that?"

"It's the truth." Hood leaned back against the concrete wall, chains scraping against the floor.

"I know who you two are. The Kaiser's gonna reward me quite handsomely, I'd wager. The Sheriff was supposed to have you in hand. Well, he always was a little cocky." The man ran his hand through his wavy, trained-back hair. "I never liked him much anyway. Never really deserved to be one of the Kaiser's officers, by my estimation."

Hood sat silent again. He couldn't help but smile at the irony. The man was waiting for some kind of trap because they had taken down the Sheriff, but there was no cavalry coming. If Whiskey had to choose between Hood and Taylor, he would pick Taylor. And Hood would never begrudge him that. She was worth it.

"Who are you?" Hood asked.

"Call me Leonard." Hood was sure that was not his real name. Not that it mattered. "And don't change the subject. Where is your boy now, hmm?"

"I told you I don't know. He's not stupid enough to get himself into this kind of mess."

Leonard paused, throwing his cigarette butt on the ground and smothering it. "That would seem to be the truth, wouldn't it?"

"What does the Kaiser want with me?" Hood asked.

"I'll tell you that only if you tell me where you and John are hiding with all those supplies you took from the Sheriff."

"No hiding going on. Whiskey has them all. Not like you'll ever get to him."

Leonard whipped out an extendable billy club and swung at Hood.

He threw up his arms to shield himself from the blows which rained down on his shoulders and his ribs. Pain burst through his body from each blow, Hood screamed in his mind but wouldn't give Leonard the satisfaction of hearing any such thing aloud. Each strike only made the anticipation of the next that much more terrible. *This is just the beginning. Followed by torture, starvation, god knows what else. All for information you don't have.*

"Lie to me again! Go ahead, do it!" Leonard screamed, the words echoing in the cellar. He pulled out his pistol and pointed it at Hood's head.

"Tell me where he is and tell me where the supplies are, or you die."

Hood wouldn't die. Not yet. Not until Leonard got the info that he wanted. Hood's shoulder, his back, his forearm all throbbed in pain from the blows. He was pretty sure he didn't have any broken ribs because it wasn't too painful to breathe. He lifted up his chained hands and inspected them, too, for broken bones.

"Well, Leonard, I just don't know," Hood said plainly.

The man quaked with rage, pulled the gun away and stormed up the steps, slamming the metal doors behind him. Hood slumped to the cold floor in complete darkness. Time slid by, his thoughts circling over and over. *I never imagined I'd die in a cellar, chained to a wall. I never really imagined how I'd die at all before the fall. And I thought life in Clearwater was tough, because we had to kill wastelanders and because I had no idea if anyone else I loved was still alive. This, this is reality. You are the war machine, or you are the casualty. You fight and claw to survive every day or you die. Thinking about someone else was a luxury.*

You wanted to have Kerry, save Ian and Taylor, go hide somewhere and live in peace? What kind of moron are you? Just finding Taylor and Ian would be a miracle. Saving even one of them would be an act of god. Living in peace was impossible.

His head hung low, his chin barely above his chest. His body throbbed in pain. *I'm not cut out for this world. I know that. I've always known that. I don't want to kill to survive. I know there are good people out there. People who will band together and fight for peace. Clearwater was proof of that.* Hood touched his palms gently with his fingers, trying to enjoy the sensation of touch before he died. *And now its gone. Good people are dying off.* Just smelling the damp air, seeing the dark world, tasting food, listening to music, touching. . . someone you love. It all was incomprehensibly beautiful. He wished he had spent more time enjoying it. His eyes seemed to close of their own accord. Ian and

Taylor had to survive. Whiskey would find them. Taylor had to survive and carry on the family line. Hood didn't know why that felt important, but it did. Exhaustion took him, and he slept.

Hood awoke to the squeaking of the cellar doors opening again. It was light out. He didn't know if he had slept for thirty minutes or for a day. This time Kerry was the only one to make her way slowly down the stairs, her long legs clad in tight jeans. She didn't have her jacket on, just a long sleeve shirt that showcased the rest of her shapely body.

She was so much the object of his desire, his hatred, and even his pity. Her freedom was a cheap fake. He found himself hoping for her safety, which seemed all wrong. She didn't deserve it. She'd betrayed them. But would he do the same in her shoes? If it were his family, would he go through with something like this?

"You awake?" She stood a few feet from the bottom of the stairs.

He said nothing. The chains rattled in the darkness as he moved. *You've got some fucking nerve coming down here.* Maybe it wasn't her choice. This was probably part of Leonard's plan.

"I know you have a right to hate me." She said. The words hung in the air.

"Are you all right?" She asked nervously.

"Hell of a question," he said with a weak laugh.

"I'm so sorry for this. I wanted so badly to tell you. I really like you guys. But that asshole has my family hostage." She hung her head slightly, her body leaning to one side as she held her own elbows in her hands. "I thought I was saving them. But now he won't tell me where they are."

Hood chuckled. "What a shock. The sick bastard didn't just hand your family back and let you walk off into the sunset." This story of hers could very well be staged. He was sure that Leonard would try this ploy in an attempt to get information out of him. The question was whether Leonard was using her as a tool, and she was oblivious to it, or whether she was in on it.

"I'm not stupid. I knew that wouldn't happen. But this was the only thing I could do to keep them alive," she said.

The chains clinked with Hood's movements as he locked his fingers together and stretched his arms in front of him. *Are you doing this, now, just to keep them alive?*

"You must hate me," she said.

He nodded, staring at her.

"But I hate myself more," Hood paused. "For letting this all happen. I let Whiskey down. I let my sister down. Their lives are the price I'm paying because I wanted to chase you around."

She moved closer to him, leaning against a red metal support beam. He didn't move.

"You should have told us," Hood said firmly.

"What would you have done? Whiskey would've killed me. He already almost did anyway."

She was right about that.

"You should have told me. I might have been able to convince him to help."

"I couldn't take the risk." Her voice was quaking. She breathed in deeply to calm herself down. "I wanted to tell you. At first I was glad I found you guys because I thought it would mean my family would live. But I came to really like you guys." She gave a weak chuckle. "Even if you did make me drive that fucking truck over a bridge. You probably think I'm insane . . ."

"But. . .?" Hood said.

"Even before the world fell apart, I didn't know anyone like you guys."

Hood laughed, scratching his scruffy jaw with a rattle of chains. *At this rate there's not going to be many likable people left.*

He wanted to believe her. But sending her down here was definitely Leonard's plan to soften Hood up. Was this just part of the game?

He grunted. "You got a funny way of showing how much you like us."

She bowed her head, her hair forming a curtain on either side of her face.

"Just tell Leonard what he wants to know. If not, he might not bring you to the Kaiser whole. Leonard is a special breed of sick bastard."

"Not telling him might be what's keeping me alive," Hood said. He paused before getting into his next thought, keeping his gaze on her. "What do you know about the Kaiser?"

She leaned her head back against the beam, exhaling. "Not much. I've never seen him. He believes he's fighting some kind of ideological war, I know that. Leonard swears the man is the best thing that's ever happened to this country. But he would feel that way, since all he has to do is fight for the Kaiser and he gets whatever the hell he wants. Without the Sons of Liberty opposing them, I'd be scared to think what the country would be like."

"Can't get much worse."

The two of them both stared at the floor. Silence filled the cellar, permeating the moment even more than the smell of mildew. She pushed off of the beam, her hands behind her back, and walked away towards the stairs. She stopped at the base, turning to face him.

"Do whatever it takes to survive. If it means anything at all, I'm going to do everything I can to try and keep you alive," she said solemnly, while still keeping her eyes on him.

He stared back, waiting for her to leave.

She stood there, seeming to be waiting for a reply from him.

"If you're looking for my thanks, you're going to be waiting a while," Hood said.

She looked away from him and climbed the stairs. He watched her leave, her long legs the last things to disappear from his sight.

He exhaled deeply, hanging his head. *Taylor needs your help. Whiskey needs your help. The entire town of Clearwater needed your help. No matter what it takes, I will not let them down. I refuse to die here in this god forsaken shithole.*

He stretched his arms as far as the chains would let him, arching his back and reaching down to touch his toes. His whole body ached. He was too tense. *Stay calm, think clearly. There will be chances. You just need to find the right opportunity.*

The door swung open with a loud crack and Leonard hopped down the steps and stood in the light. Hood's chains jingled as he wiped his eyes in the dark.

Leonard clapped his hands together, and held them spread out wide, shaking his head. "You aren't leaving me many choices here." He ran his hand through his hair, meandering around in the light spilling out of the door.

"I've already told you the truth," Hood replied.

Leonard nodded with a frown of disapproval. "You hungry? Horny? Want to pass on your seed before the end, like your instincts are screaming at you to do?" He stared at the darkness where Hood sat. "We got food, women, men, whatever you want. Cooperate and you'll get to enjoy a bit more of your short life. Make an asset of yourself and you might get to keep living, though it would be in the Kaiser's keeping of course."

"The world to you must be a cold, dead place," Hood said. "And I'd guess that was true long before this country turned to hell."

Leonard chuckled, and pulled his hands out of the pockets of his suit pants.

"Before all this I owned a taxi cab company. Little place. First thing I did, when it all went to shit, was hold up the store of every piece of low-life trash on the block. Wasted every one of those greedy fuckers just because I could. Got this suit from the dry-cleaning place around the corner."

He smiled and sauntered over to the staircase, where he pulled a pack of matches from his pocket and lit a corroded old lantern. He walked over to Hood, setting it down on the floor out of reach, illuminating them both.

"It *is* a cold dead place, my optimistic friend. And you're about to get a lot more cold and dead if you don't tell me where the rest of the supplies you stole from the Sheriff are."

Hood returned the man's confident gaze in the firelight. "It's all gone."

Leonard lunged in with a punch to Hood's gut. Hood tried to block, but the shackles impeded his movement. He backed up, clutching at his stomach and slackening the chains. Leonard swung an uppercut.

Hood leaned back, lifted one of his chains over his head and wrapped it around Leonard's neck, pulling it tight.

Leonard pulled out his revolver and put it to Hood's temple.

They stared at each other for a moment before Hood let go of the chain.

Leonard took a step back, stretching his neck and running his hand through his hair again to keep it slicked back.

"Bad idea, kid. I'm trying to give you a future."

Leonard wore a devious smile. He put his hands on his hips, pushing back his suit coat. "Listen. I want those supplies. And I imagine you don't want to die right here. So let's make this a win-win."

Hood spat. "I got another idea. Let's duel, pistols at dawn and all that crap. You'll be dead before you can tickle the trigger."

Leonard rolled his eyes and walked towards the staircase. "Y'know kid, if you don't learn to work with people whom you despise, you'll never get anywhere in this world or any other."

He moved slowly up the metal stairs and stopped at the top step, leaning down to show the look of dominance he wore on his face. "Now you get to meet my new pet. We found the infected freak wandering the streets. I call him the butcher."

Hood heard moans and guttural sounds and the clatter of chains. A huge figure was forced down the metal staircase and landed in a heap at the bottom next to the lit lantern. He heard growls and it raised itself to its feet.

It was a man, hugely obese with wild, unkempt hair, his eyes scanning the cellar with a lack of recognition like a feral animal. He sniffed at the air before turning his gaze to Hood. His tattered clothes and huge butcher's apron were stained with blood. He shrieked, and charged at Hood with huge arms raised.

Chapter 9 – No One Will Save You

"Let's find out how badly you want to live, shall we?" Hood heard Leonard's voice hooting down the stairs.

"Stop!" was all Hood managed to shout before the massive man bore down on him. He dove to the side but his chains hampered him. He relied on quickness more often than not, but as the man swung his arms like clubs in a downward arc, Hood knew this was not a fight speed could win. He flung his arms over his head as the force of the blows smashed Hood's manacles into his own skull. Dazed, Hood tried to keep his focus on the beast, the firelight of the lantern casting him in demonic shadows.

The butcher clamped down on Hood's shoulders and squeezed him like a vice. He felt his bones flexing under the pressure. A gutteral scream came out of the butcher's mouth as he opened it wide to reveal broken, bloody teeth and moved close. He was trying to bite Hood.

Panic set in.

Hood managed to cross his forearms in front of his face. The butcher's open maw tangled with the crossed chains attached to Hood's wrists. The rancid, dead smell of his breath was enough to make Hood gag. The butcher bit down on the metal. He recoiled with a scream, shoving Hood away, into the wall.

Hood smashed into the concrete, his knees buckling as he slid to the ground. His chest radiated pain; his body was exhausted.

Keep it together. He's strong, but he's not smart.

The Butcher charged at him again with a roar. Hood grabbed onto one of the butcher's outstretched arms with both hands and fell to the floor, yanking downward with all his strength. The butcher's momentum worked against him as his face crashed into the concrete wall.

Blood poured out of the butcher's face onto the floor as he backed away screaming, his huge hands pawing at his broken nose. He nearly stepped on the lit lantern Leonard had left on the floor of the cellar.

He's still dangerous. You don't have room to make a mistake.

The butcher was breathing heavily and covered in his own blood. He looked like a bull ready to charge. He roared, spitting more blood. Again he hurled himself at Hood.

The chains only allowed so much room for defense. He had to wait until the butcher was close enough before he lunged forward with a kick to the butcher's left kneecap. He felt a snap as the man's knee bent backward. Another inhuman screech echoed in the cellar as the heavy man nearly fell on top of Hood.

The Butcher leaned against the wall, sliding to the floor, no longer trying to kill but clawing at his destroyed knee.

Do what you have to do. He managed to get one of the chains around the Butcher's neck, and he yanked as hard as he could, holding it tight. The huge man thrashed and gurgled, clawing at the chain. Hood shook violently as he held the chain taut around the man's throat.

The huge man flailed his arms heavily, thumping into Hood's side and his head. Hood curled down, trying to make himself small while still holding the chain tight. Suddenly the Butcher heaved himself forward, dragging Hood with him, and slammed the two of them backwards into the concrete wall. Hood lost his grip on the chain, the wind nearly being knocked out of him. He heard the Butcher's sharp intake of air as he reached back and grabbed Hood by the back of the neck. Hood grabbed for the chain but his hand slid off, the metal slick with the Butcher's blood. Another great hand planted itself under Hood's stomach and lifted him into the air.

Raw, animal horror gripped Hood. Aglow in the hellish lamplight the wide, bloodraged eyes of the wild man stared up at him. The thick fingers of the Butcher clamped down on Hood's neck causing his neck muscles to seize in response. The butcher pulled, intent on tearing Hood's head clean off.

Adrenaline surged through Hood's body. His chains rattled as he grabbed the Butcher's thick forearm with both hands and dug all ten fingers into the tendons on the soft side. The muscles in Hood's neck burned, he tasted blood in his mouth, his jaw clenched shut. Hood felt the flesh separate underneath his nails as they broke skin and dug into the Butcher's forearm. He fell from the air, the Butcher's arm giving out.

Without hesitation Hood spun himself upright and pulled one of the chains around the huge man's neck once more and pulled it tight with his whole body. Hood laced his fingers through the links in the chain and locked his grip down. Clumsy blows rained down on Hood's head as the man swung his arms backwards, but Hood pulled himself tight into a ball and pulled the chain tighter. All his senses dulled, all thought evaporated. There was only the chain and his grip. A wild uppercut swung towards Hood, glancing off the side of his head. The near miss sent a shock through his spine bringing him back to reality, but he kept his grip tight woven around the chain. *If that had landed square. . .* He leaned backwards as to avoid any more haymakers. *Focus on the chain.*

The muscles in his arms screamed, wanting to give out. His hands shook, and again the huge man's thick fingers plucked at the metal collar hopelessly. His puffy face started to turn blue and quiver wildly. Gutteral gurgles welled out of the Butcher, and with a last quake the huge man's breath gave out and his muscles went slack.

Hood let go and pushed himself against the wall, climbing to stand up. Hyperventilating, he moved as far away as he could from the bloody body of the monster, his chains clinking against the concrete floor. Then he slid down against the wall and back to the floor, shaking from adrenaline and exhaustion, his arms limp and sapped of strength.

What the fuck was that?

Hood closed his quivering hands into fists. He tried to regain his composure, propping his elbows on his knees. He breathed slowly and deliberately. His head and chest throbbed from where he was hit by the monster. Slowly the pain came back as the adrenaline subsided. But with it, a rush of victory swept over him. *I'm still alive.*

He leaned his head back against the wall, closing his eyes. *They won't stop me. I will find Taylor and Ian, I will save them, and I'm going to kill the Kaiser for putting us through this hell.*

The cellar doors swung open with a bang and Leonard walked down with two of his lackeys carrying guns and flashlights.

"Hope my monster didn't make too much of a mess down here," he said to the guys.

Hood stood up with a jingle of chains. "Well, you might need a winch to pull him out."

The flashlight beams that focused on Hood caused him to shield his eyes with one hand. Just holding up his arm was exhausting. Looking down at his clothes, he saw just how much blood was on him.

Leonard stood for a moment in disbelief. He sighed, looking annoyed. "All of this lying and not dying you're doing is really fucking pissing me off."

He ran his fingers over his mustache.

"Something to eat would be nice," Hood said. His legs felt weak.

"Why feed the dead?" Leonard said. "Last chance, Ryan Seacrest. Where is your comrade and the supplies?"

Hood managed a slight grin. "You know you catch more flies with honey than vinegar."

Leonard shook his head, motioned to the two men and pulled out his revolver.

They approached Hood, guns trained on him. One unlocked his manacles and the other stared him down, rifle raised. Fear washed over Hood again. *They're just going to execute me here.* He tried to think of something to say or do, but he could barely think. *He still wants something from you. Use that.* Hood's heart ran wild once more in his chest. With the flashlight in his eyes he could barely make out the features of the man beside him, aside from his heavy brow and wide chin. He contemplated jumping him when the shackles were off, but this was a tight squeeze and he'd be dead before he could wrest the gun from his hands.

After the shackles were off they handcuffed him and prodded him forward. They moved slow up the stairs and out of the cellar, into bright sunlight. It was a beautiful day with a cloudy blue sky. There were a number of men with guns waiting around, some joking with each other, some silent. Leonard motioned and his captors shoved Hood down the street. The nearby buildings and houses were shuttered and dark, long since looted. Looking back at the cellar, Hood could see the building had once been a bar. No one spoke as they walked. It was surreal, so much so that his mind struggled to process it. *You're being led by a firing squad.*

Hood thought about trying to run, about some kind of escape. But they had too many people and there was no cover. They approached a broken chain link fence that stood around a construction lot of dirt and gravel, with a few rectangles of cement and rebar sticking out of the earth. As they walked towards the back of the lot, the smell of death and decay filled Hood's nose. It was sickly sweet and it made him feel ill. In a fenced-off lot there was even less chance of escape. *I'm fucked.*

Be calm. There's a way out of this.

They led him to a large pit from which the smell emanated. A mountain of desiccated bodies stared up from inside. This was their dumping ground.

Hood's hands started to shake. His hunger, mixed with the horrific smell, made his stomach feel like a black hole. The men led him to the edge of the pit, where Leonard stood in front of him.

They're just trying to scare you. He pleaded with himself. It wasn't working. *This is where they will kill you.*

"All right," Leonard said, flicking away a cigarette. "You know what I want."

Hood contemplated lying to him. What could he say? He had told Leonard the truth, but that wasn't what he wanted to hear. What *did* he want to hear? Where could he send him?

Leonard raised the chrome revolver to Hood's forehead. Why hadn't he come up with a convincing lie? He was so nauseous he could barely think, and the smell of death was overwhelming.

Leonard pulled the hammer back and pulled the trigger.

Click.

Silence. Hood exhaled with a shuddering breath, doubling over. Tears came out of his eyes. He gasped, not knowing why he deserved to live or what reason he had to live aside from seeing his family again, but he desperately wanted to survive.

A sinister smile crept across Leonard's face. He opened the revolver and slowly put six bullets in it, flipping the cylinder closed with a flourish.

"Scary, huh?"

Hood said nothing, struggling to pull himself together. *The man just wants to know something. Tell him anything. Make it up. Just don't fucking die in this hell.*

Leonard took a step closer.

His green eyes were beaming with sick pleasure in his dominance.

As Hood opened his mouth to speak, he heard a familiar bird call. He'd heard it hundreds of times before. Hood looked up at Leonard and smiled back. *Get ready to die you piece of shit.*

"Okay then. I think I'll put you right over there, next to the bodies of your girlfriend's family," Leonard said, raising the revolver. Hood sprang into action, pushing the revolver aside with his handcuffed hands and grabbing Leonard by the suit jacket. He yanked the two of them backwards into the pit. They floated in the air for what seemed like an eternity before crashing onto the spongy bodies of the dead. He felt the crack of old bones beneath them. The smell of rotten flesh decaying filled his nose, his mouth, his entire being. He gagged violently. The boom of shotgun blasts fired from somewhere outside of the pit.

Next to him, Leonard vomited out a once-hearty meal. Hood was, for once, glad there was nothing in his stomach. The revolver lay on a fleshy ribcage next to Hood's head. He grabbed it and spun around. He squeezed the trigger, the shot blasting gore out of Leonard's head while he vomited again.

Quickly Hood rolled Leonard's body over himself as cover, blood and fluid from Leonard's head pouring onto his face. The tangy metallic taste forced his stomach up, trying to hurl itself out with a vengeance. He spat the blood out of his mouth. Bullets thwacked into Leonard's corpse and the other bodies around him.

He aimed the iron-sights and shot at Leonard's soldier, who was firing at him from the side of the pit. The man doubled over, collapsing to the ground. Hood fired once more, connecting with the man's head. He peered around Leonard's body and saw no more of the men, though gunshots and shotgun blasts still blared. Hood tossed Leonard's body off him, lifting himself up into a massive cloud of insects. He ran to the edge of the pit, his feet crunching down into the corpses with each step. He pulled himself out onto the flat dirt, which felt like a freshly made bed by comparison.

Hood jumped to his feet. Several of Leonard's men lay face down in pools of blood. Two men moved in opposite directions to flank a concrete piling riddled with bullet scars that Whiskey was using for cover. Hood pulled the revolver to sight, training on the closer man as he strafed across with rifle raised. There was no doubt or hesitation. Hood exhaled and squeezed the trigger, the hammer slamming down with a loud crack and the man falling into a heap.

Whiskey moved to the other side of the piling, away from the man who was trying to flank him, pushing a cartridge into the shotgun. Hood pulled his pistol to sight on the other side of the piling, about head high. The man charged around the other side just as Hood pulled the trigger. The body collapsed a few feet from Whiskey. The shot echoed across the construction yard, followed by silence. Hood leaned over, putting his hands on his knees.

Whiskey stood up, the sound of his methodical footsteps coming closer. Blue sky shone behind him and the faintest bit of smoke still trailed from the barrel of his police-issue shotgun.

"You beautiful bastard," Hood said, all the muscles in his body loosening. "You pulled it off again." He collapsed into a sitting position, arms on his knees, still clutching the revolver in his hand. *Holy shit.* Hood was scared to turn and look at the pit of bodies now that his life was no longer in danger. *How the hell did I make it out of that? How could anyone stand up to that onslaught of death?* A creeping thought in Hood's mind told him that this was not the worst of it. This was just an outpost, a serfdom of the Kaiser's. *I don't know what kind of hell there could be out there worse than this, but I hope I never have to see it.*

Whiskey looked around to scan the area, then down at Hood. Hood held up his hand for aid in getting to his feet.

Whiskey shook his head, repulsed by Hood's outstretched hand. "Don't touch me, you're disgustin'."

Hood slowly brought himself to a standing position from on all fours and looked down at his clothes. The shirt and jeans he had been wearing were covered in blood and decayed human remains.

"Any of that yours?" Whiskey quipped.

Hood lifted his arms and inspected himself. With the adrenaline wearing off, the stench was overpowering.

"Fit as a fiddle," Hood said, shaking his head in disbelief. "I can't get the smell out of my head though." He shivered thinking about it. He spat out blood. When he realized it wasn't his, he dry heaved violently, repeatedly, his body refusing to stop.

Whiskey snorted, looking around at the bodies. "You are one lucky prick."

Hood spat, though his mouth was dry and devoid of saliva. "Was that luck? Or pure skill?" Hood pulled off his shirt, wiped his face with what little of it wasn't disgusting and tossed it away.

"You're so full of shit." Whiskey said. "I smell a load in those drawers of yours."

"You're welcome, by the way." Hood slapped Whiskey in the chest of his flak jacket, moving away from the horrid scene.

"*I'm welc*– are you serious?" Whiskey shouted. "No, no, you come back and thank me."

Hood snorted. "Yeah, you really had those two guys under control."

Whiskey's face twitched. "Oh, *okay.* What were you gonna do if I didn't show up, bust out a shovel and dig your way out?"

Hood held up a middle finger. He picked up an automatic rifle from one of the dead men and walked towards the hole in the chain link fence.

"*Don't* say thanks, asshole!" Whiskey held back a gag at the smell emanating from the pit and got moving. "Yeah, nice to see you again too!"

Hood made a heart shape with his hands over his head.

Chapter 10 – Fray

Hood and Whiskey searched the nearest ransacked colonial houses outside the construction area. Hood scoured cabinets and storerooms for water to clean himself off with, while Whiskey growled complaints that they were wasting time, and needed to clear out Leonard's bar before the rest of their captors grew suspicious.

Hood felt that death was inside him, surrounding him, and he desperately wanted to cleanse himself of the stink of it. The thought that sickness and rot had invaded his body was one he could not shake from his mind. As he hustled from house to house clawing through dust covered belongings, his thoughts drifted to Leonard's bar, and Kerry.

He clenched his jaw thinking about her. They had wasted so much time here. What happens if they make it to D.C. And Taylor, Ian, the Kaiser's soldiers are all gone? *Whiskey wouldn't say it, but we both would know it's my fault. Because she lured me in to this pit of vipers. Because I was too stupid to see it. Kerry did all this for her family, and they were dead the whole fucking time. She was too stupid to see that. She'd struggled in the vain hope she was keeping them alive. By the looks of the bodies, they'd been dead a long time. She might've fucked up, but she doesn't deserve this. I might've done the same thing in her shoes.*

He hoped she was gone so she might go on living, never having to know what happened. But he also wanted her to be there. Maybe it was brushing so close with death; maybe it was the loss and hopeful naivete they shared, but passion for her welled up inside him.

He tried to shake it out of his head. It was just a distraction, an animal impulse. He wasn't going to lose focus. Not again. They had to get to D.C. *Please, let them still be there. I don't know what I'll do if they're gone.*

Hood cursed under his breath in a fit of joy and Whiskey cursed loudly in relief when they found and extricated a bottle of distilled water from a musty garage. It was hidden behind plastic two-liter bottles filled with used motor oil.

Hood tore off his clothes and poured the water over his head, the cold freshness of it gliding over him. He felt invigorated, baptized by its purity.

Whiskey reappeared in the doorway to the house from the garage. He tossed him a towel and dropped a pile of clothes onto the ground before going back inside.

Hood scrubbed himself violently with the towel, which smelled faintly of detergent and dust. He was alive. He felt foolish knowing now that Whiskey's prevailing sense of mistrust was justified. Hood knew he shouldn't feel any remorse for killing anyone who could be a threat. *We're all just animals, now. Fighting to stay alive. Do not hesitate.* Hood gnawed on his lip, the clean water tasting like heaven. *That's not true, though.* Hood scrubbed his hair with the towel, hoping to get the filth out. *We're still alive. Other people like us are still alive. The sick bastards like Leonard, they're the ones that have to die. They're the ones we have to kill. They have to be hunted down like the animals they are.*

After a few tries, he found a tee shirt and jeans in the pile that fit right. They smelled musty and old, but that was the fragrance of the gods compared to the stench of the pit.

As Hood and Whiskey hustled down the road to the bar, Hood gripped the automatic rifle he'd taken, the knurled grip somehow comforting against his palm.

"Doesn't look like there's much of anyone left inside," Whiskey said, breaking the silence.

Hood peered over the hood of an abandoned car outside Leonard's bar.

"There's more inside," Hood said.

"Do you know how many?" Whiskey looked around. The old street was quiet and still. "I'd rather not step into a shooting gallery."

"There shouldn't be too many." Hood strained to see inside of the one window that wasn't boarded up. "But I'm not sure."

"I'll take point." Hood handed the rifle to Whiskey, who gave him his shotgun.

Whiskey set the rifle on the hood of the car. Hood dashed across the street, head down, to the front door of the bar. He peered inside the window. It looked empty from this vantage point. He waved over Whiskey, who hustled up to his side. They quietly climbed the steps to the door. Whiskey nodded at him before pulling it open, while Hood slipped inside.

"That took awhile," he heard a man say. "Did the kid talk?"

They don't deserve to live. Hood strode through the open double doors of the foyer with the shotgun against his shoulder.

A bearded man stood at a small table with a deck of cards in his hand. He lunged for a pistol on the table and Hood fired twice, deep booms echoing through the room as the man fell backwards over his chair.

Another man rose up from behind the bar in Hood's peripheral vision, raising a submachine gun to sight. Hood spun and fired twice in his direction as he dove to the ground.

The man fired in a wild spray and ducked back behind the bar. Hood's heart fired off in his chest, but he was not hit.

Whiskey sprinted across the length of the bar and leaned over it, firing at the crouched man.

The sharp ringing sound stuck in Hood's ears as he climbed to his feet. The room fell silent otherwise. Hood pointed the shotgun at the staircase, his hands sweating on the grip. Whiskey circled the bar and gazed down at the man, who was wheezing from gunshot wounds. No one came down the stairs.

"Don't shoot." Hood heard the man behind the bar gasp. Hood peered over the bar. He had dropped his gun and was clutching a wound in his chest. Whiskey stood over him.

"Mercy!" The man uttered.

Three rapid shots cracked the air from Whiskey's rifle. "Too late for that," Whiskey muttered. He leaned down and picked up the SMG.

"I think we're clear," Hood said, still keeping the shotgun in firing position.

Whiskey walked up beside him and fired another round into the prone bearded man.

"Sick bastards don't deserve it this easy."

Hood glanced at the corpse of the bearded man. It was strange how unhuman a body looked. On the table was a game of solitaire. Didn't look like it had been going too well, either.

Whiskey motioned to the stairs. Hood raised the warm shotgun to sight again as the two of them approached the staircase. The rest of the bar was open space, dotted by tables covered in everything from clothes to half-eaten meals and bullet casings.

Hood walked up the stairs to the first floor landing, pointing the shotgun at the painted black door at the top. Whiskey followed behind. They climbed the rest of the stairs slowly, the old wood creaking under their feet. Behind the door, a child cried, and was quickly hushed.

Whiskey kicked the door open and they both sighted their guns into a room of women and children huddled together. There were probably twenty of them.

The room had a number of beds and dressers and looked well lived-in. The women were dressed in tight fitting clothes and stared with terror at them both.

"Hold up your hands!" Whiskey shouted. "Don't do anything and we won't hurt you."

A sharp-eyed, thin middle-aged woman with partially dyed blonde hair leapt to her feet with a pistol in two hands. Two shots cracked from Whiskey's rifle and blood splattered onto the women and children behind her who started screaming.

"Like I said," Whiskey uttered, wearing an expression of deep displeasure at having had to do what he did. "Don't do anything." The children were crying loudly, the women staring mutely at the two of them.

"The men are dead," Hood said. "You're free."

No one moved, or said a thing. Then Kerry stood up from the corner of the room and walked forward.

"I know these guys. They aren't going to hurt you," she said, looking apologetically at Hood. Hood glanced at her as he snatched up his belongings from a table against the wall. His head swam. She moved deliberately, confidently, with a blank expression on her face that emanated nervousness. She watched him, waiting for a response. Smooth, delicate cheeks, calm blue eyes, like the first time they met. Though that was all a lie. An act. Maybe she was nothing like what he thought she was. Or maybe she was just like him, fighting in the hope to save family.

She thought she could just stride up to them and act like everything was fine. That was bullshit, and yet . . . he felt the desire to throw himself on top of her.

He closed his eyes a moment. *Would you see the truth in her shoes? That her family was dead the whole time? Or would you want to believe they were alive and you could do something to save them?*

He wanted to hate her for what she did. But she reminded him of home somehow, that life he loved before everything went to hell. Maybe that was why he wanted to forgive her. His mind conjured up images of the two of them sitting on the couch in his parents house, binge watching an epic series together. That didn't make any sense. That world was gone.

Whiskey lowered the rifle, strode purposefully to Kerry and grabbed her by the arm. He moved towards the stairs as she cursed at him to let her go, struggling against his grip.

"Wait, *wait!*" Hood yelled and followed them down the stairs.

Kerry was pleading to reason with Whiskey, unsuccessfully trying to wrench free of his hold on her. He ignored her all the way out the front door. As Hood burst through to the outside world, Kerry was kneeling in the parking lot and Whiskey had his pistol to the back of her head.

"Stop!" Hood yelled. "Wait a goddamned second!" He put down his rifle and backpack and held out both hands to Whiskey.

"Remember what I told you," Whiskey responded, unrelenting.

Kerry was crying softly.

"She was trying to save her family. She didn't have any other choice!" Hood shouted, holding Whiskey's enraged gaze.

"How do you know that? Is that what she told you when they had you locked up like an animal?" Whiskey looked almost crazed. "She almost got you killed. And me, too, in the process. Does that mean nothing to you?"

Hood reached out and put his hand on Whiskey's pistol. Whiskey shoved him away.

"One of these times I won't make it out, or no one will be there to save you," Whiskey said. "I don't forget that pit full of bodies so quickly. People like them die because of people like *her*."

"Those people die because of guys like Leonard and the Kaiser," Hood shouted, pointing at the bar. "This is not on her head."

"There will always be evil fuckers like them."

Kerry turned her head. "I'm just--"

"Shut your mouth!" Whiskey screamed, pushing the pistol into the back of her head. The wind howled, tossing her hair against the gun and Whiskey's hand.

"You're not putting these things into perspective," Hood yelled, moving quickly into Whiskey's personal space. "What would *you* do, huh? Let's say that fucktard held a gun to Taylor's head, what would you or I do? You gonna stand up to that? Or are you gonna do whatever it takes to keep her alive?"

"You've bought every little line she's fed you, from the minute you met her," Whiskey said venomously. "You think I don't know what it's like to be young? Every hot piece of ass looks like The One. This has nothing to do with her. This has to do with you being a lost kid who can't face reality."

"What reality is that? That no one else deserves to live besides us?" Hood barked.

"*Reality* is that if we don't save Taylor, no one will. If we die out here chasing around every sad fuck we come across, she's dead."

"You think I don't know that?" Hood said. "Why did we fight for Clearwater, huh? I don't know about you, but I did it because I *believe* that there are good people out there, people worth fighting for. They don't deserve this."

As the words came out, he knew he'd heard them before. In the dead man's journal. *They're good kids. They don't deserve this.* Hood bit down on his lip. *You might have died alone fighting against us, but I won't forget what you said.*

"Look what we got for living like that. It's time we learned from our mistakes." Whiskey said quietly, staring Hood down. Hood kept his gaze.

"It wasn't a mistake. I'll never regret the way we lived in Clearwater. It was a beautiful life, even if this is the way things turned out."

"You're a damn fool, then." Whiskey said with a bitter look. "I'm sorry kid, but this has to happen." Whiskey aimed at Kerry and started to squeeze the trigger.

Kerry cried out and put up her hands.

"You can't fucking do it!" Hood screamed.

"Why not?" Whiskey raged back at him.

Hood inhaled deeply, taking a step closer to him. "John, listen to me. This isn't you. It's a gradual slide into darkness. How long before we're killing good people just to get what we need? You would've done the same thing in her shoes to save Taylor. You know that. Don't even pretend. You *know* that."

Over his own outstretched arm, Whiskey glared fire at Hood.

He returned his gaze, steadfast. The only sound was a crinkling plastic bag wrapped around a fence pole in the wind.

"I swear . . ." Whiskey shook his head. ". . .You're just like him," he said at length. The pause and the tone of his voice implied he had something else to say, but he stayed silent.

Hood shrugged in exhaustion. *Just like whom?* He'd never heard Whiskey say anything like that before.

Whiskey put down the gun. "This is the second time. You're going to regret this." He spat towards Kerry, and walked into the street.

Hood rubbed his eyes with his thumb and forefinger, exhaling deeply. He wanted so badly to sleep. He wouldn't get to anytime soon.

Kerry collapsed onto all fours, breathing heavily, tears falling off her face onto the pavement.

"Are you okay?" Hood asked.

She nodded. He reached out a hand. She looked up and grabbed it, and he lifted her to her feet, though her expression told him she didn't want to be standing.

"Why didn't you run?" Hood said in a flat tone.

She hesitated. "I don't have anything left to run to."

"He would have killed you."

"That might not be worse than being alone."

Hood stared at her, but when she stared back he broke eye contact, watching Whiskey's retreating form as he strode down the road.

"You're welcome," Hood said with more venom than he expected.

"I didn't want to do this to you guys. I never wanted it to be like this. I didn't have a choice. You have to know that," She said, looking down at the pavement.

Yeah, I know. "We can't stay here. Try to take it easy around him. He's not exactly going to be forgiving," Hood said to her.

"I don't blame him," she said quietly. "I did a horrible thing to you two."

"Yeah, you did." Hood picked up his backpack and rifle. "We all have done horrible things."

She looked forlorn. She glanced at Whiskey, then back to Hood, pulling her hair out of her eyes, running her hand over her head, fidgeting as she brought up the subject. "So my family. . ."

Lie to her. Tell her you didn't find them. Hood looked her in the eyes. Eyes that were desperate, hopeful, scared of a response. He shook his head slowly. "They're dead."

She seemed to stare through him, her eyes glazing over. She nodded, bowing her head in response, her hair curtaining around her face.

"I just. . . I thought maybe. . ." She swallowed, holding her left forearm with her right hand, her thumb rubbing it compulsively.

"Thank you for saving my life. . . And believing I'm worth saving," she said finally, looking away at the empty road dotted with stripped-down, abandoned houses. *Worth saving. You almost got us killed. Left Taylor and Ian alone to fend for themselves. But yeah, you don't deserve to die.* Despite the anger he felt, Hood couldn't deny the good he saw in her. Better people have done worse. And there are more people like us out there, worth saving. *Like Taylor.*

Hood slung his rifle over his shoulder, sniffing. "You've got a second chance. Do something with it."

She made no response, engulfed by her thoughts.

"I'll give you a minute. We'll be just up the road."

Hood headed off to follow Whiskey. *This was some kind of miracle.*

His feet carried him on will alone down the road towards the truck, an immense feeling of relief washing over him. Hunger finally started to overtake the nausea.

Sooner or later our luck will run out. I can't hesitate. Too many more of these and we'll all die. They weren't far from D.C., Whiskey had told him. Behind him, he heard Kerry break into sobs. His heart went out to her. Part of him wanted to turn back, give some sort of comfort to her. *God, I hope to never have to feel what she's feeling right now.* But he did not stop, eyes fixed on the truck.

Chapter 11 – Wasteland

It was like Ground Hog's Day. Whiskey stared out the windshield, a reserved facial expression retaining what must've been a sea of doubts. Kerry sat asleep in between them, and Hood stared out the window as they sped down the overgrown interstate under a muted gray sky, desolate suburbs hiding behind thin veils of trees.

Except this time, everything was different. Kerry had silently wept herself to sleep. Whiskey had accepted her presence. He no longer saw her as a threat. A burden, maybe. But he seemed too calm for the situation at hand; D.C. was just ahead. Hood was a mixture of optimism and anxiety. He couldn't shake a strange feeling that there was something, some detail that he'd somehow missed along the way.

If everything they knew about D.C. was true, it wasn't a place he wanted to come home to. The city was now a graveyard. Anyone with a half a mind stayed away.

It was strange that the Kaiser would be there. There had to be a reason behind his presence. Was he hiding there to strike out at the Sons of Liberty up north?

None of it mattered, really. They just had to get to the church of the Epiphany. Or so the Sheriff had said. This whole ordeal was hinging on the fact that the Sheriff wasn't lying, or misinformed about where the Kaiser was after the sacking of Clearwater. *Chasing the words of an insane old bastard.*

Whiskey pulled the old pickup to a stop. A wall of destroyed cars on the road stretched before them, and it wasn't something they were going to be able to navigate around. Whiskey cursed and threw the truck into park, getting out. Hood got out of the passenger side and blinked his bleary eyes. The moment they'd been closed had felt so good. He wanted to lie down and sleep. The strong winds that blew the dust from the wrecked capitol across the stygian river didn't help.

"How much stuff are we going to bring?" Hood asked, resting his forearms on the roof of the truck. As always, his automatic rifle hung at his side.

"We should stay pretty light. Just food and the necessary tools. Bring the masks, too, and some rope. I'll try to hide the truck somewhere before we go."

"Do you think we should get a few hours' sleep before we go?" Kerry suggested, hopping out of the truck.

Whiskey turned around to face her. "No, we shouldn't, because it's already taken forever getting' here. Do you want to take a guess as to why?"

"I'm just saying ... maybe sleep for thirty minutes. You guys look like you're falling down in exhaustion."

"Just don't go anywhere," he said, getting in the truck and slamming the door, driving off the road.

Hood looked at her and shrugged. "You sure you want to do this with us? We don't know what exactly we're going up against, here."

She took two steps and looked up at the muted sky, inhaling deeply. "Yeah. I'm sure."

"Good. I have one thing to ask you. Consider it a road to redemption, if you care for that sort of thing."

Kerry worked her mouth. "Okay. . .uh, what is it?"

"If something happens to me and Whiskey, I want you to find my sister. However long it takes, find her. Look out for her. Not that she'll need it."

"How will I know her? You're going to have to be more specific."

"Her name is Taylor Huntington. She looks like, well, she looks like the girl version of me. But pretty, brown hair. . . You'll know. She's one of a kind. Tell her I love her--we love her. And that I know she's strong enough to survive."

Kerry nodded slowly. "Okay."

"Can you promise? I know this is asking a lot." Hood asked. He felt a bit lighter, just asking. Imagining Taylor captive in the Kaiser's empire for the rest of her life made his chest tighten.

"I promise."

She stared at him, and he tried not to look at her, instead gazing at the barren rows of headstones that were Arlington Cemetery. It felt strange talking that way, talking as if he was going to be dead. But he needed to say it. She owed them, and this was the best payment she could give.

"I figured there was some reason you guys brought me along." She looked down at her boots.

"We need all the help we can get. Whiskey knows that." He climbed up to the roof of one of the ruined vans cluttering the road. "Besides. I know you're not stupid enough to try to fuck us over again. I'd pull the trigger myself if you did." The George Mason and Williams Bridges ahead of them had both collapsed into the murky Potomac. They'd have to walk north through Arlington to get across.

"I want to help," Kerry said, "You guys are trying to do something good. It's been a long time since I could say I've done the same."

"Hey, if helping us eases your conscience, two birds one brick," Hood said, staring past the river to the ruined city ahead of them. It looked unearthly, seeing so many great buildings reduced to scarred rubble. "Check out the view."

She climbed up onto the van and stared.

"Wow." She rested her hand at the base of her neck, taking in the full scope of the fragmented remnants of the city.

"Yeah."

"It's kinda beautiful," she said. "If only it weren't so horrifying."

Hood looked at her.

134

Her eyes focused on the horizon, like she was searching for the right words.

"It's like the ashes before the rebirth. I can picture what the city might look like hundreds of years from now, overgrown and reborn."

That would imply that humanity wouldn't be around or able to rebuild it. Hood searched Kerry's face. Her expression wasn't one of resignation, like someone waiting for the end. *Is she just with us out of fear of being alone? Or does she believe we're going to survive?*

Even if all went flawlessly and they saved Taylor and Ian and whoever else, what would they do afterwards? Find some remote place and try to live a quiet life all over again, hoping they could hide away from it all?

Hood wondered how long this would go on–if this part of history was the end of history. It seemed that humans and the planet were running a race that only one of them could win. He shook the thought out of his head. He didn't have the time or the energy for the philosophical right now. *Don't get ahead of yourself. There's enough for you to fight in front of you.*

He hopped down to the ground and sat on the hood of the ruined van. The suspension creaked, as if it wanted to give out to the meager pull of gravity alone. Kerry slowly came down off the roof and stood next to him, still staring at the city across the river.

"I've never been to D.C.," Kerry pulled loose hairs out of the corner of her mouth. "Even before the bomb, I'd never been," she said with a hint of wistfulness.

"I grew up there," Hood said. "A great city."

Kerry nodded in agreement. She looked down at the ground, shielding her face from the wind in the collar of her jacket.

"Ground zero is far northwest of the national mall and most of the city."

"What exactly are we going to do?" Kerry asked.

"Rescue Taylor and Ian from the Kaiser's men. If they're still there. We'll scope it out when we get there and come up with a plan."

Hood sighed. "I just hope they're okay." *I really want to know how you got caught up with the Kaiser, Ian. There better be a damn good reason.*

Ian saved Taylor's life that day. Hood knew that. Maybe the two of them had already escaped together. *God, I hope so. If only there was some way to know.*

Hood bit down hard on his bottom lip, staring down at the cracked road beneath him. He fought off the surge of doubt that followed. He'd never felt further away from everyone he cared about.

She sat down on the car beside him, folding one leg under the other. "Why do you think we survived?"

Hood knew what she meant. He thought the same thing. *Why would I live when so many others died?*

"I don't know."

"When I was young, and I didn't get the job I wanted, or if the guy I liked started dating my friend, I'd just say 'Everything happens for a reason.'"

Hood sniffed a blast of cool salt air blowing off the Potomac. She took a deep breath. *But?*

"It feels so stupid looking back on it. From this perspective, it's like saying everyone who died, or had something terrible happen to them deserved it somehow, as if tragedy was their destiny. But I still want to believe it's true. Maybe we're still alive because there's something we're supposed to do," she concluded, picking flaking paint off the hood of the car as she stared across the river.

"It's comforting to think like that."

"What do you think?" she asked, rubbing the paint flakes off her fingertips.

He licked his dry lips and looked up at the clouds, which moved sluggishly. "The way I figure it, I didn't blow up with my city when the bombs dropped, so every day past that one has just been gravy." He managed a morose smile. "It's all just fuckin' random. It's easy to say we're supposed to be alive, because we are still alive. The dead can't say shit." Hood scratched behind his ear. "Maybe the real

136

tragedy isn't dying at doomsday but surviving long enough to not know what to do with yourself."

Kerry let out a thoughtful hmph, hopping off of the car. She strode down the road and looked over at the river. She intertwined her fingers and raised her hands above her head in a feline stretch. Hood watched with an unintentional possessiveness that comes with physical attraction to a girl. *Don't let yourself get pulled in. She's fucked you over once. You might think she's good, but she's only proven she can't be trusted. She's just another body to help you get Taylor and Ian back.* Did he really believe that?

"Why don't you hate me?" she asked finally, turning to see a reaction. *Mind reader.*

Hood removed his rifle from his shoulder and laid it across his lap. "Who said I didn't?"

"You open up to everyone you hate?"

"Nah, I guess not," he rubbed his nose twice.

"You could be dead because of me." Kerry said. She seemed almost perturbed that Hood didn't outwardly hate her. It didn't match her own guilt. *Well too fuckin' bad.*

"Oh, really? Well in that case," Hood lifted up his rifle and pointed it at her, making gunshot sounds with his mouth.

She froze for a moment, then laughed, moving the hair to one side of her face.

Hood smirked. *Act cute all you want. You've got to prove yourself.* He looked over his shoulder and saw Whiskey walking back, rubbing his neck. Hood stood up, stretching his legs.

"I think I knew, deep down, that there was no hope that my family was still alive," Kerry said, her face turning solemn. "But I wanted to believe I could save them."

Hood nodded slowly as Kerry turned to face the river and the broken city. *Don't we all.*

◆ ◆ ◆

The hill in front of them was slow and gradual, a worn path between the innumerable white gravestones. They moved quickly and quietly. Whiskey and Hood both scanned the horizon with guns partially raised. Kerry walked ahead of them. Whiskey had decided he wanted to be able to see her at all times. She strode forward, noticeably uncomfortable.

Whiskey refused to let her have a gun, which was unsurprising, given that he had just tried to kill her. The three of them continued down the path towards the bridge. The sun was setting and the Lincoln Memorial was visible past the river.

The reality of coming home hit Hood as they strode softly past the stone obelisks with eagles atop them, onto the Arlington bridge. A number of cars were burned down to the frame, the rims digging into the dusty asphalt. One humvee had smashed through the stone railing and was half hanging off the edge of the bridge. Broken bones and scattered skeletons littered the pavement. Only around half of the black, dormant street lamps still stood upright.

"Okay, I'm willing to admit that I'm scared," Kerry said aloud.

"There's nothin' left here. The only people we gotta look out for is the Kaiser's men," Whiskey said calmly, gesturing to keep moving.

It looked like the city he once called home, if it had been thrown through a nightmare. It almost didn't register as reality. *That doesn't matter anymore.* They were so close now. The church of the Epiphany was just northeast of here, if he remembered correctly. His mind conjured memories of his first time at the national mall, staring up at the monuments and wondering what they meant, as he held on to his mother's blue woolen mitten.

He threw the thoughts into the void of his mind, focusing on the smell of dust and the motionless hellscape ahead of him. The once-golden statues of men on horseback on the other side of the bridge were black with dirt and ashes. The trees surrounding the Lincoln memorial were dead or ripped from the ground, huge shelves of earth clinging to their roots and jutting into the air. Concrete road barriers had been blown away or crushed underneath the treads of a tank that sat blackened and defunct in a blasted ditch on the hill of the Lincoln memorial. The three of them trod silently through the blasted landscape, as if making noise would cause the charred remains of the dead to rise.

Nothing moved besides the paper and plastic that kicked up with the wind. The memorial was empty, save for Lincoln, who's face and famous beard had been reduced to rubble. Someone had spray-painted black chains on him from wrist to wrist. The Gettysburg address had been altered, as well. All that remained was *These dead shall not have died in vain. . . people shall not perish from the earth.*

A chill flashed through Hood's body as he read it. It seemed to communicate that all this death and destruction was someone's idea of a future. Hood and Whiskey had never known who or what caused the collapse of the country. The infrastructure collapsed so fast that there was no way of knowing. One thing was clear, though. There was no invading army. This was someone's homegrown revolution.

The walls of the Vietnam Veteran's Memorial were cracked and crumbled, and the long reflecting pool was a shallow, murky basin of sludge, the dark reflection of the broken mall on its surface. The north side of the mall had become an impassable wall of collapsed structures and upheaved earth. The Washington Monument was scarred and blackened, but still stood tall. The closer they got to the White House lawn, it became clear that much of the impassable terrain had been crafted on purpose. Walls of debris had been piled up to keep anyone from going north. Hood cursed softly, afraid any sound he made might somehow carry across the empty city.

"The Church of the Epiphany is just past all this. It's a bit east of the White house," Hood said, gnawing on his bottom lip.

Whiskey glared at the impasse, his nostrils flaring. "Hell, it ain't the Maginot line, so let's find a spot and climb through it."

Hood shook his head. "I don't like it. If someone finds us clambering over broken walls, we're not exactly in a good strategic position. And it looks like someone destroyed all this on purpose."

Whiskey stared motionless at the jagged wall. "I don't think the Kaiser did this."

"Probably not. But he's clearly smart enough to use it to his advantage while he's here." Hood took a step forward. Something he stepped on sank into the dirt under his foot. He lifted it and saw dull bullet casings pressed into the dark earth.

"Where's the subway?" Whiskey said, looking around.

"Oh, shit, the Metro!" Hood said, spinning on his toes and pointing to the Smithsonian metro stop. He sprinted towards it, weaving through two blown out black SUVs, a filing cabinet that looked like it had been ejected from somewhere by an explosion, and a sedan propped up by a run-over mailbox. Whiskey's and Kerry's footsteps carried across the empty mall behind him. He stopped at the stairs leading down to the metro. The walls were tagged with graffiti, some artfully crafted, some of it hasty scribbles of hate and rage.

Hood stared down at the landing that led to a metal gate and the dormant escalators in the dark. Whiskey and Kerry walked up beside him, Kerry registering the carnage there with a sharp intake of breath.

Hood hefted his rifle onto his shoulder. "Look at it this way, we found someone."

The landing was splattered with blood, and what had once been a body lay torn apart, a bloody ribcage showing amidst the mess of flesh. The nauseating sweet smell of decay was everywhere.

Kerry gagged, covering her mouth.

Hood himself had to fight the urge to heave. Immediately his brain conjured up Leonard's mass grave.

Hordes of flies spun around the corpse. It had been there a while. Above the fenced- off entrance, someone had written in blue spraypaint: *Salvation lies through the darkness.* It was markedly different in tone from the words scrawled onto the descending walls. Though one other tag stood out from the others. It was spraypainted in big white lettering, rivulets of dried white paint coming down from where it was stenciled: *STAY AWAKE, STAY ALIVE.*

"Do we really have to go down there?" Kerry asked, covering her nose and mouth with her hand.

Whiskey, too, looked askance at Hood.

"This goes straight to the church," he told them. "It's not far at all."

"All right then," Whiskey said, holding his shotgun ready with both hands. He nodded at Hood, looking at his backpack.

Hood pulled off his pack and opened it, pulling out the flashlights and gas masks, handing them out. He produced a roll of duct tape and carefully taped a flashlight to the underside of his rifle. He tossed the roll to Whiskey, who wasted no time taping his own flashlight to the side of his shotgun barrel. They hung the gas masks loose around their necks.

"I don't know about this. . ." Kerry said, watching them prepare their weapons. "I don't know what would do . . . that," she said, looking at the mangled corpse.

"Scavengers," Whiskey said, turning on the flashlight.

Kerry turned to Hood with a pleading look in her eyes. "Even you must think this is insane."

Hood took a deep breath through his nose, looking down the stairs into the dark. "I'm kinda curious, aren't you?"

"Admit it, you're scared!" Kerry said, pointing to the corpse. "That is *not* natural!"

"Of course I'm scared," Hood said. "Who isn't, anymore?"

Whiskey walked down the steps to the steel gate that sealed shut the entrance. A metal desk, a dumpster and a refrigerator sat in front of it, keeping it closed.

"Give me a hand with this?" He called back to Hood.

"Come on," Hood said to Kerry. "You'll be fine. I promise." He strode past the mangled body, heaving at the refrigerator as it squeaked and squealed against the concrete.

Kerry stared at him in consternation. "You're awfully quick to make promises!"

Hood flashed her a smile, and said nothing. One by one, he and

Whiskey moved the obstacles out of the way of the gate and pulled it open. Whiskey stepped inside, the beam of his light jumping back and forth from wall to wall. *You're either with us are you aren't.*

Hood paused for a moment, glancing back at Kerry. Her hands were in balled fists at her side, and on her face was a pleading expression. She didn't want to leave them. Otherwise she already be gone. *If you want her to prove herself, this is your chance to let her. She can't do much empty handed.*

He reached into his bag and felt the metal of the Glock 9mm. He grabbed it and strode to Kerry, placing it in her hands. Her warm hands wrapped around both the gun and his own. He hated how good just the feel of her hands on his was. She looked into his eyes, a mixture of surprise and fear in her own. "Point it at the bad guys," he said, winking at her and making a shushing sound, nodding towards Whiskey. He turned and went through the open gate and down the motionless escalator. *Don't make me regret this.*

At the bottom, he turned and looked back at Kerry once again. *Desperate times.* She cocked back the slide of the pistol and held it for a moment before she let it snap back into place. Then she tucked it into the back of her jeans, shook her hands at her sides and exhaled. With slow, deliberate steps, she followed them down into the station.

Chapter 12 – Descent

The beams of light from Hood's and Whiskey's guns danced inside the dark subway, crossing occasionally as they scanned back and forth. Their footsteps echoed with a metallic clank on each step down the escalators. Inside the metro, the ceiling was a like a huge concave waffle, rectangular indents running the length of the walls. Hood remembered thinking that as a kid. His familiarity with the station only made the broken landscape harder to take in. This couldn't be home.

They walked around the same bend as he had hundreds of times, down another set of escalators. The same escalators he lost his Hot Wheels truck in when he was a boy, crying on the train ride home. Maybe it was still down there, somewhere, covered in dust. At the bottom ran a long hallway. It was pitch black except for the flashlights. Piles of refuse and makeshift sleeping mats hid along the walls. The air was dry and acrid, like old dust in a bone-dry river bed. There was no sound but their footsteps, which echoed in the dark so loudly that he was sure people in Georgetown could hear them. He felt like an invader in a tunnel on some foreign planet, as if some giant bug monster would jump out and eat them, something out of Starship Troopers.

Hood exhaled slowly, closing his eyes. *You're in no danger. At least not from the architecture, anyway. The place isn't going to collapse on you. It isn't going to collapse on you.* He repeated, hands starting to sweat.

The long causeway toward the trains was littered with signs of life: Empty food wrappers, water bottles, beer cans, dirty newspapers and even an old ratty couch someone had brought down. Much of the refuse looked as though it had been torn apart.

Whiskey held the light on something on the floor and approached it cautiously: a puddle next to a metal subway bench. As he got close, he knelt down and shone the light around them. Hood sighted down his rifle and scanned the empty subway. Nothing was there.

"Is it blood?" Kerry asked.

"Keep it down," Whiskey whispered. "Speak only loud enough to be heard." He sniffed at the air, then touched the liquid, looked at it in the light, and smelled it again.

"It's water," Whiskey said quietly. "Clean water." Whiskey pointed his shotgun directly above them. The ceiling had no leaks; no droplets oozed through the cracks.

"Someone was here," Hood replied in a hushed tone.

"We don't really know that. This place looks as empty as the rest of the city. I think we should go back," Kerry whispered.

"We're not going back," Whiskey responded gruffly.

"We don't even know if the way through is clear. It could be a dead end," Kerry retorted. "We are literally and figuratively in the dark."

Whiskey turned around and pointed his shotgun into her face, the light blinding her. She shielded her eyes.

"I don't know why you're still here, or what exactly you intend to do with the rest of your short life, but you would be dead already if it weren't for Hood. If you don't agree with our decisions, then leave!" Whiskey growled.

Hood stepped up and pushed Whiskey's gun down.

"I just want to help," Kerry said.

"Oh yeah? And why is that? So you can sell us out to someone else

144

down the road?" Whiskey barked.

Hood moved between the two of them and patted Whiskey on the chest repeatedly, reiterating that they needed to stay quiet. The darkness around them felt overwhelming.

Kerry stood her ground, her feet residing in the halo of light from Whiskey's downward-facing shotgun.

"You may hate me, but you two are the only people I can trust. The closest thing to family I have left." She hung her head.

Whiskey glared at her, searching her for some sign of weakness, some hint of a lie. He hefted his shotgun and turned to continue. "You're not my goddamned family," Whiskey said.

She didn't answer.

Hood believed her. Enough to give her a gun, anyway. She had done terrible things, sure. But she wanted to redeem herself. It was also valuable having someone around who owed you their life. Just thinking it felt ugly, but it was reality. Was her life just a chip to bet? *Don't pretend like that's the only reason she's here. Don't pretend you don't feel the way you feel.*

"We have to stay quiet," Hood reiterated.

He could feel her eyes on him as he scanned the empty corridor. He faced her and offered a halfhearted smile of reassurance. "Come on," he said quietly. "Let's keep moving."

He walked forward silently, sighting down his rifle again, using the light to show the way. Whiskey was a few steps ahead of him, doing the same.

The corridor became an open balcony with steps down either side to the train platforms below. Hood saw nothing but rubble and refuse on the platforms, and the empty black train tracks below.

Whiskey grunted. "Anything?"

"No," Hood responded. "Both of the train tunnels have been sealed up with rubble. It looks like they wanted to block the exits."

"One of them on this side is open," Whiskey said. "Heading north."

"Isn't that the way we want to go?" Kerry asked.

"Yeah," Hood replied.

A cockroach scuttled across the floor, illuminated by the light from Hood's rifle. The three of them inspected the tunnel entrance, aglow from Whiskey's light.

"Doesn't that seem a little too convenient?" Kerry said.

Whiskey stared at the tunnel, clenching his jaw. His hesitation was response enough.

But Hood wasn't about to back away now. Not when they were so close.

"It doesn't matter," Hood said.

"What station does it lead to?" Kerry peered at it.

"Metro Center," Hood said, shining his light on the faded subway map on the wall. "If I remember it right."

Whiskey said nothing as he walked down the stairs to the platform on the north side, scanning the ground ahead of them. Hood followed behind him. A few rusty cans and some dirty plastic bags greeted them, the only inhabitants of the space. A soiled newspaper sat in a crumpled ball against the wall. Hood wondered what the date was today. It was hard to keep track.

Whiskey hopped down onto the train tracks. A skittering noise made him whirl around. Two rats ran down the tracks in the other direction. He let the shotgun rest at his side and rubbed the back of his head.

"I hate rats," Kerry said. "I'd rather see snakes."

Hood jumped down alongside Whiskey and shone his light into the open tunnel. Rubble had once blocked it, but it was strewn about as if the wall of refuse had been torn down. Wooden cabinets and a metal table lay against the platform, pieces of a garbage puzzle that had walled up this exit. Had someone dug it up to get in . . . or get out?

Whiskey stepped over the pile and into the tunnel. The light skated over years of filth, though the tracks gleamed from decades of use. The third rail sat dark and quiet, no longer carrying fatal amounts of electricity to make the trains move anymore. Just a piece of history. Hood looked over his shoulder.

Kerry still stood at the entrance of the tunnel.

Hood jogged over to her.

"I don't want to be here," Kerry said."There's something wrong with all of this."

"It's okay. It's just dark," Hood said, trying to reassure himself, even though his heart was pounding. What if the tunnel was structurally unsound and collapsed on them? He urged her on, but she wouldn't move. "I won't let anything happen to you. Come on."

He grabbed her hand and led her into the tunnel. She followed behind him, and he let her hand go and lifted up his rifle to keep the light ahead of them. Whiskey hadn't waited, and they needed to catch up.

The air felt thicker and cooler as they kept moving. The sooty walls of the tunnel appeared undisturbed, and nothing could be heard except their own footsteps.

"Something smells funny," Kerry said. The air had become somewhat foggier.

"Put on your masks," Whiskey ordered, a few steps ahead of them.

Hood secured his gas mask and Kerry did the same.

The sound of their breathing was the only sound in the tunnel. They crept forward carefully as they focused on every foot of dirty track the lights revealed.

Whiskey halted. A train sat dormant on the tracks ahead of them, blocking the way.

They inspected it with their lights.

"There." Whiskey pointed at the wall to their right. There was an inset cubby in the walls that lead to a utility room. The door was open slightly.

Hood shone his light back at the train cab.

"We can probably get into the train through there." Hood said. "Walk through."

Whiskey wasn't paying attention. He held his gun up to sight, and slowly walked towards the utility door. Hood raised his rifle and followed behind him. They stepped up into the cubby and Whiskey looked over at Hood to see if he was ready. Hood nodded.

Whiskey swung the door open slowly with his left hand. The room was empty except for a small desk and a chair next to a switchboard of some kind. Most of the space in the room was taken up by a big, boxy machine that led up to the ventilation shaft.

Hood jerked his head in the direction of the open vent. A person could fit inside, though it wouldn't be comfortable. The vent cover lay on the ground, bent with the screws ripped out.

Behind the mask, Whiskey's eyes narrowed and his breathing quickened.

This was the first time Hood had ever seen Whiskey show fear.

"We're so close." Hood said. "We just gotta be quick and quiet."

"Let's take the train." Whiskey said, looking up at the vent again before turning away. He closed the door behind them.

Kerry stood in the dark, her hand on the pistol behind her back.

"What was in there?" she said quietly

"Nothing," Whiskey said in low tones. "We'll have to go through the train."

"What if it won't open?" she posited.

"Then we'll crawl to the other side," Whiskey grumbled.

Hood jumped up onto the train, and yanked the door handle hard. It budged a little, and on the second try, slid open.

"No crawling for us," Hood said through his mask.

"Not yet," Kerry retorted.

Whiskey climbed onto the train.

Hood waited for Kerry.

"After you, milady."

"How chivalrous. Do me a favor and keep that light off my ass and over my shoulder where it belongs?"

"Don't flatter yourself."

She turned to face him, her face obscured by the monstrous mask. "My eyes are up here," she deadpanned, pointing at the alien-looking plastic eyepieces of her mask.

Hood stifled his laughter, the sound reverberating in his own mask.

She paused, clenching her fists. She exhaled, the sound more pronounced through the mask filter, the only sound in the empty tunnel. She climbed onto the runner and into the train. There was something comforting to her visible trepidation and attempts to diffuse it with humor—like he wasn't alone with that itching feeling in the back of his neck. *I feel it too. But we have to keep on,* he wanted to say. But he wasn't sure giving it words would help.

Hood grabbed the handle beside the door and hoisted himself inside.

Hood walked beside Kerry through the cab. Dust swirled in the foggy air. An empty sports drink bottle lay on the floor; a faded tabloid magazine on the seat. The metal poles for standing passengers shone in the light.

"You ever imagine you'd be doing something like this?" Hood said just above a whisper. She seemed to be expecting something with every step.

"Not ever." She searched the darkness for unseen terrors. "Based on my master plan, about now I'd be engaged to a handsome musician, planning to have kids in a few years."

It was an indulgent bit of sentimentality.

Hood had never really been a big-picture guy. He'd never known what he wanted to do with his life. He still didn't—after they rescued Taylor. And Ian. If he needed rescuing. Hood raised his rifle to his shoulder as they crept through the cab.

The thickening fog made it harder to see. Whiskey opened the stainless-steel doors that led to the next cab. It was similarly abandoned, empty aside from scattered refuse. Whiskey quickened his pace, walking past the rows of silvery posts to the door of the third cab. They finally reached the engineer's car, the seat empty and the control panel dormant. The dials, control lever and gauges were covered in dust. The windshield had been removed, and the dust spiraled in the light of Whiskey's flashlight out of the train into the tunnel.

Whiskey leaned over the console, looking down at the tracks below. Hood stepped forward as Whiskey slung his shotgun over his shoulder and climbed over it, dropping down with a crunch onto the fractured latticework of the plexiglass windshield.

Kerry followed, eager to keep moving. She, too, dropped down onto the tracks with feline grace.

Hood handed her his rifle, and she illuminated the matted steel finish of the train as he climbed down. The shattered windshield ground against the tracks under his feet.

She handed him back his rifle. They walked down the murky tunnel, Whiskey twenty paces ahead of them. The air was thick with whatever fog surrounded them. As uncomfortable as it was, Hood was grateful for the gas mask suctioned onto his face.

The three of them made little noise as they pressed on, the walls black with grime and the rails shining from the flashlights. Fetid puddles lay outside the tracks. There was an uncomfortable moisture in the air, like the station had slowly come alive, and they were deep in its belly.

"Come look at this," Whiskey said aloud.

Hood and Kerry hustled forward. Whiskey stood at the entrance to the next station. Light came through a gaping hole in the ceiling. Vines and a large tree clung to a shattered chunk of sidewalk that hung down into the station, its branches growing upward in a slow-motion attempt to reach the outside world.

On the collapsed overhang sat a wrecked missile, huge, with nothing but empty chambers open on either side. It was clearly a chemical weapon.

Boom. A distant rumble resuonded in the dark.

The three of them looked around, Whiskey pointing his shotgun light into the open train tracks.

Hood looked up at the escalator, into the concourse.

Boom. Boom. Boom. The echoing grew closer.

Hood pointed his rifle light upwards, illuminating a vent just as the cover burst off.

A humanoid figure flew at him, screeching, crashing down onto him.

Every nerve in Hood's body came alive as he fell into a heap on the ground. *What the fuck is that?* His mind screamed, his heart raged in his chest as he fought to push whatever it was off of him. Hands clawed his face and shoulder, pulling his mask off. He reached up to grab the creature's arms, flailing wildly. He rolled onto the train tracks, trying to get away, but it had wrapped its legs around his torso from behind, was ripping his hair out and trying to gouge out his eyes.

Hood lurched to his feet and threw himself, back-first, into the wall. The creature—a woman?—screeched even louder, and fingernails dug into his neck. Searing pain wracked him as teeth dug deep into his left shoulder.

Whiskey and Kerry shouted something indiscernible. He felt the teeth clamp down again into the meat of his shoulder as he heard a deafening gunshot.

The creature went limp, sliding off him to the floor.

Kerry stood next to him, pistol in hand. She was screaming at him, but her voice was muted from the high-pitched ringing in his ears. He inspected his shoulder; his torn shirt already bloody. Pain consumed him.

Flashes of light blasted from Whiskey's shotgun as humanoid figures collapsed in front of him.

Hood's rifle lay on the tracks, the cone of light illuminating the dirty gray wall. He picked it up as Kerry grabbed his arm, pulling him to his feet. Disoriented, Hood ran alongside her, the gas mask hanging around his neck.

The three of them climbed onto the platform as a veritable horde of feral humans charged towards them from the far tunnel. Something clawed his shoes from below. Terror galvanized him, and he ran.

Whiskey pushed shells into his shotgun as the three of them headed up the escalator. There were no thoughts. The primal urge to run as fast as his body was capable quickly snapped into a desire to cut down that which hounded them.

At the top of the escalator, Hood turned around. Filthy people with torn clothing and crazed eyes surged onto the platform and ran towards the escalator. He lifted his rifle butt to his shoulder and squeezed the trigger, firing on full auto as the stock quaked on his shoulder.

He cut the feral humans down as they climbed the escalator, a mass of bodies piling into a heap that the others screeched at and fought each other to climb over.

He fired the clip empty. The pain and the adrenaline pumping through his body demanded retribution. He removed the magazine, flipping it over and tapping it against the body of the rifle before loading and cocking it.

Kerry pulled on his hood, screaming at him to keep running. He could barely register her words, but he forced himself to follow her. Whiskey was ahead at the exit.

Twilight shone through the closed gate ahead of them. Rubble, office furniture and an uprooted mailbox were piled against the fence on the other side of the metro exit. Whiskey shot the padlock on the fence until the chain broke.

"C'mon, hurry up!" Kerry shouted.

Whiskey cursed at her, trying to pry the fence open.

Hood turned to face the subway tunnel. His mind slowly started to clear. The words of the man they'd found in the church, Donte, came back to him . . . *Turned you into an animal while you was still alive.* It was a chemical weapon.

A few of the ferals made it up the escalator and ran at them. A woman in a summer dress, a man in a suit. Hood was not about to be anyone's dinner. He lifted the rifle and shot the two of them down. Another man in jeans and a torn shirt came at him. He smashed his face with the butt of the rifle, then pulled out his knife and stabbed him in the heart. The man stared up at him with wide, sightless eyes, baring his shattered teeth as he fell.

"Come on!" Kerry shouted.

Whiskey had opened the gate enough to squeeze through.

Kerry was holding it open.

"Go!" Hood shouted. "Go already!"

She hesitated before sliding through the opening. Whiskey put his shotgun barrel through the fence, firing at the incoming ferals.

Hood ran to the gate, threw his rifle through, then pushed his head through, using his hands to leverage his torso. His shoulder screamed in pain. He looked back to see a naked feral man lunging at him. Hood kicked the man away. Whiskey unloaded on the man with his shotgun.

Kerry grabbed his free hand and pulled as hard as she could, leaning backwards. Whiskey fired away through the gate openings.

Hood felt something clawing at his legs as he burst through, falling forward onto the concrete. Kerry stumbled, then picked up his rifle and held it out to him.

"Let's go, close it up!" Whiskey shouted, jamming the gate shut again and holding it closed. Hood climbed up onto the pile of broken concrete and wedged himself between two huge chunks, pushing as hard as he could with his legs. His left shoulder shrieked louder than any words could. He pushed the concrete chunk forward, it slowly rolled off the pile and crashed up against the gate. The three of them hurled every piece of rubble they could find up against it amidst the din.

Hood ran up the stairs out of the station, following Whiskey and Kerry. The three of them stopped to look back at the metro. A horde of the crazed ferals pushed against the flexing gate, but it held them back. Hood gasped for air, hands on his knees, the feel of his heartbeat thundering in his ears.

"Jesus Christ. . ." Kerry panted, pushing her hair back. "I told you that was a fucking bad idea!"

Hood gritted his teeth. "They're . . . *animals*."

Whiskey pulled the last two shotgun shells out of his flak jacket and pushed them into the body of the shotgun. "Well, we found *somebody,*" he grunted.

Chapter 13 – Epiphany

"It's just up the road," Hood said, the narrow street heavy with stillness. The city was dark, a carved-out husk of it's former self.

"Keep your eyes open," Whiskey said with a quiet vehemence.

I feel it too, big guy. What if she's not here? What if no one is here? Hood gnawed on his lower lip. *What do we do if she is here?*

Kerry walked up beside him, looking at his wounded left shoulder. "Are you alright?"

"Yeah," Hood said. "As good as you can be walking out of a nightmare."

"Whiskey," Kerry said. "Hold on a sec."

He looked annoyed at her request, turning to face the two of them.

"We need a second. I can bandage him up."

"You all right, kid?"

"Yeah, I'm fine." Hood shrugged, pain shot through his shoulder and up his neck.

Kerry shook her head. "You're still bleeding."

Whiskey glanced back up the street, his gaze lingering. He bowed his head. "Alright. Let's take a minute. Get him cleaned up." He moved towards the nearest storefront, a dark electronics store. He pulled open the door, raising his shotgun, moving it in a sweeping arc as he surveyed the scene.

Kerry met Hood's gaze momentarily before turning her head to scan the street and the rooftops. Hood watched her movements, taking in her every curve. *She really is looking out for you.*

"You saved my ass back there," Hood said, waiting for her blue eyes to meet his own again. "You saved all of us. We would've gotten overrun by those ferals."

"Payback." She flashed a smile. "I'm just glad I got the chance to do it. I really. . ." She took a deep breath, looking aside at the pavement. "It killed me to betray you guys. You have to know that. I thought I was saving my family."

"I know. It's alright," Hood managed a faint smile. *This is why, Whiskey. This is why we can't lose ourselves. I saved her, she saved us. Now we can save Taylor and Ian. This is what we are fighting for. She's just like us.* Somehow, despite all the hell they had put each other through, their mutual survival was proof that Hood wasn't wrong. *We can live like this.*

"I hated myself for it. I hated myself right after I met you guys. I was praying you'd be someone I could hate to make it easier. But you guys are easy to like."

Fuck it. What the hell are you waiting for? Hood moved towards her, his feet acting on his own until he was standing in front of her. His heart was racing like he was a kid again. She looked up at him, from one of his eyes to the other. He wrapped his arms around her, her lips soft against his own. He took his time, wanting the feeling to last. His shoulder seared, but the pain didn't matter. *We're in the open, we're vulnerable,* a voice in his head said. *He shut it out. I'll take the risk.* He pressed her body against his, and she slid her hands up his back between him and his backpack. She was a good kisser. Patient, enjoying each moment.

"It's clear," Whiskey said from the doorway. Hood and Kerry stepped away from each other slowly. Hood scratched behind his ear, and Kerry ran her thumb and middle finger across the top of her head, pulling her hair back.

"Come on," Whiskey said, shooting Hood an I-knew-it look.

"Yeah, just wanted to help her out all right," he murmured as he turned back inside. Hood couldn't stifle a laugh, and Kerry gave him a humorous smirk. *What are the chances you'd find a girl you like this much in this world?*

The thought brought the hammer of fear down on him. *She's another person you can lose. Another tragedy waiting to happen. Someone else you can't protect from this war.* The two of them moved through the doorway inside. *Shut the hell up, brain. I won't let you ruin this. Not right now.*

Kerry took in the dimly lit scene, ambient daylight from the storefront the only thing keeping away the darkness. Dusty shelves of phone chargers, cases, USB cords and Ethernet cables undisturbed. *We're still alive. We've made it all the way here. Just enjoy this, even for only a few minutes.*

The store remained largely intact, much to their surprise. Fear and death must have taken the city quickly for there to be no looting. It felt good to peel off his shirt, except of course for the intense pain in his shoulder. Kerry zipped open her backpack and removed a first aid kit.

Hood snatched an unopened pack of double A batteries off a hook, tore them open and pushed them into a portable CD player as Kerry tried to tend to his injuries. "This is the greatest discovery we've ever made," Hood said to Whiskey, intently focused on the outside world.

"Stay still, for God's sake," Kerry said from behind him, prodding the gouges in his shoulder and neck with swabs of hydrogen peroxide. Hood tried not to wince, failing miserably. He took a swig of vodka from a bottle they'd found in the back office of the store. He tossed it to Whiskey, who barely caught it before it hit the floor.

"You almost done?" Whiskey said to Kerry, taking a drink from the bottle while staring out the wall of windows, into the street. He wiped his mouth with his forearm.

"Stop moving around!" Kerry pleaded, grabbing Hood by his good shoulder. "You're gonna pull your wounds open."

Hood plugged in earbuds, snapped the CD player shut and pushed the play button. The CD whirred up to speed as the music started. He recognized the song, his mom and dad used to play it in the house when he was young. "This is the best thing ever. I can't believe this place still has CD players. Whiskey, check this out."

"I'm good." Whiskey said quietly.

"This is *music* were talking about here. Real music. Not Billy howling over a a shitty old guitar he found."

"How can you even think about somethin' else right now?"

"We just survived a horde of human animals. We are minutes away from the Church. This is it, big guy. We've made it all the way here. Just take a second while I'm getting put back together to enjoy this with me."

Kerry was wrapping bandages around his shoulder. "Where did you find that? I want one." Her voice did little to contain the sound of childlike excitement. Hood pointed over to the darkened shelves of electronics.

"See? She knows what's good. Come on, you're gonna love this shit. My dad loved this song and you're old, so yeah."

Hood held out an ear bud. Whiskey stared at it like it was a foreign animal for a moment, before taking it and placing it in his ear. Hood jacked up the volume to max level.

"...You *the* still real fun, hrmm hrmm tears, You're still real fun I want somethin' somethin' here!" Hood sung aloud badly. He didn't know what 'in key' was, but he knew he wasn't.

"Stop it. That's not even close. You're ruinin' it." Whiskey nodded his head with the music. "I do love this damn song," he admitted. "Call me 'old' again and you're gonna be pickin' your ass up off the floor."

Hood laughed, plucking the strings of an air guitar.

"We're still havin' fun, and you're still the one!" Hood sang.

For the first time in a long time, he felt normal. He felt like things might just be okay. Not that that was true. Reality was they were moments away from everything they had fought for. There was no sequestering the nerves that the Church of the Epiphany was just down the street, that Taylor and Ian might or might not be inside. Or that they might not be able to rescue them.

I'll do whatever it takes to find her. If she isn't there, I'll keep looking from one end of the continent to the other—and so will Whiskey.

"Maybe I should be gettin' myself one of these." Whiskey said, looking towards Kerry. "Hey, grab me one!"

Hood turned to see her reaction. She was intently sifting through rows of CDs.

"They have some awesome shit here!" She exclaimed.

Hood pulled a gray tee-shirt over his head that said *Bigfoot was born blurry* and a black hoodie over that. Then he shouldered his backpack with a grimace.

"Where in the hell did you get that shirt?" Whiskey said, chewing on a handful of trail mix.

"What? I found it at the abandoned T-shirt kiosk awhile back. Pretty great, huh?"

Whiskey scoffed, shaking his head." Your shoulder all right?"

Hood picked up the Vodka, taking another drink before he tossed the empty bottle away. It clanked against the floor and rolled up against the wall. "Burns like a bitch, but fuck it, still alive. Right?"

Whiskey chuckled. "For now."

An excited Kerry showed the two of them the plethora of CDs she'd procured. Hood plucked a few albums from the rows as they left the store and tossed them into his bag. It was something to look forward to, extra incentive to stay alive long enough to enjoy them.

The last light of the day was fading away. Anticipation, excitement and worry all rattled around Hood's head as the three of them headed down the abandoned streets in a euphoria that was giving way to raw fear the closer they got to the church.

The buildings showed ancient signs of struggle, some sporting flamed out windows, while others had collapsed entirely. The dusty scent of abandonment drifted through the air. They crept up the side street around the corner from the church, wildly distrustful of the utter silence that gripped the empty city.

Hood directed them up a narrow alley between tall corner buildings. The rotten smell of decayed garbage surrounded them as they crept ahead, guns at sight. Hood tucked the rifle stock tight against his right shoulder. *Is there really no one around?* He thought he should feel relieved, but it only made him more nervous.

They entered the back of a sports bar across the street from the Church of the Epiphany. The air in the bar was stale, the only sound the soft thud of their footsteps as the crept ahead to the windowfront. There it stood. A narrow, white gothic-modern tower of a church. Plain, sparsely adorned with an arching bright red door. It was sooty, but otherwise unscathed between the boxy windowed buildings on either side of it. *Why here? Maybe the Kaiser was a religious man.* That thought had never crossed Hood's mind. *Hard to picture such a ruthless bastard to be religious. History is littered with them though.* No, it didn't make sense. There had to be another reason. *Is anyone even inside? Did they leave this place behind?*

The only thing that moved was a hanging sign that swung back and forth in the wind. Kerry sat down on a stool, looking around at the once-upscale bar that was now covered in a layer of dust. She leaned over the bar, pulling a bottle of rum out of the rack. Hood couldn't help but enjoy the view.

"No charge? You're too kind." She said this to nobody, pulling a rocks glass off a stack and wiping it down with her shirt before pouring the rum. Hood turned back to face the doors. Whiskey stared at the church, jamming his thumbnail between his two front teeth and gnawing at it.

"Doesn't seem like anyone's here," Kerry said, inspecting her glass.

"Maybe. Or they want it to look that way," Whiskey muttered.

Hood's stomach turned. The Sheriff had said it. He'd said they were going to the Church of the Epiphany. He bit his bottom lip, wondering how far their search might take them. Probably into the heart of the Kaiser's lands. For what felt like an hour, they surveyed the solemn church.

"Stay here." Whiskey said, gripping his shotgun. "I'll make a sweep. If they *are* here, they got to have sentries."

"You think that's a good idea?" Hood asked.

"I won't be long. If I draw some attention and they come stormin' out, it might give you a chance to sneak inside."

Hood nodded slowly. "Yeah, that might work."

"Just hang tight. We need to find out more before we go chargin' in."

"What should I do?" Kerry asked, hopping off her barstool.

"Stay here. With eyes glued to that church." Whiskey produced his Glock. He checked the magazine, replaced it and pulled back the slide.

"Guys, it looks abandoned," Kerry said. "I know you might not want to hear that."

"Yeah, it does look like it. But if we're wrong, we don't get a do-over." Hood shifted his left shoulder. The wounds burned with every movement. It was bearable, but the pain urged his mind away from the task at hand. He ignored it.

"If we get split up, meet back up near Metro center. Somewhere out of sight." Whiskey said.

Hood nodded.

Whiskey turned and headed out the back of the bar.

Ahead, the church lay dormant. The trees planted in the gardens around it clung pathetically to life, sporting only a sparse few green leaves on their thin branches. The bright red front doors were closed, and the last light of the day was gone.

"Well, considering we have time on our hands. I'm making peanut butter and jelly sandwiches." Kerry pulled off her backpack and tossed it onto the bar. "Best part of having all those supplies to ourselves, is we get to eat the good stuff whenever we want," she grinned.

"Silver lining," Hood said wistfully. Hood hadn't thought much about eating, but his stomach was calling out for food. That seemed to always be the case, though. *You've got the metabolism of a*

hummingbird, like your father. Sending the grocery bills through the roof!
His mother's voice echoed in his head.

It was years ago, and he'd been eating a bowl of cereal after polishing off some leftover ribs at two in the morning when she came into the kitchen, bleary-eyed in her pajamas. She just sat down next to him, watched him eat, told him she was proud of him. Hood remembered it vividly, because he thought she was going to be pissed, thought a life lecture was coming.

What the hell was there to be proud of anyway? He had no job, no idea what he wanted to do, student loans out the ass, and he stayed out all night getting drunk only to come home and eat his parents' food. But she just smiled and said she was proud of him. *I wish I could tell you guys that I'm still alive. I wish I could just sit down and talk with you guys about anything, about nothing.* Being a parent must be a special kind of hell at the end of the world.

The smell of peanut butter and the sight of double-stacked graham crackers with jelly oozing out of them snapped him into reality. Hood took the sandwich, looking at Kerry. She sported an impressive look of self-satisfaction.

"Try it. It's pretty goddamn delicious. As delicious as you can possibly get nowadays." She took a bite, nodding with raised eyebrows. "Ahm tellig you," she said through the peanut butter, covering her mouth.

She wasn't wrong. He devoured the entire thing in moments, the sweet cracker and jam complimenting the salty peanut butter magnificently. He pulled off his backpack and produced a canteen of water, washing it down. He held it out to her.

"Thank you, sir!" She grabbed the canteen and took a drink. "It's the little things, right?" She inhaled in appreciation, dabbing the corners of her mouth with her fingertips.

"Yeah." A faint smile crossed his face as he stared out once again at the church. He felt her gaze lingering on him.

"Isn't weird to think. . .we've come all this way, and your sister is either just across the street or miles and miles away. But we don't know which."

"Schrodinger's cat." Hood muttered to himself.

"What'd you say?"

"Nothing. . . It's stupid." Hood shook his head.

Kerry leaned her hip against the doorframe, looking out the window, her arms crossed. Hood glanced over at her for a moment.

"Y'know, I think he's getting used to me." Kerry said, nodding towards the back of the bar.

"Yeah, I think so too." *He's smart enough not to turn down help we need, even if it takes some persuading.* "He's a good guy, y'know. He just doesn't trust easily."

"Well, he hasn't tried to kill me in a while. So I'm taking that as a positive sign."

Hood chuckled, brushing his mouth with the back of his middle and pointer finger. "Thanks for patching me up, by the way."

"I figure now we're even." She sounded satisfied.

"Let's get it straight: you still owe me."

"What? How do you figure?"

"Well, I saved you *twice*. And you didn't have to fight a fat Frankenstein while chained to a wall."

"Oh, get over yourself," She waved him off. "I should've let that bitch eat you."

Hood laughed, rubbing the scruff on his jaw.

"And it shouldn't count that you saved me from your own psycho friend! That's like wearing clothes made of bird seed and blaming the pigeons for eating you alive."

"What? What kind of analogy is that?" Hood furrowed his brow.

"It's *my* analogy. The point is, we're even, okay, asshole?" She waved her pointer finger back and forth from him to herself.

"Oh, okay. So you'll be leaving us then?" Hood said.

She paused, biting her bottom lip. "Maybe I will."

Hood smiled at her.

The back door swung open with a clank and a squeak. The two of them whipped their guns to sight and pointed them down the

163

hallway in the back of the bar.

"Don't shoot, Robbie," implored a familiar voice. A voice from home.

Ian stepped into the hall. His eyes met Hood's. His short cut blond hair was shorter than Hood remembered, and he looked so much older, carrying more worry in his face. His boots, gray jeans and thick long sleeve shirt looked well-worn. Ian slung his rifle onto his back and ran towards him. Hood dropped his rifle, running to meet him. They embraced each other, Ian pounding his fist against Hood's back.

"Ah!" Hood grimaced at the pain, inhaling sharply. "I fucked up my shoulder."

Ian released Hood from his bear hug. "Shit, sorry bro." Ian shook his head in disbelief, a look of euphoria on his face. For a moment the two of them stood there, at a loss for words. Ian carried himself in a different way now. This life had inevitably changed him, as it had done to everyone. But just seeing him made Hood feel like the person he was in his old life still was alive. And he loved that feeling.

"I can't believe it's you. I can't believe you're here. I saw you guys enter the area, I was on watch. I got down to ground level as soon as I could. How did you guys get this far into the city without being seen?" Ian said.

"We went through the Metro."

"You serious? There's a horde of feral motherfuckers down there."

"Yeah, we found that out. Hence the shoulder," Hood nodded towards his wounded side.

Ian clicked his tongue. "You sick bastard! From emo kid to badass!"

Hood laughed. "Haven't quite shaken the emo kid part yet."

A toothy grin grew on Ian. "Of course."

"You don't know how good it is to see you." Hood clapped his hand onto Ian's shoulder. *If he's here, Taylor has got to be here too. He wouldn't stay far from her.*

Ian face turned solemn. "I do though. I've been alone in all this."

164

Alone? What happened to Jen? Hood wasn't sure he should ask about Ian's wife, fearing the worst. And he had a thousand other questions. "I saw you at Clearwater. I saw you take Taylor. Where is she? You're working for the Kaiser?" *I want hours just to talk. What happened? How did you end up like this?*

"Yeah. It hasn't been easy." Ian looked down at the polished floor of the bar, working his mouth. "I had to get her out of there. I didn't want the other soldiers to get a hold of her. She's okay."

She's still alive. Hood felt a surge rise up through him. *This wasn't for nothing.*

Kerry stood by the bar, holding her forearm. She looked nervous, unsure of what to make of the encounter.

"Kerry, this is Ian." Hood moved towards her, gesturing towards his foster brother.

"Hi. Ian. Nice to meet you," he shook her hand, turning to shoot a devious look at Hood. "I see you still have great taste."

Hood scratched the back of his head. "I see you still have no filter."

"Some things don't change." Ian shrugged.

"Do you—" *Boom, boom.* Muffled echoes of distant gunshots stopped Hood.

Shotgun blasts.

If they were Whiskey's, those were his last rounds. Kerry's scrutiny turned to Hood to see his reaction, her face a picture of cold fear.

"Whiskey." Hood said aloud, as if saying his name would keep him safe.

"Is that the guy you guys came in with?"

"Yeah. He's Taylor's guy."

"He probably ran into the other patrol."

"Oh shit." Kerry hid herself behind the doorframe. Hood made himself flat against the wall. Six armed men filed out of the side door of the church, moving swiftly down the street with guns raised, heading west.

165

Ian grabbed Hood's arm. "This is our chance. Taylor's in the church. We can get her and get the hell out of here," Ian's voice carried an unexpected intensity.

"What about Whiskey?" Kerry said pointedly at Hood. "Are we going to leave him behind."

Hood cursed. *This is our chance. This is what he would want. He would kill me if he knew I came for him when I had the chance to free Taylor.* "This is what he wanted. He'll be okay. We'll find him after." Hood said, trying to sound calm. *Will we?* Hood's heart wanted to leap out of his chest.

Being scared is better than not being scared enough, Whiskey had said to him on their first raid together.

"I'm coming with you." Kerry said, visibly steeling herself.

"No, stay here. Take my rifle. You know how to shoot it?"

She nodded.

"I need you to unload on anyone who chases us if we come running."

"Okay." She exhaled forcefully, putting the rifle butt against her shoulder, taking aim at the window.

"Come on." Ian urged. "We have to go now."

Hood pressed himself up against the door, and turned to look back at her.

"If this goes to hell . . . don't forget what you promised about Taylor."

She nodded slowly, working her mouth. "I haven't."

Hood nodded, pushed open the door and crept outside with Ian. Everything was dark. The only cars in the road sat sunken into the pavement with blasted tires and blown out windows. He pulled out his .38 and cocked the hammer, the two of them walking without a sound across the street to the church. *If we can just all make it through this.*

The air smelled of dust and the only sound was the squeaking of the paddle sign as it waved with the wind in front of the church. *All Are Welcome!* Hood scoffed. They approached the short steps that lead to the red wooden doors. With a nod, Ian pulled one open by its black metal doorknob and Hood stepped inside. The double glass doors in the foyer were open. Inside, orange glow from candlelight lit up the interior of the white stone church. There were brown wood pews and arched ceilings. The smell of death and incense filled the air.

Carefully, Hood walked down the aisle. Ian followed behind him. The silence broke with the metallic clank of the front door closing.

Two bodies hung from ropes attached to the wooden supports running the length of the ceiling. His heart dropped what seemed hundreds of feet through his body.

He could only make out the silhouettes of the bodies. One was a man and one was a woman. Part of him wanted to turn, run out the front door. But his legs carried him slowly ahead. *God, don't let the woman be Taylor.* Hood turned to look at Ian. His face was placid, and he nodded ahead.

The woman wasn't Taylor. He could tell as he got closer. But something about the two of them was very familiar. He looked up at their faces, nearly underneath them now. His muscles froze, his feet stuck in the ground.

Mom? Dad? It didn't register as reality.

What? How, why are you here? Who did this?

Hood sank to his knees. *What the fuck?*

Hood choked on a sob, holding the back of his head in his hands, still grasping tightly onto his black .38.

"They were waiting for you." Ian said, moving towards the rows of red-cushioned seats in the east wing. "Waiting for you to come home."

Hood looked up, blinking away his tears. "What are you talking about? What is this?"

"Does it matter?" He said calmly, standing next to Hood as he stared up at them. "They're dead."

Hood's mouth fell open. "What the fuck do you mean, asking me if it matters? Of course it matters! What's wrong with you?!"?

"The old world is gone, Rob. We can't go back. We can never go back."

Ian shrugged. Then he smirked, a morose, condescending smile. "You're still holding on to the way things were."

How the fuck can you act like this? Suddenly he knew. *"You* did this?"

Ian pulled the rifle off his back, placing it on the bench of a pew. He gnawed his upper lip, looking up at the bodies, his expression calm. A look of grave acceptance. "I had to, Robbie."

No, this isn't real. This isn't you. This is a lie. Hood rose to his feet, glaring at Ian, his eyes demanding the truth. Ian sighed, putting his hands on his hips.

"You don't know what I've been through, Rob. It was only days after the world went to shit. A pack of escaped criminals came into my house in the middle of the night. They beat me within an inch of my life, left me to watch as they raped and killed Jennifer. Her eyes begged me to do something. But I couldn't stop them.

"They left me to die. Left me with my shame, my utter destruction of self. I waited for death, but it did not come. Something inside me snapped. Painstakingly, I tracked them down for weeks. Slaughtered them like animals in their sleep, reveled in their blood. I still dream about it sometimes. I dream that I kill them first. I dream that she's still alive." Ian ran his hand over his head.

"Afterwards, all I wanted was death. For days, I blamed the people who'd destroyed the country, I blamed those who had survived, I blamed death for not taking me, I blamed the entire world. . . My mind pulled apart a thousand whys until a realization came to me: this *is* our world, we created it." Ian hung his head. He nearly grimaced, like this great idea was the source of his guilt. Not anything else he had done.

"Who are you?" Rage burned behind Hood's eyes. "You're not my brother."

Ian inhaled laboriously, ready to continue. He seemed to accept Hood's rage, his disbelief, expecting it. "My whole life, I've been

168

clinging to something. My parents died when I was young, and I turned to your family for meaning. As I got older, I fell in love with Jennifer, and I was obsessed with starting my own family. I couldn't see anything past it. We all entrench ourselves in our own little lives–while humanity free-falls with its eyes closed, unable to see the ground rushing up to meet it."

Ian met Hood's stare, his face plain, expressionless. "We finally hit the ground. But some of us are still here. It's up to us to change things."

Hood could taste the tinge of blood in his mouth he was grinding his teeth so hard.

Taylor was right. Of course they came back home. That was the only place they had hope of finding us. Mom, Dad, I'm so sorry.

"Do you understand?" Ian asked. As if what he'd done was within comprehension.

Ian's eyes were flat, depthless, a deep abyss. Like someone had drained the life from the brother he'd grown up with. He wanted to put a bullet in the head of the man that was supposed to be his family. The man he'd loved so much growing up. *Just a few minutes ago in the bar he was the brother I remember. Pretending not to be this madman.*

"Where is Taylor?" Hood said, his jaw set as he looked upon the countenance of someone he loved, someone he hated.

Ian sighed.

"I need you to really listen to me. I need you to see the truth. We need to rise up, Rob. We need to kill our instincts. We're something greater than animals. We kill others, or at least don't care if they die so long as our own children survive. But what happens when the whole world acts this way?"

Ian held out his arms, a gesture to encompass everything. "This. We get this world. This is not a tragedy. It's not an accident. It's not a statistical outlier. It's an *inevitability*. This is history's legacy. That's why we have to start anew. We have to kill off the idea of family, and replace it with the idea of humanity."

He was insane. Ian was absolutely out of his mind . . . and to him, it was the truth. To him, it was clarity. The thought scared the hell out of Hood. *That's what you believe? That's why you did this?*

"Where. . . is. . . Taylor?" Hood repeated with venom, his low voice resounding in the empty church.

Ian exhaled forcefully, scratching the back of his head as he looked down at the floor. "Fine. I know you're worried about her. She's not here."

"She's alive?"

"Yes, she's alive."

"Where?"

Ian bit his lip. "Don't you think you're getting ahead of yourself?"

Hood stepped into Ian's personal space, grabbing him by his shirt. "What the *fuck* is wrong with you? You took Taylor away from our town, and you're clearly working for the Kaiser. I come here and find you spouting this fucking nonsense. *Wake up*, Ian!!"

Ian started laughing. It echoed throughout the church.

Hood let him go, taking a step back. *I don't know how you let yourself become this.*

"I'm sorry what happened to you. What happened to Jen. But this. . . This isn't you."

"You still haven't figured it out?" His foster-brother smiled. "You're emotional. I get it. I know I'm going against my own ethos, bringing you here and giving you special treatment. But we aren't family, technically. You know me. You're smart. You're clearly very capable, and you have great vision. On top of it all, I love you, Rob. We grew up together. I want you to join me."

"You're wrong. This. . . these sick ideas, they're wrong. You can love your family and care for them while still caring for others. Fuck the Kaiser. Help me free Taylor!" Hood tightened his grip on the .38 at his side.

Ian shook his head, wearing a thin smile. "I *am* the Kaiser, dummy."

Hood stared at him. His brow furrowed. *No, how could. . . that doesn't make any sense.*

"Derp." Ian tapped the side of his head.

"There are a great many survivors out there who share my ideals. I didn't build this empire through brute strength alone. Sure, the low-level guys are pretty mindless, just animals picking the right alpha to follow. But the revolution is real. This is our chance to re-make the world, Rob. I want you to be a part of that."

Hood's hands shook. *This isn't real. This is a nightmare.* A chill raised the hair on the back of his neck, and the burning pain in his bandaged shoulder started to itch. *You did this? You did all of this? You killed Lucky, Billy, Doug, Tommy, and everyone else; you sent that man to attack our camp only to let him die alone. All of this was you? How many people have died because of you?*

Hood's entire body began to shake. Ian continued on, undaunted.

"I was hoping that putting you through all this might have made you see the truth. I could've just had you killed at Clearwater. But think about all you did to get here. How many people did you kill? For what? To make yourself feel better when you found Taylor? Who says she isn't happy and thriving on her own? Set yourself free, Rob. Help me set us all free."

Hood raised his .38 to sight on Ian. "Fuck your Kum-ba-yah bullshit. Tell me where Taylor is."

"She's safe with me. Don't worry." Ian looked up at Hood's parents. "She isn't hanging from anything."

Hood squeezed the trigger. Ian dove behind the altar. The shot echoed through the church.

"You're making a mistake, Rob. You're not thinking clearly. I wasn't either after I lost Jen. I thought you might handle it better than I had, though."

"You're a *lie*." Hood said, baring his teeth. His blood roiled through his body and his grip on the .38 was sweaty, the sidearm quivering in his shaking hands.

"We don't have to do this, Rob. Just leave. Walk out the door.

Come find me later, when you've had time to think. I know you know what I'm saying is true. It's not easy doing the right thing. This isn't about living for yourself or Taylor anymore."

Hood aimed perfectly down the sights, at a spot over the altar. The only sound was Hood's quickened breathing. The candles in the apse flickered.

"Okay Rob, if this is how you want to do this."

Something flew up into the air from behind the altar: a grenade. It soared through the air, spinning towards him. Hood cursed, leaping from one row of pews into the row behind it. He flattened himself on the seat. Two shots echoed as Ian fired from behind the altar.

The great roar of the grenade was deafening. The pew he lay on shook from the shrapnel that blasted into it from the other side. Hood looked down at himself, vaguely surprised to see himself unscathed.

He jumped up with pistol raised, leaping backwards as Ian fired. Hood fired back, three times in rapid succession -- one bullet caught Ian in his left trap muscle. He gurgled in pain, clutching it with his free hand. Hood took aim of Ian's head. His finger hesitated before the firing threshold. It was a face he'd associated with nothing but love his entire life.

Ian's eyes were wild with pure survival instinct now. He raised his pistol and fired back. Hood kept his body low behind the pews. He ran crab-like towards the entrance, popping up behind the last pew to open fire. Ian strafed bullets across the western transept.

Pain burst through the edge of his ribcage, and Hood doubled over. He pressed his left hand against the wound, the whole side of his body radiating pain. He moved towards the entrance. *Kerry, I hope to God you're ready.*

A grenade clattered to the ground at his feet as he reached the vestibule. A sweeping cold fear gripped him. He flew to the front door, blasting it open with his shoulder as he dove. The world shook around him, and his mind went dim, unaware.

He lay face down on the concrete outside, a pool of warm blood beneath him. He lifted himself to his feet, his side screaming in pain. His blood slowly funneled down the seams in the sidewalk. Nothing made sense. He struggled to remember what was.

This is you. You must move. He stumbled forward, forcing each step across the street, moving towards the bar. Someone he knew was there. An unfamiliar voice shouted from somewhere. It was down the street. He glanced over towards it. A group of uniformed soldiers in blue helmets moved towards him with rifles raised.

"I just want to find her." Hood said simply. "That's all," he slurred. "I'm no bother to you."

He collapsed onto the sidewalk in front of the bar, closing his eyes.

Chapter 14 – Refuge

The awakening took Hood by surprise. He'd been in a dark and dreamless sleep, and coming to felt like being thrown back into existence. The light fixture in the ceiling had useless dusty bulbs in it. Morning light poured in from curtain-less windows, illuminating the sparse room. *Where the hell am I?*

He slowly picked himself up from the stained mattress on the floor, a deep stinging coming from his side and his shoulder. The plain white shirt he wore concealed bandages wrapped against his midsection. He dug for memories of what had happened. He felt a momentary hope that it had been a dream, but he knew it had been real: the fight with Ian, his parents swinging from the rafters. The explosion.

He stared into the buckled crack in the sheetrock underneath the window. *How did I end up here? Wherever here is.*

"Hello?" His voice creaked.

Footsteps came quickly from another room. Kerry appeared in the light from the open window, tucking her hair behind her ear. She stared at him. He couldn't tell if it was reflected light or moisture in her eyes.

"I thought you weren't going to wake up."

He managed a faint grin. "Ta-daaaa."

She moved to the mattress, kneeling on it to hug him. It took him by surprise. He wrapped his arms around her, resting his nose on her shoulder. She had a distinctly feminine smell.

"Where's Whiskey?"

She broke off the hug, leaning back onto her heels.

"I don't know."

"Where are we?"

"A refugee camp in Annapolis. It's where the U.N. remnants are stationed." She rested her hands on her thighs. "What happened in there? In the church?"

Hood stared at her thin fingers, her fingernails frayed and uneven at the ends from where they'd been bitten or peeled short. *The church.*

The images ran through his head. The picture of his parents hanging quietly struck him in the gut.

They were waiting for you to come home, Ian had said.

Hood turned his head away from her, feeling a stinging in his eyes and his nose. He wanted to get away from these idle thoughts. His legs wanted to yank him up off the mattress, run out the door, start his search anew for Taylor, for Whiskey, for both. . .

No, fuck you, don't run from this. Don't push it away. This is reality. They are dead. You are alive. Look her in the eyes and tell her.

He turned to face Kerry. Her backlit, kneeling figure on the mattress was a blurry watercolor already.

"I didn't even get a chance to bury them. They're still hanging there." Hood's words cracked.

"What? Who?" Kerry said, placing a hand on his back.

"My parents. They fucking came home for us. And we never came back." Hood sank his head into his hands, the warm tears rolling down his face.

Yes, this is real. This is how you should feel.

Hood's mind raced to Lucky, Billy, Whiskey, everyone he knew in Clearwater. It all felt real, all at once.

They are all gone and you have to keep going. For some reason they had to die and you get to live.

"Who did it?"

"Kaiser." Hood let his hate out on the word.

"You saw him?" It was a poorly contained astonishment.

"Ian is the Kaiser. He's. . ." Speaking it aloud still felt insane. That it wasn't possible. But in his heart, he knew it was the unassailable truth. Growing up, Ian had been brilliant–but his worldview had always been quite different than most people's. On some level, he knew how he could become what he is now.

Hood always sought tranquility; Ian sought answers. He was always desperately searching for something, and never seemed to accept the explanations people wanted to give.

Except for starting a family. Ian was only thirteen, lying on a lumpy bed in his uncle's cabin in Maine when he told Hood late one night: *I'm going to be there for my son, for my daughter.*

Memories flooded Hood's mind unabated. Ian climbing up the tree next to the school at night, Hood hopping from the branch onto the roof, his heart pounding. The two of them lying on the roof, looking up at the city-lit purple sky, drinking a backpack full of warm beers together.

Dad singing *Wild Horses* to him when he had a fever so high he slept on wet towels. Staring up at Taylor's guilty fawn eyes the summer she spiked a volleyball so hard into his face and said: the good news is, now you have something to talk about with that hot girl working in the infirmary. His eyes burned.

Kerry's expression was stoic despite its soft intensity.

"Part of me wanted Whiskey to pull the trigger that day," she said. "The weight of it all is just unbearable." Her words were soft, matter-of-fact. They carried no guilt or angst. "But you find something to hold on to. To carry you through the sea of hopelessness."

"I'm not made for this. I have to kill who I am in order just to have a chance to save anyone." The words poured out of Hood without thought. *This is the truth. There is nothing left of what I want the world to be. Either become the demon you have to, or die holding onto your halo.*

"I don't believe that." Kerry looked down at the mattress, her hair spilling from behind her ears beside her face. She hesitated, looking

176

Hood in the eyes. "*You* were what I held on to."

Her cheeks reddened, but her face remained calm, deeply accepting of the truth.

He hadn't realized the depth of her strength of will–whether she'd always been this way, or she had become something greater through her own losses. *How long has she had to fight through hell alone? She's lost everyone, she's been hated, mistrusted, betrayed. And still she stays strong.*

She flashed a sheepish smile, still looking at him. He couldn't look away from her. He leaned over, reaching his hand out and touching her neck, his thumb on her cheek. The pain radiated in his ribs and his shoulder as he reached for her. Her chest rose and fell as her breathing quickened.

His own heart was running wild.

He pulled her head to his, her soft lips brushing the corner of his mouth; then he kissed her slowly, drawing her closer to him. He pulled her on top of him as he lay down, feeling the dimples in the small of her back, holding her neck as they kissed. She held onto his neck with both hands, kissing him passionately. He ran his hand over her curves, approaching the front of her jeans, where he pulled the button open, sliding his hand south.

Her breath caught as he touched her. She pulled off her shirt and he eased her onto her back. She held onto his forearms as he lowered himself down to kiss her. The pain in his body seemed farther and farther away. She reached down and grabbed hold of him, and he bit her bottom lip. Hood held her close, and thought nothing of the future.

◆ ◆ ◆

Feeling slowly came back to Hood, the aching in his shoulder and his ribs more pronounced now. He exhaled slowly until his lungs emptied, feeling a satisfying tingling in his brain. The clouds in the sky outside the window moved sluggishly, the sun muted behind them. Kerry lay on her side, her arms and legs around him. He rubbed his cheek against the top of her head. Her hair got caught in his scruff.

"Mmm," she murmured.

"Was it good?"

"Really?" She looked up at him.

"I want to know."

"You can't tell?" She furrowed her brow, but smiled.

"I think so," He smiled back. "Actually, I don't know."

"Idiot." She nuzzled into his chest.

"Would you tell me if it wasn't?"

She paused. He felt her eyebrows move against his skin. "No."

Hood laughed, rubbing the hair on the top of his head. He felt the desperate desire for amnesia, wishing he could just lie in this room and that it would become the scope of the world as he knew it.

"What should we do now?"

"I think we should lie here a while longer." She ran her finger along the edge of the bandages around his ribs. "If you keep throwing yourself at everything, you're going to get killed."

"I just have to do a better job of getting out of the way." He wrapped his arm around her, running his finger softly over the rise and fall of her spine. "I have to get out of here and start tracking down Taylor again. And Whiskey. Will you come with me?"

"A promise is a promise." She rolled onto her back, closing her eyes and leaning her head against his arm.

"Good. I'll need your help. And I don't mean as my portable triage unit."

"You're lucky my mother was a nurse."

"I was thinking more of your ability to point a gun at things and pull the trigger."

"And my dad loved to hunt."

The sun reappeared from behind the clouds. Hood lay his forearm over his eyes.

How the hell am I gonna do this? His mind thought back to Ian. To his wild visions of a new world. A world he was trying to birth with violence.

An idea snapped into Hood's mind. *Of course. He wants me to join him. If I do, I can locate Taylor and find some way to get us out of there.* The idea was tempting. But he was sure escape wouldn't be easy. The journal of the dead man he'd found was a testament to that. He needed to know more. Whatever he was going to do, he needed to track down Ian and his Kaiser militants again first.

"We're probably going to die," he said to Kerry.

"Long full lives don't really happen anymore."

"Are you sure you want to help me do this? You don't have to. I wouldn't blame you if you wanted to go live your life."

"I am living my life. Do you still doubt me?" She turned her head, her eyes searching him.

"No. I think I know who you are."

"Good." She returned to her resting state.

Hood placed his hand on her side, feeling her chest expand with each breath. He was grateful she was with him. Grateful for the warmth as she lay next to him. He was drawn to her will, her ability to survive. *You're being selfish. Bringing you with her is going to get her killed. You can't save her. You can't even save yourself.* She looked utterly peaceful, undisturbed by the moment. *Grow up. She's making her own choice. You care about her. You want her to be here. Embrace it.*

Maybe they could really do this. Maybe they could make it out alive. *Mom, Dad, I won't leave Taylor alone out there. I promise, I'm going to get her free of this mess.* He wanted to find Whiskey. He'd need his help. *Is he even still alive? Of course. He had to be. He'd be looking for Taylor too. Are we just animals desperately protecting our own?* Ian's insane theories swirling in his head. Hood didn't care what the truth was. It didn't matter. All he knew was that he would fight to be with the ones he loved. An unwelcome thought entered his mind: *Being in your company hasn't kept the people you love very safe thus far.*

"I'm doing what I can." Hood said aloud without realizing it.

"Mhmm," Kerry responded. "Can you do me a favor?"

Hood looked over at her. She opened one eye to look at him. "Can you stop talking and sleep with me?" She paused. "Sleep *beside* me," she corrected.

Hood smiled. "Yeah."

He closed his eyes, shifting to get comfortable next to her.

She rolled over on her side.

He felt the blood wriggling through his veins near the glancing shot he'd taken between his ribs. He grimaced. The area throbbed, refusing to be ignored. *Ian shot you. Ian killed all your friends. He killed your parents. He's killed countless people you'll never know. He took Taylor just so you'd have to hunt him down. So you'd drag yourself through hell. Because he wanted you to see the world how he saw it.* Despite his thoughts, Hood couldn't shake the image of a young Ian lying on the roof beside him, staring up at the sky with the most serene countenance, a beer can resting on his stomach.

The brother you knew is gone. He's dead. He's just the Kaiser, just another person who snapped under the weight of the world. Except he's leading armies. Waging wars.

For a brief few minutes before they entered the church, he wasn't, though. *Don't pretend it's not him. He's still Ian. You may live long enough to confront him again. Will you be able to pull the trigger if you have to?*

Hood lurched into a sitting position as he awoke, looking around the room. Kerry wasn't beside him. He'd dreamed deeply, but he couldn't remember about what. The tension in his body and his mind told him the dreams hadn't been peaceful. Something about being hunted, and a green book that he kept trying to read, but the pages were blank.

"Kerry?" His voice rattled.

Silence.

The daylight had diminished, but yet remained. Slowly Hood hoisted himself upright, the linoleum tile flooring cool on the pads of

180

his feet. His side and shoulder ached as the blood rushed away from the wounds. The bathroom door sat open, the dingy pale blue room dark and empty. He walked to the kitchen of the open floor plan, and peered into the bedroom in the back. It featured ransacked armoires and a bed frame with no mattress.

He moved slowly back to the living room, stepping over the mattress to the couch where his backpack lay. Inside he still had the C.D. player, the journal, a bag of peanuts, a nearly empty jug of water, two unused tee shirts and his bloodstained hoodie. Of course, his weapons were gone. They had refused to let him take them inside the refugee camp. He couldn't help a moment of panic at their loss.

He closed his eyes, purging his mind of his racing thoughts. *You're on an even playing field in here. But obviously, you'll have to find something before you put yourself in harm's way.*

Hood nabbed the bag of peanuts and wolfed them down without regard, washing the distinctly nutty taste away with the cool, metallic water. *Kerry should be back from wherever she is soon. Then we can set our sights on leaving this rat cellar.* He sat down on the couch, reaching his hand into his pack. He caressed the soft exterior of the dead man's journal. He plucked it out, pulling it open to a random page.

Sometimes I want to throw myself into the refuse trolley filled with fish carcasses and get dumped out onto the fields for fertilizer. Instead I have to dream up some way to strap Danny and Kim to my back and Shawshank my way out of here.

Not that it's going to happen. I don't even think the kids want to leave. Why would they? They get to be around other kids, and sure . . . they have to work hard but they don't have to kill anyone. Not yet anyway. By the time they do, they'll probably believe they're fighting for the right side. They don't have a clue what horrible things I've done. I did them because if I didn't . . . What, they'd kill me? The hell do I have to live for, anyway? My best reason for surviving is I'm afraid to die.

181

I saw the Kaiser today. I couldn't believe it. He's just a damn kid. Probably twenty years younger than me. I kept expecting his officers to just nod at each other and shoot him in the back as he strolled around the courtyard, talking to someone I've never seen before. But it didn't happen. The way they look at him, it's like reverence. They were more protective of him than they were of themselves.

They really believe this nonsense? They believe we're going to change the world? They say, "We're fighting our war to destroy all war."

Bullshit. You're fighting a war because you think you're smarter than everyone, because you think you're special, that there's some reason you survived it all. But you're all wrong. Human history is just a bag of shit hurled from a catapult. It's been soaring through the air for awhile, but at some point, it's hitting the wall.

Hood closed the journal again. He tried to remember the man's face, but his features remained blurred. All he could recall was dark hair.

How many people are you going to kill in your life? Even if you have no choice?

He snapped the thought off in his head. He needed to kill the doubter. *Channel your inner Whiskey. You want to survive? You want to save the ones you love? Then put the philosophy on the shelf and push the shelf out the window.*

Ian had truly built his own empire. When Hood had imagined the Kaiser, he imagined a ruthless old despot at the head of a war machine. Maybe Ian was ruthless, but he ruled with the mind, with indoctrination and hope. It was more powerful than brutality and fear. The one thing more desirable than immediate survival was a future. History was littered with people doing horrific things under the guise of righteousness.

Slowly, the sun set, the orange glow coming in at a sharp angle from the westward-facing windows. Hood's mind veered between restlessness and contemplation as the time crawled. Kerry had been gone far, far too long.

His jeans lay in a heap next to the bed. He pulled them on, tossed his pack over his right shoulder and shoved his feet into his shoes as he bolted out the door and hurried down the barren stairwell. His side reverberated in pain with every step.

Outside the front door of the dingy apartment building, the refuse-littered street sat empty, except for corridors of orange sunlight between the packed houses. A forlorn feeling seeped through the entire area, and down the road loomed tall rigid fences with razor-wire curled atop them, a pair of blue helmeted soldiers on the other side. The stumps of chopped-down trees were visible everywhere that buildings weren't.

Across the street, an aging man in dirty pleated pants and a golf cap sat on a bench outside his home, with a cardboard sign next to him that read: *Bet me on a game of chess.*

Hood started towards the man at a walk, his wounds aching with each step. Fear and impatience turned it into a hustling run. The old man looked up at him as he grew close, trying to hide the fear in his eyes with a stern expression.

"Take it easy, fella. I didn't think anyone wanted to play chess *that* bad." The old man chuckled at his own joke.

"Did you see a girl come out of that building? Pretty." Hood asked, his words accusatory despite his intent to remain calm.

"Oh, I've seen her. I knew the minute she came in. You must be the fella that guardsman was carrying in with her." His voice carried a hint of condescension.

Hood grabbed the old man by the collar of his brown cloth jacket, lifting him to his feet. His body seemed to be acting on its own.

"You knew *what* from the minute she came in?" Hood said, staring into the man's yellowed bloodshot eyes.

"Hey now! Take it easy, Piss n' Vinegar. I haven't done a thing. I just sit on my bench and watch."

"If you want to live to touch another bishop you'll tell me what the fuck is going on in this rat hole, old ass man."

The guy's hat fell off onto the bench behind him as Hood gripped

183

him, the wispy gray hair on his head poking up into the air. He stared up at Hood with wild eyes.

"You're not the first rogue to get thrown in here and go off lookin' for those they take from him. It ain't gonna end well for you sonny. I'm tryin' to help ya."

"She's gone? They took her?"

The old man nodded. A chill ran through Hood's body. *I'm not losing her, too. I won't let them touch her. . .* The thoughts were overrun by his doubts. *You've been sitting around inside for hours. You don't know what they've done or where she is.* He felt every muscle in his body coming to life, ready to fight.

"Well they've fucked with the wrong rogue this time. I don't want a sermon, just tell me *who and where.*"

The old man smiled, baring worn teeth that still clung to his gums somehow. "What, you think slavers wouldn't get their paws into a place like this? It's free merchandise. They don't need nothing from the old and the sick though. Keep your eyes about, young fella."

"Where are they? I'm not asking again."

"School, down at the other end." The old man slowly nodded down the street.

Hood released his grip. The old man shakily smoothed out his jacket, still grinning at Hood. It left a bad feeling in his stomach. *This place is no refuge.* His feet carried him down the sidewalk of their own accord, though he felt desperate and vulnerable without a weapon. A gun had become a part of who he was, his definition of personal security. Now he was in a foreign cage without one, alone.

The road curved, nearly every darkened building showing signs of life though few people were out to be seen. The smell of urine and waste emanated from an abandoned gas station. As the road straightened, two sour-looking figures cast wary glances at him from across the way, the unappealing smell of bad meat roasting atop their barrel drum fire.

He turned away to see the face of a ragged child staring at him out the murky window of a derelict house. Ahead, a patchy dog clawed and gnashed at a plastic bottle as it rattled across the street. As Hood drew closer, its head snapped up to look at him, and it dove away down an alley. *He doesn't want to end up cooking on top of that barrel,* Hood thought in disgust.

The slavers could be anywhere around here. You need something, anything you can use in a fight. This sort of thing was more Whiskey's cup of tea. The only thing Hood had going for him was that he was quick. He wasn't about to try to overpower a group of slavers, that was for damn sure.

The road leveled off, and Hood could see the elementary school down the street. The charred storefront on his left had exploded long ago. Shards of glass glimmered in the tall grass and the sidewalk ahead of him. His mind spun into a whirlpool of ideas. He bit his bottom lip in consternation. *Could it work?* The sound of a scraping footstep spun Hood around.

A young boy gazed wide-eyed at him from around the corner of the building. He turned and ran up the cross street. Hood sprinted after him. The kid dove down the first alley, but Hood's long strides caught him quickly. He grabbed the kid by the arm. He tried to get away, then turned and looked at him with tears in his eyes.

"Don't sell me off. I just needed to sneak out and find medicine for my ma. Please, I made it all this way, just let me go!" The boy pleaded.

"What do you know about the people in the school?" Hood whispered.

The boy shut his eyes tight, shaking his head in denial of reality.

"Tell me, and I'll let you go." Hood grabbed the kid by both arms.

"Slavers, under the Kaiser, that's what my Dad said. Dame Pria the man eater, he calls her. She has a gun. The only one in the whole camp. She and her men, they grab people and sneak them out of the camp to some other place."

Hood looked the boy in the eyes, searching his freckled face for a lie.

"Tell me everything you know."

◆ ◆ ◆

Hood moved slowly up the short steps from the sidewalk with the last light of the day, heading towards the front of the school. He felt even more naked without his backpack or Hoodie. A slaver lay back on the staircase in front of the door, his elbows resting on the top step.

"Well, now." The words slid out of the slaver's cracked lips. They were surrounded by an unkempt chestnut goatee. He stared at Hood from beneath bushy eyebrows.

"I'm here to see Dame Pria."

"Oh, okay then." The slaver said with a laugh. He stood up, pulling a machete by the handle out of the leg of his pants. He moved the polished blade to Hood's neck, observing his reaction with a raised eyebrow.

Hood remained still.

The slaver took the blade away and slapped Hood on the ass with the flat of it. "Well then, get on inside, honored guest." The slaver made a grand gesture to the door with a devious smile.

Hood moved towards the heavy double doors and swung them open. Inside, the trophy cases were shattered and empty, and displaced couches sat on either side of the hallway, each complete with lounging slavers. He heard the distinct echo of a basketball being dribbled in a gym somewhere nearby.

One of the slavers, a man with a braided red chin-beard, menaced Hood from his recliner.

"You lost, boy?"

"I'm here to see Dame Pria." Hood said as loudly as he could. *This is all going to go to shit if she isn't here.*

A chorus of the slavers' laughter echoed as they all rose to look at Hood.

"Well, you're lost now." Braided beard said with a look of pity in his eyes.

186

Footsteps heralded the approach of a woman from one of the rooms. The slavers all stood up as she appeared, eyeing Hood coldly. She was a tall, middle-aged, not unhandsome woman, with a hawkish nose dominating her face. Her black hair was bound back behind her head, and she wore a low-hanging gun belt around her stonewashed blue jeans. In it, snugly holstered, was a pistol.

In the land of the disarmed, the one woman with the gun is queen.

"You're no one I work with." Dame Pria said.

"No, I'm not." Hood said.

"Well, this is interesting. What are you doing here, boy?" She moved slowly towards him. Two of the slavers flanked Hood. He held up his arms, and they thoroughly patted him down before moving away.

"I've heard you're the only people here who don't live like rats."

She gave Hood a once-over, slowly pulling her pistol from its holster as she sauntered closer.

"You're a pretty thing. Don't make a lot of boys lookin' like you." She bit her bottom lip as she stood a few feet away from him. "Someone's gonna pay *a lot* to get their hands on you," she whispered, smiling. "I *love* it when they pay a lot."

"I think you'd rather keep me around for yourself." Hood grinning back at her with an equally cold stare. She raised an eyebrow. "I don't need you to tell me what I need." She pressed the pistol against his forehead. Hood looked up at it, then back at her with another nonchalant grin.

"I know you're probably sick of the, ah. . . handiwork . . . of these ugly bastards." Hood said. "Take me on and I get to not live like a rat, and *you* get a lot more pleasure out of this hell hole." Hood shrugged. "I call that a win-win."

She bared her teeth at him. "Or maybe I'll just use you up and blow your head off for being an arrogant fuck."

"That would be my least favorite of your choices," Hood said.

"Let me see what you got." She said, pressing the barrel harder against his head. "And I'll decide whether you get to keep breathing my air."

Hood held up his hands, and then moved them towards his jeans, unbuttoning them. "You're going to like what you see."

Hood unzipped and then reached into his boxers. In one motion, he gripped the glass shard he'd secreted there and pulled it out of his trousers, pushing away her pistol hand with his left and driving the glass shard into her eye.

She screamed as the pistol went off.

He drove the glass deeper into her head, ignoring the pain as the glass sliced into his own palm. She let go of the pistol to clutch at her eye, and he flipped the pistol into his bloody right hand. Then he shot her in the head.

She collapsed into a gory heap.

The slavers stood dumbstruck as he held the raised pistol. They gripped baseball bats and pipes and one of them had a sword. The guy looked ridiculous.

"You all get the privilege of deciding whether or not you die today." Hood said. "The pretty girl you guys took this afternoon. Is she here?"

The slaver closest to him shook his head, eyes ablaze with anger.

"You smuggle slaves out of the camp—I need a map to where you send them."

All of the slavers cast glances at each other, but stood motionless. Hood aimed the iron sights at the closest slaver about fifteen feet away. "I know you have a map of the area. I need it."

The slaver gripped his bat hard, fighting against his rage. Hood kept his grip firm but easy on the pistol as he focused on the man's head. The slice in his palm from the glass screamed in pain against the grip of the pistol. His blood dripped from the handle of the gun to the floor. The slaver opened his mouth to speak.

Hood fired.

The man's head exploded, spraying another slaver five feet behind him. The only sound was the body slumping to the floor and the ringing in his ears from the shot that echoed in the halls.

Hood pointed the pistol at the gore-covered slaver.

"He must not know what 'map' means. Do you know what 'map' means?" Hood said to the gory man. The man nodded, turned and ran down the hallway.

"That's better. You all keep working on your snowman impressions and I'll be on my way in no time," Hood said, surveying their faces. Some stared back in hate, some in horror. Not all of them were grizzled wasters. Even if they were doing the devil's own work. None of them said a word, frozen in place.

The gory man hurried back down the hall, holding a map over his head.

"That's the place right there. It's down the highway." He pointed to a marked spot on the worn, folded road map. Hood snatched it with his left hand.

"You're not lying to me, are you? If I go there and there's no slavers, I'm going to have to come back here. And I'm going to be pretty unhappy about it."

"It's the one. It's the place. I swear." The man said, his close-set eyes wide.

"Good." Hood backed away from them all to the front doors. "Well, it's been real. Next time try opening a lemonade stand or something."

Hood turned to face the front door. He paused a moment. *The guy outside definitely heard the gunshots.* Hood pushed the door open and dove forward in a somersault. The machete scraped against the concrete as the man swung it down hard. Hood flipped onto his back with pistol raised, firing three times fast at the machete man as he lunged towards him.

The shots made a three-step ladder up the man's chest and he collapsed onto Hood's legs.

Hood kicked him off, the once-smug slaver gurgling on his own blood. Hood stood up, taking one last glance at the school before hustling away. He pulled his backpack out of the scrub brush beside the ivy-overgrown house, then tucked the pistol into his pants, the barrel warm against his body.

His right hand shook steadily, still bleeding out of his palm where the glass had sliced into him. He tore off the sleeve of his shirt and wrapped it tightly around the wound. As the adrenaline faded, the pain rushed back into his shoulder and his side while his hand throbbed.

Hood climbed the steps into an old apartment building the young boy had told him about.

Muffled voices argued in Spanish from an apartment as he walked down the empty hallway with filthy walls and peeling paint. He quietly went down to the basement, where an old laundry room featured a boarded-up earthen hole. It lead down to the sewers and out of the camp. His mind floated to Kerry, Whiskey, and Taylor, wishing they were with him as he splashed down into murky water that rushed down the slope of the sewer.

You're not alone. You'll never be alone. I'm coming. I'm not giving up until they kill me.

Chapter 15 – Deliverance

It was a long, quiet walk along the road. Too long and too quiet. Not one haggard soul had he seen after leaving the camp.

The route on the map was simple. He wished it were more complex, giving him something to focus on. Instead his days were filled with hunger and wild imaginings as to where everyone he loved had gone. His nights were filled with dreams of searching frantically in dark mountain forests only to have the mountain split open, heaving fire and swallowing up distant familiar figures until he could only turn and run. Being hungry gives you bad dreams.

As he got closer to his destination, he tried to focus on Kerry. In his gut, he was steeling himself to the challenge of freeing her from the slavers. But fears and questions ran free in his mind–where was Ian with Taylor? What had happened to Whiskey? Were any of them still alive?

One thing at a time, he'd remind himself. They're more than capable of taking care of themselves. You won't find them if you get yourself killed by some wastelanders while you daydream.

A sickly looking deer with patchy fur galloped out of the treeline beside the road, bounded across its cracked surface and into the thick layer of trees on the other side. Hood was so surprised by its appearance that he couldn't even line up a shot on it until it had vanished once again into the tree cover.

Goddammit.

His stomach rumbled in frustration. He consoled himself by thinking it would take too much time to skin and cook the thing. But he had found very little food in the few abandoned roadside stops he'd seen thus far. He eyed the woods, considering whether to give chase.

Stay on the road. You know how to get to the camp from here, and you could get lost in those woods.

He urged his body forward, drinking some water out of the bottle in his pack, which only made his stomach feel more empty.

What if you never find any of them? The thought barged into his head. His heart sank at the idea that might have seen the last of those he loved. He wanted to refuse the possibility, but he couldn't.

If that's the way it has to be, you keep moving. You keep searching for any sign of them. You keep living and surviving and you fight because there is good in the world worth fighting for.

Hood desperately hoped someone, anyone, would come out of the woods. Friend, foe, he didn't care. There was too much time to think.

There's no one out here because they all get captured or killed by someone or another.

He was far enough north now that he was probably near where Rangers from the Sons of Liberty would come through. He was almost to the borders between which the Kaiser's militants and the Sons held sway.

There was a crazy, expansive empty feeling to being alone, walking for days through this country he knew to be so huge. It gave him the sensation of being lost even though he knew where he was going. There were wasters and soldiers and slavers that would prey upon him, but the silent emptiness of the road in the woods felt as though it would engulf him, that it would never end.

As the long walk continued, he checked the Beretta he'd taken from Dame Pria. It was a beautiful pistol, but he only had three bullets left. *It's okay, he said to himself with a grin, just don't miss.* He felt a confidence bordering on cockiness.

You're acting pretty tough for a kid who got touched up pretty good in his last few fights, Whiskey's voice said in his head.

Hood chuckled.

You're laughing at yourself. You've reached crazy territory.

Despite his aching injuries, Hood felt sharp. He felt ready now. He just hated the wait.

As each day wore on, he'd check the map for his progress far too often.

He realized he was close when a rusted exit sign for a nearby podunk town appeared amidst the tall roadside weeds. The trees slowly gave way to empty 'civilization' once again.

The mall on the highway service road was really more just a collection of large retail outlets surrounding a parking lot. The wind blew garbage bags and papers swirling into the air and skidding across the pavement. The waning sun offered little warmth.

He paused in front of the shattered glass doors of a huge warehouse-style store, scanning the area for movement. He didn't know what he was hoping for. According to the map, this was the place.

He hid outside and watched for movement for an hour. Nothing so much as moved. If it was empty, where were the slavers? Where was Kerry? Had Pria's slavers lied to him?

Pistol in hand, he stepped through the remnants of the door, ducking under the handle that ran across the midsection. The shattered plexiglass sheets crunched under his shoes. He moved forward cautiously, the building only barely illuminated by ambient light from the front doors. Racks of clothes lay knocked on the floor, and cash registers were smashed on the ground. Once proud retail items were strewn about everywhere. *This looks just like every other ransacked nightmare frozen in time.*

Hood balled his free hand into a fist. This couldn't be the place. Had he read the map wrong? No. But there didn't seem to be anyone here.

He looked up at a sign hanging from the ceiling, directing him to the back of the store for the sporting goods department. Quietly he walked between a row of shelves holding a host of different kinds of shoes. The samples were all scattered across the floor, laid low with impunity. Hood tried to imagine a timeline for this place. He could only imagine the kind of anarchy that had ensued when the panic truly set in, and people realized they were on their own for survival.

Without a sound he turned the corner and hustled over to the hunting section of the darkened warehouse. The display cases were empty, devoid of shotguns. A large amount of blood stained the carpet.

On the other side of the counter he found several empty casings on the floor. In the cabinets below he found a case which was probably once full of shotgun ammunition, now only a few boxes remained. If he could ever find a shotgun they'd be useful. He tucked two boxes away into his backpack. The place was picked clean of weaponry. That was not a good sign.

He hustled down the aisles, looking for anything of value. Only stacks of garbage bags were left, along with bottles of laundry detergent, soaps and cleaning supplies. He found a garden hose and slung it over his shoulder, and tossed a bottle of soap into his bag. He could cut off a section of the hose; it would be perfect for siphoning gas. If he could find a functioning car.

A faint clicking sound echoed through the warehouse. It was rapid and soft, but incessant. Hood crouched low and quietly hugged the back wall of the building as he passed aisle after aisle, getting closer to the sound.

It was so dark he could barely see, but he recognized the faint smell of gasoline. As he approached the back corner of the building he saw a dormant generator. The clicking sound stopped. Hood froze. He could hear something sniffing, then growling.

The clicking started again. It was an animal's claws on the tile. He could smell the pungent odor before he could see anything. The clicking sped up greatly. Dogs barked. They were coming after him.

He saw one of them only as it leapt for him. He jumped back into the aisle, and it skidded on its claws against the floor. He raised his pistol and shot at it as it turned to face him, teeth bared. It yelped and fell into a heap. Another one crashed into his back, clawing and trying to bite down into his neck only to sink its teeth into the hose slung over his shoulder.

Hood spun around and it flew off of him, hose still in its mouth. It landed on all fours, dropped the hose and lunged at him. He fired at the animal but missed his mark. Its jaws nearly snapped off the front of his nose and he fell onto his back. It leaped onto him once more. Hood reached out to grab it by the neck to stop it from sinking its teeth into his face. He tried to position the pistol for a clean shot but the animal flailed so wildly he could barely keep it away. It foamed at the mouth, the warm spit dripping onto Hood's neck. It reared back to dive in for the bite.

In that second of reprieve Hood whipped the pistol into position and shot it through the neck. Blood spilled out of it onto Hood. It struggled for a moment before going limp. Hood tossed it to the floor, pulling himself to his feet. He leaned his hands on his knees as he caught his breath, adrenaline racing through him. The slide was locked back on the pistol. He was out of bullets.

Why in god's name would wild dogs be in this place? He turned back to the generator. Near it was a pile of refrigerator shelves. He followed the cord from the generator to the wall of food storage refrigerators. The smell seeping out was putrid.

Blood covered the floor.

But worse, the plexiglass doors of the refrigerators displayed at least a dozen human corpses flayed and hanging from meathooks. Some of the limbs were missing. A tall table used as a chopping block sat covered in gore just inside the wall of refrigerators. Hood threw his hand over his nose and mouth to cover it. His stomach tried to leave him repeatedly.

The bastard wasn't lying. This is the slaver's den.

They would be coming back here. He needed to leave now.

But how many more people will they kill and eat if you leave?

"Would the extremely loud motherfucker please come to the front desk?" A raspy voice echoed through the warehouse. "I'm afraid we are not open for visitors, sir or madame. And I *do hope* it is a madame!" It boomed again with sardonic courtesy.

Hood looked down at his pistol, devoid of bullets. He cursed under his breath, looking around the warehouse in desperation. He ran quietly on the balls of his feet down the nearest aisle and climbed up as furtively as he could manage to the top of the shelves and lay down among stacks of boxes, staying motionless. He waited. Time seemed to take forever. He felt that his breathing was louder than a foghorn.

He could hear several men murmuring to each other, and could see three flashlight beams illuminating different parts of the store. Slowly they scanned the building, moving closer and closer to the back where he lay. He had to be calm, wait for the right moment, and hope they didn't find him before then. Maybe if he waited it out, they'd leave again.

Fuck that. You have to kill them all. A thought sent a shock through his body. Kerry had been taken here. He imagined her kicking and screaming. *What did they do to her? What if they killed her? What if they. . .ate her?* The thought nearly impulsed him into leaping off the shelves. *Get a hold of yourself. She's still alive. She has to be. But these sick fucks forfeited their right to live. You kill them, you're saving lives of god knows how many people they'd dice up.*

He shook with anticipation. He never took pleasure in killing anyone. He'd struggled with it for a long time. But he had a desire to kill these men. He wanted to see them dead. *Are you getting numb to this?* No, this was something different. This is more than just killing to survive. *The bastards need to die.* The desperation of it all caused his heart to race, and he tried to breathe as softly as possible. *Relax, he repeated to himself. Stay calm. You have to be smarter than them.* He turned his head and saw the men inspecting the refrigerated corpses in the back wall. He could hear them better now. *How could she have escaped this?* His fear resounded in his head.

"Think they'll still be good?" one man with a twangy voice said.

"Haven't been hangin' long. And we gots' gas now," another deeper voice responded.

"Whoever it was, he kill' them dogs," The raspy voiced man said as he walked over to the two them.

"You think he got out?" twangy asked.

"Naw, we sealed off all the vents. She's still here," Raspy replied. "Ain't that right, beautiful?" he shouted.

"It ain't a girl, dumbass. Wishful thinkin'," deeper voice quipped.

They resumed their search. The longer it took, the more comfortable they got, the more they spread out. They'd regroup, murmuring to each other, "Maybe the motherfucker did escape," only to set out again more relaxed than before. Finally one of them walked around the back of his aisle and sauntered past him. The other flashlights were on the other side of the warehouse.

Hood jumped down, landed on his feet and pressed the pistol into the side of the man's head as he spun around. Hood grabbed the barrel of the sawed-off shotgun the man held with his free hand before the man could point it towards him.

"Let it go," Hood said quietly. The man didn't move. "Let it go." he repeated in a low growl.

"If ya shoot me, they'll hear and come kill you," Twangy said.

"And you won't be around to see it." Hood tugged on the shotgun and the man let it go. Even in the dark he could feel the man's sideways gaze. Hood could smell the nervous sweat on the man, eyes wide. Hood slid the shotgun handle into his left hand. The man shoved him as he adjusted his grip, turned and ran.

"He's over here!" Twangy shouted. Hood hefted the shotgun as he regained his footing, firing twice as the man was about to turn the corner. Two echoing booms. Twangy's body collapsed onto the ground. Immediately Hood ran farther back into the warehouse, getting to one knee and ripping a box of shotgun shells out of his backpack.

He grabbed a handful and jammed them into his hoodie pocket.

He put two shells in his mouth, stood up, opened the shotgun and threw the empty shells across the warehouse. They hit the ground with a distant echoing clatter. He loaded two more into the barrels and spun around the corner to the furthest back aisle. He peered around the corner. He could see the flashlights coming, scanning aisles as they hustled down.

Quietly he climbed to the top shelf again. The flashlights worked in Hood's favor. He could see wherever they were and their peripheral vision was worthless in the dark. Again, he'd play the waiting game. They discovered their friend's body and cursed, moving together quickly, scanning the aisles. *Don't try to get away. You're going to die here.*

He waited until they were about an aisle away and stood up slowly. He pulled the shotgun to his shoulder and fired both shots into the men. One of them cried out.

"I can't see nothin'!" Deep voice screamed. "Oh God, I'm blind. Rog, where are you?"

The other man had retreated. He'd figured out what was going on, and turned off his flashlight. Hood hopped down from the shelves, reloading. He put the two empty shells in his mouth, not wanting them to make a sound on the floor. The heat from the plastic casing burned his lips, the smell and taste of gunpowder filling him. One of the bodies in the refrigerators had looked female. His mind struggled to process the information, the possibilities. *That's not her. It's not.* He pleaded with himself, while his need to kill the last slaver surged within him.

He knew where the man had last been. And he knew he'd be scared. He'd be on the move. He'd be retreating. Or at least, that's what Hood was banking on. *There's nowhere you can run, you sick fuck.*

"Rog, I can't fuckin' see. Don't leave me like this!" Deeper Voice continued to cry out. There was no response.

Silently Hood crept past the dying deep-voiced man, weaving through the aisles towards the entrance.

He looked around the corner near the front of the store. The light of the sunset came through the front doors, and Hood could see Raspy, a thin, squirrelly man with tattoos on his neck and hands backing towards the doors, frenetically scanning his surroundings.

Hood realized the man didn't know if he was facing one or more enemies.

Hood took the two shells out of his mouth and threw them over Raspy's head. They clattered on the other side of the warehouse and Raspy spun around to face the sound, turning his back to Hood. Hood snuck up behind Raspy and fired.

A spray of blood covered the checkout counter behind the man, the deep boom echoing. Raspy fell to his knees. Hood fired again as he stepped closer, the man collapsing to the floor.

Hood reloaded, walked over to Raspy and flipped him over with his foot. He had a braided chin beard and thin straw hair. The man looked up though dying, terror-stricken eyes, chest rising and falling laboriously. Hood leaned over him.

"Don't fucking eat people." Hood pulled the trigger, blasting the man in his chest.

"Was that you Rog? Did you get the sumbitch?" Deep Voice boomed from the store's interior.

Hood reloaded one barrel and walked back towards the man.

"No."

"You're the god damned devil!" Hood didn't respond, moving towards the man. He could hear his breath racing, before he switched from ranting to pleading for his life. "I swear I didn't do nothin'. They gave me no choice. I had to help 'em."

Hood walked past the blinded man, picked up his automatic rifle and slung it over his shoulder. He retrieved the two gas cans the group had brought and walked back to front of the store. When the man heard him walking away, he started thanking god loudly.

Hood picked up Raspy's hunting rifle. He lifted it, got Deep Voice in his sights, and fired. The man lay still, his lies dying with him. Hood turned on his heel and marched to the front door. *That wasn't Kerry in those refrigerators.* He wasn't about to go back and check. If found anything, her hair, some of her clothes. . . He ducked under the doorhandle of the shattered window door and stepped back outside. *No. She's too good at survival. You know that. She's still alive.*

Hood was so focused on Kerry that he almost didn't see them.

A semicircle of men with rifles pointed at Hood flanked one side of the building, the sun setting behind them. They all wore deep red armbands and were well-outfitted with combat vests and automatic weapons, though they weren't in uniform.

"Drop it all," one man said.

Fuck me. Hood dropped all the guns onto the asphalt with a clatter. *You've got to be joking.*

"Making quite a commotion in there, partner," said an olive-skinned man with a salt-and- pepper beard and slicked-back, dark hair.

Hood couldn't believe his bad luck. *I wouldn't mind something going right for a change.*

The wind blew and a cloud of dirt billowed over all of them.

They haven't shot you. There's a way out of this.

"Who else is with you?" The same man asked at length.

"About forty dudes with mini-guns, so you guys should leave," Hood replied with a grin.

The man chuckled, and nodded at the skinny black soldier next to him. The soldier hustled to the other side of the building. Another group of armed men with the same red armbands walked around the corner. Damn, there were a lot of these guys.

When it rains, it pours legions of bastards who could kill you.

"It's clear," one of them said to the first man. He inclined his head towards the entrance, and they all moved inside.

"So you just killed some of the Kaiser's slavers all by your lonesome?" The man with slicked back hair motioned to Hood's bloody clothes.

"When you say it like that, you make it sound easy," Hood quipped.

The man took his left hand off the rifle and rubbed the side of his head.

"You should come with us." It was not as much of a suggestion as a statement of fact.

"Why do I get the feeling I don't have a say in the matter?" Hood asked. "Besides, I don't even know who you are."

The man continued to size up Hood. "My name is Gene Mercadier, Captain of the Deliverance of the Crusader, 21st infantry." He flashed a smile. "We are The Sons of Liberty. And we are the rebirth of this country."

Yeah, you and everyone else, Hood sighed.

Chapter 16 – Crusader

It wasn't so much that Hood didn't know what to expect from the Sons of Liberty. He had heard some things that were vaguely positive about them, the dead man's journal, for one. But he'd long since abandoned thinking his expectations would meet reality. He had a bulldozer's finesse when it came to guessing the future.

They took his guns and left him with his backpack after searching him thoroughly. They handcuffed him, and he marched uncomfortably in front of the 21st as they moved away from the slavers' den to their hidden Humvees in the woods. The soldiers made fun of each other as soldiers always do. It reminded Hood of his crew in Clearwater, and he couldn't stop the longing he felt for those days. *I'm still alive, guys. I haven't forgotten you.* A few of the soldiers ribbed Hood as he walked in front of the company, calling him "Bad Meat"—they thought he had been captured by the cannibals and fought his way out. Hood just looked at them, smelled himself and gave a disgusted look, which inspired some laughter among the ranks. *Maybe if I get them to like me, they won't kill me.*

Though they hadn't mistreated him, Hood feared execution. He knew nothing of the Sons outside of hearsay, and he felt that he was being lulled into a false sense of security. He thought of every possible escape opportunity or bargain he might be able to negotiate. All of these options were weak, but he refused to have none.

"Where are you taking me?" Hood said to Gene, who walked among his soldiers.

"You'll see," he said, looking straight ahead.

Hood was terrified of the response to his next question, but it was better than staying silent. "Why am I here?"

Gene said nothing, though he seemed to be in contemplation.

"The Crusader will know what to do with you."

The Crusader? Like, THE Crusader, leader of the Sons? Hood was dumbfounded. *Why would he want me? Why is he here?* At the very least, this meant Hood's death wasn't predetermined. *Only a possibility. Great.* Hood tugged at his handcuffed wrists. *Make yourself valuable.*

When they reached the Humvees hidden atop a tree-covered hill, Captain Mercadier spoke to his men away from Hood. He could hear little of what was being said. Several of the soldiers kept their gaze on Hood with their fingers hovering on the triggers of their rifles. Their faces showed surprise at Gene's words, but they saluted him nonetheless, splitting up into predetermined groups. Some of them climbed into Humvees and drove away. Four more soldiers came out of the woods to meet Gene. He discussed something with them in a low voice, and headed off deeper into the woods with one of the soldiers. The other three stood watch over Hood, a guy and a girl, both black, and a white guy, all wearing former U.S. army uniforms, except they had a red lion patch on their shoulders. *They guardsmen for the Crusader?*

"Nice day," Hood said, looking up at the blue sky between the trees. The three of them just kept their rifles sighted on him. Hood looked down at his bloodstained clothes, and realized how insane he must've sounded. "You guys take a vow of silence, or. . .?"

The three of them glowered at him.

"Alright. Good talk," Hood said, nodding sardonically.

A two-way radio beeped on one of the soldier's belts. *"Bring him."* it crackled. Without hesitation they ushered him deeper into the woods. Southwest, if Hood's sense of direction was right. His heart began to pick up speed. *Oh man. What the hell am I supposed to do here?*

The walk seemed to take forever, every second an eternity. *Do whatever it takes. Say whatever you have to say. Just don't die here. Taylor, Whiskey, Kerry, they're alone if you die here.*

Slowly, the woods opened up into a clearing among the trees, a bustling hub of Sons' soldiers. The three guardsmen ushered him past rows and rows of tents. This was a small army, complete with supply train. *If they're letting me see all this, this is either going to end badly, or really badly.* They brought him to a larger tent with its own area sectioned off naturally by the boughs of pine trees. Sitting on a tree stump was a barrel-chested, middle-aged black man wearing a plain white tee shirt tucked into his belted slacks, and a decorated military jacket on loosely over that. His eyes flashed up at Hood from behind rectangular silver rimmed glasses, his head and face closely shaven save for a goatee peppered with gray.

He leaned down to grab a metal pot that sat above a small fire, pouring the steamy black liquid into a plain coffee mug.

"I don't know what I'm going to do when we run out of coffee." The man said, his voice soothing, almost fatherly. "That for me, will be the real doomsday, I think."

Hood had no idea what to say, or what to make of this interaction. *You bring me here to talk about coffee?* He wanted to say.

The Crusader scrutinized him, blowing on his mug. "Not everyday some kid mows down some of the Kaiser's slavers."

Hood shrugged. "Caught me on a bad day."

The Crusader chuckled. "What's your name?"

"Hood."

"That's your real name?"

"It's made of real letters, isn't it?" The words just seemed to flow out of him without thought. *Okay, I guess this is how I'm playing it.*

The Crusader laughed. *Thank god.* "Alright then, Hood with real letters. Why did you kill them?"

"Because they deserved to die," Hood said.

"Just making the world a better place, huh?"

"I guess so."

"So what's the real reason?" his eyes searched for any hit of a lie.

"I'm looking for someone." *Might as well tell the truth when lying won't do you any good.*

The Crusader smiled, rubbing his thumb back and forth on his mug before taking a sip. "Aren't we all?"

Small birds chirped in the trees, and the cool wind blew evergreen air that swished through the pine needles. *Who are you looking for?* The Crusader measured his words.

"I think I know who you are, Hood."

"Oh yeah?"

"We knew of this small group who was stealing from the Kaiser for some time down south. Had a knack for getting away with it. We considered contacting them to see if they wanted to work together. Earlier this month scouts told me the Kaiser had tracked them down and destroyed their town. I think I made a mistake by not offering them my protection. Caution getting the better of me." The Crusader took another sip of coffee, profoundly at ease. "I think you are one of the survivors."

"Why do you say that?" Hood said, keeping his face stoic. *Just chess pieces on a chessboard, huh? Son of a bitch.*

"Call it a feeling," The Crusader rested the coffee mug on his knee. "Not many survivors even try to oppose the Kaiser, those that do usually don't stay alive. And you seem to have a talent for staying alive."

Hood scoffed. "Feels more like a talent for nearly getting myself killed." *And getting people I care about killed.* Hood fought back a grimace.

"That's one way of seeing it." A soldier carrying a message walked into the area. The Crusader gestured for the man to give it to him. The man handed it over, gave a tired salute and walked off. The Crusader's dark eyes scanned the message behind his silver glasses before he turned his attention back to Hood. "So. Who are you looking for?"

Taylor. Whiskey. Kerry. Ian? Yes, I want to find him. To kill him. Can you even bring yourself to pull the trigger? No, there's only one thing that matters now. Finding the others. Getting them the hell out of this mess.

"My sister." Hood said, the words feeling heavier than he expected. *How could you do this to her, Ian? To me? To Mom and Dad?*

"Was she taken by those slavers?"

"No. The Kaiser took her from Clearwater the day it was destroyed."

"Ah." A satisfied smile grew on the Crusader's face, accenting the creases around his eyes. "So I was right. You are one of the survivors. Good! So why did you seek out the slavers?"

"Following the trail of breadcrumbs. Trying to track down where the Kaiser is now."

"To do what, exactly?"

"Get her out of there."

"You think you can do that?"

"What, should I just lay down? Go start a new life somewhere? Leave her to die?"

The Crusader nodded as if he already expected Hood's sentiment, expecting it. "It is a rare sort of man that knows the stupidity, the impossibility of a task, and is yet compelled by the depth of his loyalty to undergo it anyway."

"I think many would do the same." Hood felt profoundly uncomfortable and confused by the scope and intent of the compliment. *What is your game?*

"Some? Yes. Many? No."

Hood itched the side of his head with both cuffed hands. The Crusader's guardsmen brought their rifles to sight on Hood when he moved.

"Easy. . ." The Crusader raised a hand to his soldiers. They lowered their rifles. "This young man means us no harm." He rose to his feet, moving slowly beside the small fire. "I think God is giving me a chance to redeem myself for the destruction of your brave town." He cocked his head. "Either that, or you are the Devil's own

206

weapon on earth. Either way, I'd be in poor judgment to overlook you for a second time."

The smell of poorly seasoned food being cooked wafted over from the camp. Hood's stomach groaned in desire. He lifted his cuffed hands, gesturing with them slightly. "Well, I know when a choice isn't mine to make."

He smiled at Hood, drinking his coffee. "I think even if you came to us as a free man, you'd see the wisdom in working together. After all, we have the same enemy."

It still didn't seem possible, that Ian, his Ian, was on one side of a war for the remnants of a destroyed country. I don't think you all understand. I've seen him throw up. I've played Contra with him. We could never get past the fourth level without cheat codes. I've seen him stub his toe, I broke his finger playing dodgeball. Hood wanted to shake the thoughts out of his head. I guess Stalin once cried to his mom and played with toys. It just doesn't make sense. Wake up bro. Wake the fuck up. That's not who you are.

But it was. This was reality. "What do you want from me?" Hood said with as much calm as he could muster. Fatigue started to overtake the adrenaline. His wounds ached, his muscles sore.

"You've set some things into motion, killing those slavers. Surely their death will draw the Kaiser's attention to this area. And as you can imagine, we've gone to great lengths to try and keep the fact that we are this far south away from him as long as possible. . ."

If I know Ian, he knows you're here. Hood worked his mouth. *Kid could stare down a needle to the eye just to win a bet.* Not that Hood could say a word of that to the Crusader, though. If he knew Hood's connection to the Kaiser, this could get real ugly.

". . .There is something I think you are well suited for. And if we want the plan to work, we need someone like yourself that has no known connection to us. You have forced our hand into doing this now. Only fitting you should be a part of it." He finished his coffee, placing his mug on a gray rock beside the fire. "Oversee a country as long as I have, you notice the patterns in the weave that stand out. The uncanny coincidences. You learn not to ignore them."

This guy sure loves to hear himself talk. Hood met the Crusader's easy gaze. *I can't deny the air of greatness that surrounds him, though. You'd be dumb to underestimate him. Or to take him at face value.*

"How will you help me get my sister back?"

"Talk to Gene. He will accompany you. Do what he says, prove yourself worthy to him, and we will afford you the rights of our own. And you will get the chance to track down your sister."

You clearly don't mind taking advantage of your leverage, huh? It felt just as likely that he'd kill Hood, if the task he was about to undertake wasn't already a suicide mission. *Not like I have much choice. Who knows, maybe he truly is testing you, trying to enlist you in his war.* "What's your name, by the way?"

"Crusader. Spelled with real letters." He wore a wry smile. "Richard. Richard Leone. You could ask anyone that. Life has not granted me the anonymity it has given you." His tone carried the faintest hint of longing for a simpler life.

"Grass is always greener, huh?" The Crusader met Hood's gaze, a knowing, piercing look, before he pulled open the flap to his tent and stepped inside.

One of the guardsman walked Hood back through the quiet bustle of the woodland camp to a folding table outside an open row of tents. Gene and other members of the 21st sat around it wrapped up in their own discussions while eating hot food, a few of them rolling dice and cursing their luck. Gene rose out of his seat at the sight of Hood, moving to talk to the Guardsman, who relayed a message before he turned and walked away.

"Well." Gene said, green eyes beneath bushy eyebrows. "I had a feeling I'd see you again."

Hood nodded towards the food. "Any chance I can get some of that?"

Gene smirked. "Yeah, of course." He moved to one of the tents where a cook doled something out into a metal bowl and dropped a hunk of something onto a beaten plate. Gene walked back, setting it in front of Hood.

"Stewed vegetables and salted meat," Gene said as if it were filet mignon. Hood climbed into a seat beside the other soldiers who shot conspicuously skeptical glances at him. "You're going to want to soak the meat in the stew. Damn near inedible if you don't."

"You ask me Captain, that's throwing good meat after bad." One soldier said with a toothy grin. The soldier beside him roared. Hood sank his teeth into the meat after he dipped it in the bowl. Even with his hands cuffed he stuffed the food down ravenously. *Slow down. You're going to choke.* How long had it been since he had a hot meal? Even one as tasteless as this felt like heaven.

"So what Cap, is Bad Meat a part of the 21st now or somethin'?" One soldier said through a thinly rolled cigarette as he pulled off his boots.

"That remains to be seen." Gene said. Hood could feel their eyes on him, but he didn't care. *This might be your future. This might be your only way to get Taylor, Kerry and Whiskey back. The Crusader had a point. It was damn near impossible to try to undertake this on my own. If it means pledging myself to fight for the Sons to get them free, I'll do it.*

Hood put the spoon down into the empty bowl, feeling rejuvenated. The soldier across from him with grease lines on his scruffy face kept him in a cold stare. "The fuck you lookin' at?" The man barked.

Hood ignored him, looking up at Gene, expressionless.

"If you're done, come with me," Gene directed to Hood, nodding away from the camp. "J.R. is acting command of the unit while I'm gone," he said loudly to the nearby members of the 21st.

"Where you goin'?" One soldier asked. Hood noticed that Gene was carrying Hood's backpack along with one of his own as the two of them walked together towards the treeline.

"Hey, keep 'em forward Cap!" another member of the 21st hollered at Gene.

"Keep 'em forward." He called back over his shoulder.

Chapter 17 – Wayward

The two of them stood alone on the wooded hill outside the camp. Gene approached him, producing a key to unlock his handcuffs.

"Didn't feel right putting bracelets on a man willing to fight the Kaiser's meat-eaters all by his lonesome. But I had to protect my men."

Hood scrutinized Gene's face. He looked unaffected, if not time-worried, as he untied his red armband and hung it up on a tree.

"What is this?" Hood said flatly, regarding the situation in it's entirety.

"I'll just lay it out there. Don't really have time for the long form. The Kaiser shuttled a refugee right past the slavers' den to a way station on the route to his stronghold in Greenridge University. He rarely does that. But when he does, it's usually an important slave, one that the Kaiser himself wants. Usually women. Pretty ones. He took this one right from the U.N. camp not long ago."

Kerry. Hood thought. It has to be Kerry. "How do you know all this?"

"We've been watching them for a long time. Since way before we mobilized down here. Any good officer knows information wins wars."

"So you just let them hang around, buying and selling people, cutting 'em up for meat." Hood said, unable to hide his disgust. *This is not a productive line of inquiry.*

"Believe me. It didn't sit well. But orders are orders."

Hood watched intently as the Captain removed any and all paraphernalia that held significance with the Sons. It wasn't much. Other than the armband, it was only captain's insignias pinned on his collar, which he stuck unceremoniously into a nearby tree.

"Okay, so. . .We're looking for this woman? What's special about her?"

"Nothing. Aside from the fact that she's being shipped straight to the Kaiser. Probably the last one to do so, given that the war is truly about to begin."

The Sons are about to make their move. Hood rubbed his wrists, enjoying their freedom. "I won't lie, I don't like that you guys have been so free to trust me and tell me all this."

Gene snorted. He seemed to be enjoying Hood's complete lack of guile. "Believe me, if the Crusader thought you were a threat to our efforts, you'd be dead. By the time the Kaiser could get his hands on you, there's nothing you could tell him that he wouldn't already know. Best case scenario, we pull this off and you prove yourself an asset to the Sons. Worst case scenario, we die."

Hood laughed, rubbing his neck. "You alright with that?"

"It's worth the risk. You do what I say without question, we can pull this off."

"And if I don't?" Hood said, forcing the issue. Gene gave him a wry smile.

"You've survived this long. I think you know how to avoid bad decisions."

Gene scanned the area, moving suddenly towards a patch of thick brush. He moved some artfully placed branches aside, and backed out a mud-splattered dirtbike.

Hood pointed at it, squinting skeptically. "Ain't that thing gonna make a hell of a lot of noise?"

Gene smiled. "Nope. It's electric. Moves like a ghost."

"Damn. The Sons have power?"

"Only some. We're working on more sustained sources," Gene

said. "Come on, we're losing daylight. I need you to drive. Just don't do anything dumb." He waved his pistol for effect. The safety was off. "I'll tell you where to go from here."

Hood inspected the bike. They had painted it dark, woodland colors. Where the two-stroke motor would have been there were large battery boxes.

"Are you going to tell me what we're doing exactly? Just gonna find this chick and have a cup of tea?"

"I'll fill you in when we get there. Have you driven one of these things before?" Gene said. He strapped both bags to a rack on the back fender.

"Yeah. Well, not an electric. But my cousin had one."

"Good."

Hood mounted the bike, settling his hands into the hard-contoured grips of the handlebars. Gene saddled up behind him, pistol in his free left hand.

"You see from here that intersection to the southwest? Head for that."

Hood nodded, and opened the throttle. The electric motor spooled up slowly, but after a few seconds it accelerated like a whip. The only noise coming from the bike was a slight whirring and an occasional whining noise when he took the bike over rough terrain. Hood wove the bike down the hill between the trees, bounding over roots and uneven ground. The wind rushed against his face and he squinted to keep his eyes free of dirt. They moved faster than he might have expected as they cruised under the darkened canopy of the tree cover.

When they emerged into the empty intersection, Gene pointed with his pistol down the westward path. The road was empty, the leaves and dirt billowing away from them as they sped along. The ride was smooth and the wind howled in his ears. For a moment his mind was pulled free from the clutches of fear for his family, fear of the man with the gun sitting behind him, fear of the war-sundered land he now lived in, and he couldn't help a grin. *Damn, this thing is fun.*

The sensation of riding the bike was nearly identical to a memory of when he was eighteen. Visiting relatives in the country, he and Ian had taken his cousin's dirt bike down an empty forest road and into town to see the new Batman movie that had blown everyone away. It was one of those rare days in which nothing extraordinary happened, but life just felt perfect.

"Up ahead there will be a break in the tree line, a path going south. Take it into the woods and up to the ridge," Gene called over his shoulder.

Hood leaned the bike as he angled it onto the dirt path that led back into the woods. It sloped upwards over a short hill. He opened the throttle at the crest of the path and launched them into the air, his heart beating wild in his chest, his feet tingling. The bike bounced hard as they hit the earth.

"This thing can fly!" Hood hollered over his shoulder.

"Keep us on the damn ground!" Gene yelled in his ear over the roaring wind, prodding Hood in the ribs with the pistol.

The daylight was fading fast, and dusk was upon them. Hood urged the bike ahead, climbing up the path until they were riding along the high ridge Gene had mentioned. They could barely see across the expanse of overgrown fields in the fading dusk.

"See that road over there? On the south side of it, not far west, is a cabin. That's the way station," Gene shouted over the rushing wind.

"What would you have done if you hadn't found me?" Hood shouted back.

Gene paused. "Would've figured something out."

Whatever this is we're here to do, it's my ass he's putting on the line. That's the only reason he wouldn't use his own men instead of me. Because it's a suicide mission. The only thing Gene seemed to take more seriously than his commitment to the Sons was the lives of his men. *You've got to admire his loyalty. It must be nice to believe in a cause you're fighting for so wholeheartedly. Even if it does make him a heartless bastard.*

Night fell as they neared their destination. They hopped off and

Gene unstrapped their packs before hiding the bike in a patch of brush. Wordlessly he urged Hood forward towards the cabin, which was really more of a summer house nestled in the woods.

The short uncovered porch featured a black wooden front door, surrounded by planters with dead plants hanging out of them. The cedar siding of the house still retained its reddish color despite general wear and tear on the house; entire sections of the siding were gone, showing ripped vinyl and decayed wood beneath.

A dirty jeep sat in the earthen driveway, and a faint light could been seen between the cracks of the boarded-up windows.

Hood and Gene hid in the dark behind tall maples, staring at the house for an eternity. Hood's eyes wandered, trying to check the whole dark scene for any signs of movement. The only sound was the incessant chirping of Katydids. There was no wind.

"There's someone on guard. You can be sure of it." Gene whispered. "They're out of sight somewhere, but they are there."

Hood nodded, though he wasn't sure Gene could even see it. They had done similar watches in Clearwater and out in camps in the mountains. He'd spent plenty of nights up in trees with nothing to do but wait. Usually no one came. The hard part was staying awake. Hood was hoping whoever was on guard would be having the same problem.

The time crawled. For hours, no sign of movement. Hood's mind examined thousands of hypothetical scenarios, preparing him with a survival plan for each one, weighing its realism and efficacy. The tension of staring at the house for so long left him with an itch of uncertainty.

He made a habit of looking behind them, scanning the trees around them, feeling keenly uncomfortable staying in the same place for so long. Anxiety crept up on him, making his blood throb faster. Maybe it was a culmination of walking the thin line of survival for so long; the anticipation of putting himself in harm's way for the Son's machinations tore his mind asunder. He felt an animal primacy taking over.

He didn't just want to get away, he wanted to kill everyone who was a threat to him. He wanted to comb the earth for Taylor and Whiskey and lay low anyone who might get in his way. These were all strangers around him, strangers who did not fight his fight. He wanted to act, but he was forced to wait. And wait. And wait. *Fuck this. I should just kill him. But he has a gun. What is it we're here to do, asshole? What game are you playing?* Hood tried to shake the rage out of his own head. *He's not an evil man. And I am not a machine. I can't just kill my way out of this. There's always a way to survive. Use your head.* Gene was on one knee behind a tree, watching the house intently, anticipating something, like he was steeling himself. *But maybe I'm wrong. Maybe I will have to kill my way out of this.*

"It's time. I need you to move into the clearing by the house until they spot you, then draw them out into the woods. This is here for you." Gene moved two trees back into the woods and hung Hood's Beretta by the finger guard on a broken twig of a branch. "When it's over, I'll meet you back by the bike."

"What? You want me to just go out there? Why do you need me to do that? What is it we're doing here?" Hood whispered.

"Don't question your orders. And don't get yourself shot." Gene pointed his pistol at Hood in the dark. "Go now."

Hood hesitated a moment. If he had some semblance of a choice before, he had none now. *This is fucking crazy.*

Feeling Gene's impatience, Hood moved out from behind the tree cover and walked toward the clearing around the cabin. He tried to move quietly in the darkness, but dried leaves and twigs crackled and snapped under his feet as he reached the clearing. *They're there on purpose.*

All of the hair on Hood's nape stood on end. *Someone's taking aim at you.*

A shot cracked the night air as Hood sprinted forward, towards the house. He felt no burst of pain and surged euphoria for it. He pressed himself flat against the rough cedar shake of the house.

There was silence, then the sound of shoes scraping on bark. Hood pounded the cabin with his fist once and sprinted back towards the tree-line. Another shot cracked the night air, but he felt no pain. He moved from tree to tree frantically until he found the hanging Beretta.

The sound of creaky hinges and cracking twigs came from behind him. He pulled back the slide in the Beretta and dove deeper into the woods. He grabbed onto a low-hanging branch and swung himself up into the tree, quickly climbing up three branches and leaning up against the trunk with full vision of the area below. *I'll play your game better than you can.*

Patience was the sure way to win; stay silent and motionless until the enemy was sure he'd gone away for good. Unless the man was stupid or desperate, he wouldn't go charging into the woods. He'd move slowly and deliberately, but after enough time everyone lets their guard down.

The problem was, he didn't have enough time. Whatever the Sons had planned with Kerry, it wasn't good. *What the fuck could they possibly want her for? Do they know something I don't?*

Hood saw a dark figure dart from one tree to another. He lifted his Beretta to sight and waited for movement. None came.

This is taking too fucking long. The pressure made Hood feel that he would burst. *Whatever it is they need her for, it's sure to get her killed. That's what the reality is. They will kill her. You can't just fucking pretend it's going to be okay.* Hood grit his teeth.

Fuck it. He clenched his free hand, embracing the reckless adrenaline.

He jumped down from the branches to the forest floor with a thump. He raised the pistol towards the right side of the tree.

The man popped out to the left side.

Hood swung the pistol to sight on the man and fired as fire flamed out of the barrel of the man's rifle. The figure slumped into a heap on the ground as Hood's left ear radiated in pain.

He reached up with his left hand, and it came back wet with his blood. *Holy shit.* His body shuddered. A few inches to the right and he'd be dead.

Another gunshot rang out and Hood dove away from the tree, getting up on all fours and sprinting up the gradual slope to the south. The searing in his ear and his shock at the near miss kept him locked in place behind a tree. *Don't stop now. You don't have time. You have to take a chance.*

He turned and sprinted diagonally from tree to tree, scanning the darkness in the direction he'd come from. He heard two shots and saw gunfire down the hill to the northwest. He spun around the next tree and opened fire towards where he'd seen it.

This would be a good time for my luck to kick in.

Hood heard no groans, saw no collapsing body after his shots. He had only a handful of bullets left in the clip, if it had been full to start. He peeked around the tree.

A figure shuffled southward in the dark.

Hood tried to sight on the man but saw no clear shot; too many trees in the way. There was something familiar about the figure's movements.

Hood reached down and felt for a rock. He found a palm-sized one and hurled it southwest. It thumped and rustled along the ground while Hood sprinted north down the hill. He trained his eyes on where the figure had been. Something shifted on the ground as shots cracked the air.

Hood jumped to the side, skidding onto his back through the rough dirt and raising his pistol between his knees. He fired back at the figure on the ground twice before the slide clicked back empty. The figure rolled behind a tree.

Hood jumped to his feet and charged at the tree. Pure rage and a desire to survive drove him. He was only feet away when the figure leapt out from behind the tree, swinging his rifle like a club. The man was bigger than he'd expected. The blow glanced off Hood's bad shoulder as he crashed headfirst into the man, the two of them sprawling onto the ground.

Hood wrapped his hands around the man's thick neck. The man

grabbed Hood's face and pushed him away with incredible strength. The two caught each other's desperate, wild gazes. They both let go of each other.

"So you're still alive," came Whiskey's familiar gruff, southern-tinged voice.

"*Whiskey?*" Hood backed off, falling back into the dirt. "What? What the fuck?"

Whiskey pushed himself to a sitting position, dusting off his long-sleeved shirt. "It's over, kid. We lost. We can't fight a war machine on our own. Taylor is alive. I've seen her. This is the only way I can keep her safe."

"The fuck are you saying?" Hood shouted. "You think fighting for the Kaiser will keep her *safe? He's using you! He's. . .*" *He's trying to get to me.*

"Whatever it takes. This is what we have to do to survive."

"No." Hood shook his head, eyes ablaze. "What about Clearwater? What about all our friends that died?"

"They're dead. There's nothin' we can do for 'em now. It was a dumb thing, trying to live like we did in Clearwater. We should have left it behind." Whiskey pulled himself to his feet. "I knew it too. I knew somethin' would happen. But I couldn't convince people to leave. Or join up with the Kaiser. Everyone would have thought I was crazy."

Hood spat. "Fuck that. I'll never regret what we were doing. We were trying to live a good life, Whiskey. We were fighting for *something.* My only regret is that we got caught."

"Look where we are now, kid." Whiskey picked up his rifle. "Come back with me. Taylor will want to see you. We're not free, but we're alive. And we might live long enough to get out of this."

You won't. Ian will kill you once he has me. And he'll keep Taylor hostage. . . But if I do join. . . If I pretend to come around to Ian's sick ideals, maybe we can all live. The thought made him feel sick. *Fuck that. That's what he wants. Indoctrination takes time. He wants you to think there's no other way.* Hood's mind lurched back into the moment. "Is

Kerry here?" He jumped to his feet. Whiskey nodded slowly. "This Sons bastard I was with, he's here for her. We've got to stop him!"

"Of course," Whiskey said, eyes fixed in the dark towards the house.

"What!?" Hood barked.

"The Sons are trying to infect her. The Kaiser takes slaves to these houses before they bring them in to check them for disease. But if the Sons inject her with something without being caught, she'll take it straight to the Kaiser, or at least his officers." Whiskey's words held a tinge of hope.

How did I not see that? Gene sneaks in after I draw them out, infects her with something lethal and contagious. Turn a sex slave into a biological weapon. The thought ran chills of rage and disgust though his whole body. Images of her being poisoned, being taken advantage of. . . by Ian. Then dying a slow, painful death alone. . . Hood turned to run towards the house. Whiskey grabbed his arm, and Hood spun around to face him.

"I know it's wrong. I know she don't deserve it. You were right, she is a good person. But listen to me. *This is our only chance."* Whiskey's eyes locked with Hood. Hood didn't even realize he was baring his teeth.

"You're wrong. I will not let them do this," Hood ripped his forearm free from Whiskey's grasp.

"There are no more good options here, Hood!" Whiskey retorted. "Maybe there never were any to begin with. But if the Sons want to set us free, I say let them."

"If it were Taylor instead, what would you do?" Hood raged.

Whiskey stood motionless, staring at Hood in the darkness.

"If it were Taylor, what would you do!?" Hood repeated with venomous emphasis.

"But it's not."

Save our own. Let the rest of the world die.

It was Ian's own depiction of humanity.

Don't make him right. He killed Mom and Dad and Lucky and Billy and everyone we've ever cared about. Don't you fucking make him right! The thoughts raged inside him and something snapped.

Hood swung a balled right fist that connected with Whiskey's temple. He stumbled backward. Hood hurled himself at him, sending him crashing to the ground. Blood from Hood's wounded ear slid down his neck and soaked into his shirt.

He swung his fists down repeatedly on Whiskey's head. Whiskey held up his arms to shield himself from the blows, not even attempting to fight back. *Fight me you bastard. Just like that, you give up? You were stronger than that. This isn't you.*

Hood grabbed the rifle from the grass and raised the butt high in the air, ready to bring a final, crushing blow down on Whiskey's cranium. His body seemed to be carrying out its rage without him, as if Hood was a distant observer.

He froze, breathing heavily.

"Do it." Whiskey said quietly. "I can't fight no more. I'm sick of losing it all. Kerry will carry death to the Kaiser and Taylor will be free of all this." He let out a long exhale. "I can go ahead and die knowing that."

Hood fought hard against his body's will to bring the rifle down onto him.

You bastard, you fucking bastard how could you give up? You just let him win? We were fighting for something more than just survival, Whiskey. Maybe you weren't, but I was. What the hell is the point of living if you have to kill yourself to stay alive?

Hood bit his bottom lip and squeezed the stock of the rifle so hard he wanted the wood to splinter. Something gave way inside him. He let go, the rifle clattering onto the nearby root system of a tree. Wet warmth filled his eyes. Sensation surged back into his body as the adrenaline faded, the pain from his wounds dragging him back into reality.

I can't do this anymore. I can't make these choices. It's too goddamned heavy. All the friends and family and strangers who died for me to keep on living. And for what? I don't deserve to live if I can't do something to make their deaths mean something.

Like the sun rising in his mind, clarity struck. Hood blinked, trying to focus in on the idea and never let it go.

I am still alive because I can stop this. Because Ian is wrong, and I'm the only one who can stop him without killing countless innocent people. Family isn't the root of all war. Family is the solution to all war. Everyone who fights to live a good life and care for others is family. Whiskey is my family. Kerry is my family. Everyone from Clearwater was my family. The dead man from the journal who was fighting for those kids was my family.

Hood stood up, running both hands over his head. Whiskey slowly picked himself up off the ground. *Kerry. She's here. She needs you.* Hood burst into motion, running back westwards towards the cabin.

It's too late. You know it is.

He dashed into the clearing and up to the porch of the cabin, the black door left open.

No. I don't accept that.

The living room showed signs of struggle. The room was disheveled; the floor was littered with an upturned end-table, picture frames, magazines and kitchenware. A sectional couch sat facing a dusty, long-inert T.V. A pair of boots protruded from behind the couch. Hood hurried over, his stomach sinking.

It's already done.

But it was a man's figure that lay face down on the floor. It was Gene.

Hood could hardly believe it. The boards were pried off the back window above the kitchen counter and stood open, the curtains lightly swaying in the night air.

She got free.

Hood knelt down next to Gene. He still had a pulse, but was unconscious. In his right hand was a small metal case. Hood took it from him and opened it. Inside was an empty syringe and a sealed vial of liquid. He started to laugh.

The hell was I worried about? Hood ran his hand over his face. He looked down at Gene again in disbelief. *Damn girl, how did you manage this?*

Whiskey appeared in the doorway.

"She made it out," was all Hood said.

Whiskey peered over at the man as he moved inside.

"Who was he?"

"Infantry Captain for the Sons."

"That girl is tough as nails."

Hood smiled. "Yeah she is."

Where have you gone? Would it have killed you to wait around a few minutes? She had already taken Gene's backpack and his pistol. *Nothing can keep you down, huh? I think I'm in love. Come back to me, I'm yours forever.*

Whiskey reloaded his rifle, cocked it and aimed it at Gene.

"Don't," Hood said, holding out his hand.

Whiskey looked incredulous. "A second ago you were charging in here to stop him."

"He's a good man. Maybe a bit overzealous, but he's not evil."

"He used you." Whiskey followed this sentence with a grunt, annoyed to have to state the obvious.

"Under different circumstances, I could've easily seen us fighting on the same side."

Whiskey slowly lowered the rifle.

"Okay, kid." He nodded. "If you say so."

Hood met Whiskey's gaze. *We've both come a long way, haven't we?* Whiskey's face carried more exhaustion than it did before, his dark eyes heavy, unmoving. There was a certain acceptance between the two of them, silent amends being made.

"Do you know the way to the Kaiser?" Hood said.

"Yeah."

"Between the two of us, I bet we can get Taylor out of there."

"The place is a stronghold, Rob. Deep in his territory."

"We have to try."

"If we fail, we're all dead."

Hood smiled. "Isn't that the way it's always been?"

Whiskey shook his head, the wood floors creaking gently with his steps. "We've been playing with fire a long time. Just come back and join up with the Kaiser. We can ride out this storm together until we can find a way out."

"There's no way out." Hood said, feeling the cool wind wafting in through the open window Kerry used to escape. "Other than death. Believe me. I know the Kaiser better than anyone. He's Ian. My Ian. He's not just going to let us slink away some day."

Whiskey's eyes shot over from his perusal of the house to meet Hood. "You're kidding."

Hood snorted. "I wish."

"Ain't that some shit. What are the chances?"

I don't think it's chance. "I refused to believe it for awhile. But truth be told, it makes sense. He was always a ballsy kid with unconventional thinking. And a natural leader. People were drawn to him when we were young. I used to joke he was the mayor of our generation in D.C. Kid knew everyone."

Whiskey bit his lip, sighing. *Let's finish what we started, Whiskey. I know you're scared. You're scared we'll fail and she'll die and it will be our fault. But this is our only chance.*

"The last two of Clearwater crew are still alive. So lets make the boys proud. Let's get Taylor the fuck out of there." Hood said, grinning at Whiskey. He chuckled.

"You tryin' to hype me up?"

"Hell yeah I am."

"Well, it's workin'." Whiskey cracked his neck, working the blood back through his body as he stretched. "Besides, I wouldn't want you gettin' roughed up out there on your own. Looks like you got tagged a few times since I last seen you."

"It's good to see your geriatric ass again." Hood clapped him on the shoulder. "You been playing a lot of bingo and shuffleboard?"

Whiskey clicked his tongue, turning on his heel as he shook his head. "I shoulda just let you guys keep on your merry way the day I found you two years ago."

Hood laughed loudly. Pain shot from the mending wound in his side "What, and miss out on all this fun?"

"You need help, kid."

"Not anymore. I've got you." Hood smirked, grabbed the keys to the jeep off the dining table and tossed them to Whiskey, who nabbed them out of the air. "We might be able to find Kerry out there on the way. I've got a dirtbike we can load into the Jeep, too. Let's end this shit."

◆ ◆ ◆

You're okay. You're okay. No one is chasing you. Kerry dashed ahead through the overgrown woods, her heart pounding in her ears, her eyes searching frantically for signs of anything that might stop her in the dark. She slowed to a stop, looking back in the direction of the way station. At least, not yet.

She moved around to the other side of a mossy oak, leaning against it with one hand to catch her breath. The air was abuzz with the chirping of cicadas and god knows what other gross insects. She didn't mind only hearing them, though. They weren't trying to kill her. *Who the hell was that guy? What did he want with me?* It wasn't anything so primal as lust. That was an easy thing to read in a man's eyes. But the man was determined on something else. Something he seemed almost guilty about. If he knew she was adept at turning handcuffs into bangles, he might've had less hesitation. *Didn't expect a pipe to the head. I hope he doesn't wake up anytime soon.* Still, she had to thank the man. If he hadn't drawn out the Kaiser's soldiers she never would have had an opportunity to escape.

She pulled on the straps to the man's military rucksack, tightened it against her shoulders. Her wet palm held tight against the rough grip of the pistol she'd taken from her assailant. The safety was off. She had to be ready. She took a deep breath and broke into a run, wanting to put more distance between her and anyone that could be looking for her. *Where the hell am I going? What direction is this, even?* She took comfort in knowing it was deeper in the woods, which felt farther away from mankind. The intense loneliness of her situation closed in on her, though it was not stronger than her desire to escape. *I don't know where anyone is. I don't have anywhere to go. I don't even know where the hell I am.* She wanted to burn the thoughts away, but they would not relent. *I'm alone. I'm lost. I have nothing. Shut up, just keep running.*

Her lungs burned, her stomach yearned for sustenance, her hair caught in her eyelashes, messing up her vision. The harder she pushed her body, the more distant she felt from anyone who might be hunting her. So she did not allow herself to stop. *If that guy came after me, who else will? What would they want with me? It's not like I'm anyone important. When they took me captive at the refugee camp I just figured it was slave trade.*

The idea of being someone's slave again sent shivers through her. She wanted to block out the memory of being Leonard's property forever. The sick fuck had killed her family. As hard as she tried to block out those memories, she still had dreams of hunting him down, driving a knife into his chest over and over. And nightmares that he was still alive, and no matter how many times she escaped or what dark corner she hid in, he always found her.

But in that hellish time, she met Hood. She never expected it. Which was part of why she felt the way she did. He had stayed by her. Fought for her. He had believed in her, forgiven her, trusted her. Loved her. She lived in a dark place back then—when she was sent to find Hood and Whiskey, she expected cold cruelty from every survivor she met. But he had not allowed the world to make him numb and heartless. From the first time she met Hood, she felt a way she hadn't since the first time she fell in love as a young girl. She had long tried to deny those thoughts, for fear of the loss that would come with loving someone again only to lose them. But she could not deny them now, now that he was gone. *Stop it. Stop thinking about this. You're just going to make it worse.*

Her foot caught on something. She hurtled forward into the tall grass, tumbling over rocks and knobby roots until she came to a stop. She sat up slowly, bruises aching, her palms stung, scraped. Her breath was wild, frantic as she scanned the scene. *What did you think would happen, sprinting headlong in the dark?* She could barely make out the outline of trees, haggard bushes, and wild weeds. *The pistol!* She looked down at her empty palms, then at the ground around her. She crawled around the area, feeling through the tall grass with her hands. *Everyone is gone. You'll never see them again. You have nowhere to go. You're going to die alone, sick and starving, huddled in some abandoned building somewhere.* Her search grew more frenetic, climbing to her feet and crouching over the ground, clawing wildly at a huge spread of ivy.

She stood up straight, trying to discern which way she had come from. *I can't see a god damned thing.* She hung her head, running her hand through her hair gently, leaving it to rest on the back of her neck. *Why is this happening to me? God, tell me, is this hell? Having to live on without a goddamned clue, alone, everyone I love ripped from me?* Her eyes started to sting and blur, tears of self pity wanting to force their way out. *No, I won't.* She took in a deep breath through her nose, calming herself. *Take a second. You're okay. Stop acting like a crazy person. An hour ago you were the Kaiser's captive. Now you are free. That is something of a miracle.* She breathed easier now, taking in the cool, woodland air.

You are free. Do something with that. Hood might still be alive. You might see him again someday. First things first, get the hell away from wherever the Kaiser is.

She pulled off the rucksack, moving to a nearby tree and sitting down. She unstrapped the top, feeling inside. She felt the handle of something and pulled it out. It was a flashlight. *Bingo!* She felt a stack of folded papers tucked inside the bag. At a glance, she could tell that they were maps. *Alright, if I can find a town or a crossroads I might be able to figure out where the hell I am.* She dug into the bag again, pulling out a hunk of stale bread and dried meat wrapped in a cloth. She tore off a chunk of each and chewed them, savoring what she would have easily considered inedible in an earlier life. *Gotta have water in here.* She dug around once more, producing a steel canteen that sloshed as she shook it. *God, yes. Thank you, Mr. assailant. Sorry about the head trauma.* The metallic water tasted like sweet honey, the cool liquid refreshing her parched tongue.

She replaced everything but the flashlight and re-strapped the bag. She stood up straight, like gravity had less pull on her now. *This is not the end. This is just the beginning. You're going to survive. You'll find a way. You'll find other people like you. You'll find. . . You'll find whoever and whatever you're meant to find.* She clicked the flashlight on, pointing the wide beam at the grass that waved gently in the wind, looking almost like it moved of its own accord. She strode forward, feeling something solid move beneath her foot. She lifted it, and beneath her step the black pistol rested on a bed of grass, waiting for her. She smiled, picking it up, looking to see if it had gotten dirt in it. *I heard guns work best when you step on 'em first. Gets them motivated.* It was Hood's words in her head, his dumb joke in his voice. *I miss you. I'm not afraid to say that. I'm not afraid to say I love you, or that I wish you were here beside me.*

She turned off the flashlight, letting the darkness envelop her. Better to move unseen in the dark, just a figure in the shadows. Her steps made little sound, and she knew she could stay undetected by anyone who came looking. *Just like old times. No one can find you when you don't want to be found.* She tucked the pistol into her jeans, and pulled her hair behind her ears. She felt her wrist for a hair-tie, where it usually would be. But there hadn't been one there for a long time. *Damn. First thing on my list. Well, second, next to more food.*

You're not alone. You're never alone, the thought struck her, as if coming from somewhere else. She smiled in the dark. *You're never alone.*

Chapter 18 – Harper's Ferry

There was an undeniable feeling that everything was the way it was supposed to be. The cool night wind rushed through the jeep as it sped down the moonlit road with Whiskey at the wheel.

Even if nothing was the way they *wanted* it to be.

Taylor and Kerry were alive, the last they knew, but Hood and Whiskey would need an incredible amount of luck and brilliance just to have a chance to see them again.

At least he was with Whiskey, and they would face this together. Hood took comfort in that. *There's no one else I'd rather fight alongside.*

Even if these were likely the last days of their lives, Hood envisioned scenarios where everything worked out flawlessly. But he and Whiskey both knew they were looking at incredibly long odds. Neither of them put it to words, but in the long silence, Hood knew they both were thinking about it.

They were deep in the Kaiser's territory. If everything went right, they'd go largely unseen until they got close enough to Greenridge University to even get a shot at springing Taylor. If they got caught on the way, the Kaiser's militants might just execute them rather than dragging their asses back to the University Ian had made into his capital. And as the miles went on, there was a heaviness in his heart. They had found sign of Kerry. Hood knew he would probably never see her again. Chances of finding her were slim. She's too smart to stay near roads. *I wish I had just one more day with you. One more day to just be ourselves, together.*

But if Hood put it all out of his mind and stared up at the band of the Milky Way, if he soaked in the explosion of stars that lit up the sky while they hummed down the road in the dark with the headlights off, he could pretend they were back in easier days.

It was amusing to remember the early days of protecting Clearwater as easy. At the time, it had felt terrifying. Even though he'd quickly found he was good at keeping his head level in a fight, he'd been absolutely petrified during the first raids they went on.

With Whiskey's guidance though, they'd carved out a life for the little town, skirmishing with wasters for food and supplies out in the country. It had been a wild, unreal life compared to growing up in civilization. But now, he had warm memories of those days.

An empty expanse of abandoned farmland gave way to a hill covered in trees. This was followed by a river valley with train tracks parallel to the road on one side, and rushing waters that reflected moonlight on the other. Even in the dark of night, it was a gorgeous scene. Whiskey slowed the Jeep down and pulled off near the forest, driving up into a small clearing cut out for electrical wire towers. They parked amidst the trees.

"Where are we?" Hood asked.

"Corner of three states, back when that meant something."

"Maryland, Virginia. . .West Virginia? It's gotta be."

"Yep," Whiskey said, pulling the keys out of the ignition and stepping out of the driver's seat.

Hood climbed out of the passenger side, moving around to the back. Whiskey heaved the electric dirtbike out of the back with a grunt.

"My Goddamned back." Whiskey snarled. "You mind helping?"

"You didn't even ask, you psychopath!" Hood said. "Use your words. Was your mother a Sphinx?"

Whiskey leaned backwards, his hands on his lower back.

"So, we stopping for the night? What are we doin' here?" Hood asked, looking from the clearing through the words, where the latent electrical towers stood like skeletal metal monoliths in the faint moonlight.

"There's a hill up there that overlooks the whole area. We can camp there. Scope out everything and make our decision where to cross the river in the morning."

"You've been here before?"

"Yeah." Whiskey groaned, still stretching.

"Well? What is this place?"

"Come on, you'll see. It's a heck of a view," Whiskey said with a hint of fatherly enthusiasm. Hood pictured him being a father to Taylor's kid, lifting a little girl onto his shoulders, the little girl wrapping her hands around his forehead as they walked through the woods, while Taylor walked alongside them, wearing the same smile as her daughter. The thought that it might never happen weighed heavy on his heart.

There's still a chance. Fight for it. People died for you to be here. Fight for them. If you feel so goddamned guilty for surviving, then do something great with the life you have left.

Hood grabbed his backpack, tucked the Beretta into his jeans and climbed onto the dirt-bike while Whiskey was still fishing his gear out of the Jeep.

"Oh no. You're sitting on the back." Whiskey said with a grunt.

"Too late, compadre. This girl is purrin' for me." Hood patted the chassis of the bike between his legs.

Whiskey rubbed at his forehead. "Fine, whatever. It ain't that far anyway."

"That line would've been a lot more awesome if I could've revved the engine. Can't really rev up a battery. But I was tryin."

"Maybe ya should've made some *vroom vroom* noises, then." Whiskey climbed onto the back of the bike and it sank down considerably.

"Oh yeah, dammit—you're right. I fucked it up."

He couldn't see his face, but Hood was sure Whiskey was shaking his head.

"Just go. It's up the hill."

The bike didn't exactly burst into motion, with the two of them on it and the uphill route. But it picked up some speed. Hood wove it between the trees and around the rocky terrain as they climbed upward. After a short trek, the hill leveled to reveal a gray stony overlook, craggy and dotted with shrubs and stubby, tough looking trees fighting through the rock. Whiskey hopped off the back of the bike, and Hood dropped the kickstand and stepped off, looking out over the expanse below.

It truly was a sight, even in the dark.

A great river forked sharply in two around a spit of land where a very small town lay quiet and undisturbed. Two wooden railway bridges diverged on the north side of the river, one wrapping around the south side of the narrow town and the other around the north. The two rivers flowed quietly below, the shimmering water glinting in the moonlight. Stone pillars with rusted metal stubs jutted out of the south river where two other bridges had once stood. On the southern bank of the river that curved around the town was a tree-covered hill, one not as steep as the sheer cliff they stood on.

"Harper's Ferry," Whiskey said with a kind of nostalgic air. "West Virginia," he pointed at the town. "Virginia." He pointed at the tree-covered great hill on the southern bank of the river. "Maryland." He said, gesturing at the wooded rocky cliff they stood on.

"It's gorgeous."

"Yeah, it is."

"Why are we here?"

"I figure it's our best shot at getting across the river without anyone noticing. It's a tiny place, probably less attended than the other bridges and crossings." Whiskey tried to crack a stubborn knuckle unsuccessfully. "We can find out for sure when morning comes. With any luck, the town will be empty and we can scoot on through."

"Wouldn't mind some luck," Hood said emphatically. He walked over to the edge of the uneven cliff. His feet got chills just looking over the edge. "I think we're a bit overdue."

"I'm overdue some sleep," Whiskey said.

"Amen." Hood moved over to his backpack and dug out a few cans. "No fire, I figure?"

Whiskey shook his head.

"Cold beans and mystery meat it is, then." Hood tossed Whiskey a small pop-top can.

"What is it?"

"It's better if you don't know."

"What is it?"

"I'm not kidding; it tastes better if you don't know."

"What is it?"

Hood sighed, clapping his hands onto his knees as he stood up. "Cat food."

Whiskey looked at the can. "Delicious."

Hood pried open the beans and shoved a spoon into the can. Whiskey sat down on the grass, and Hood sat down beside him, placing the beans in between.

"There is no shortage of spoons in the apocalypse," Hood posited.

"We should capture them all and create a spoon empire," Whiskey said, completely serious as he stared out at the town like a conquering general.

Hood burst out laughing. "Hot damn! It only took us nearly killing each other, but you've let loose!"

"Don't ruin it." Whiskey dug into the cat food. "You're right," he said through a mouthful. "It would taste better if I didn't know."

"Told you." Hood proffered the can of beans. "Wash it down with some gooey beans and some nice murky water." He plopped down the jug of water between them.

"I think I'd kill you for a nice cold IPA." Whiskey cleaned out the bottom of his cat food can.

Hood nodded at him with a heartfelt smile. "The feeling is mutual. Maybe a nice stout."

An owl hooted somewhere in the woods, and cicadas buzzed as the crisp cool air off the river swept over the cliff side. It had an intoxicating woodsy smell of wilderness to it.

Hood choked down his cat food as quickly as he could. As watery and salty as it was, it felt glorious in his empty stomach. The beans were an upgrade. He longed for the peanut butter- and-jelly, cinnamon graham-cracker sandwiches Kerry had made.

Is it wrong to say I miss you? Hood wriggled his toes inside his shoes. Only because you can't hear it.

Whiskey leaned back on his elbows, looking out at Harper's Ferry and the gleaming canopy of stars. The incredible night sky was one of the few benefits of the collapsing of civilization. As fucked up as everything was, Hood was happy to be on this planet and not any other. If this was going to be his last night alive, it was a pretty damn good one. Save for the food. *Every night could be your last one alive. Stop thinking so damn much.*

Hood looked over at Whiskey, who seemed lost in thought himself as he looked out over the scene.

"Speaking of killing each other," Hood started, pulling Whiskey back into reality. "There's something you've never answered for me."

Whiskey nodded slowly, like he knew what Hood was going to say.

"Why didn't you shoot me when you first met me? Or just leave? You've always dodged answering this, but I know there's a reason. Ever since I've been with you, you've mistrusted every stranger we've ever met until they proved decent. Why did you trust me?"

Whiskey inhaled.

"And don't give me this 'you saw Taylor' crap, because you didn't, not at first. She was in the car."

"I don't know," Whiskey said at length.

Hood chuckled. "Saving your secret for the grave, huh?" He shook his head. "Figure it'll be a real knee slapper to tell Marlon Brando and John Wayne after you kick the bucket?"

"I'm like fifteen years older than you, so cut the old man bullshit,"

Whiskey grumbled.

"Oh man, that's been pent-up for a while, hasn't it?" Hood said.

Whiskey ran his hand forcefully over his face in annoyance, still looking out at the river.

The owl continued his serenade.

"It's just not something I like to talk about, is all." Whiskey said.

Hood leaned his head back and sighed.

"Well shit, I don't like to talk sometimes either, but I do it because I gotta get it out, and if I don't. . . Fuck man, if I was like you, our time together would have to be called The Silence Chronicles."

Whiskey laughed to himself. "And here I always thought you talked way too much."

Hood snorted. "I'd rather talk too much than too little."

Whiskey rubbed the palm of his left hand with his right thumb.

"Yeah, I think you're right." He stared up at the stars, exhaling. "I ain't never talked to anyone about this." He hesitated. "I don't know how I'm gonna feel."

Hood furrowed his brow. Whiskey leaned forward, resting his forearms on his raised knees.

"No one?"

"Not as an adult, anyway."

Hood sat in the same position as Whiskey, forearms on his knees.

"My brother died when I was young." Whiskey said it quietly. "It was my fault. We, I wanted to. . . Well, it don't matter how. But it was my fault."

Hood looked down at the rocky grass. "Damn."

Whiskey's breath hitched as he tried to talk. "I. . . It's crazy, I know it sounds crazy." He worked his mouth. "But I swear, you're just like him. You even look a lot like him. I mean, you're grown up. He was much younger, but it's almost like. . ." Whiskey looked away. "It was like when I first saw you, I stopped in my tracks. I could'a sworn. And as I got to know you, I couldn't believe it."

Hood watched Whiskey intently, giving him time to speak. *It makes so much sense. Why he's always looked out for me. Why he took on*

234

that brotherly role so fast.

"Wow," he said finally. "I never would've known."

"I never wanted to say it because. . . because I thought saying it might make it less real, make it sound dumb."

"It doesn't sound dumb." Hood said, feeling like his whole history after the collapse was some incredible feat of serendipity. "It's amazing. I'm sorry for your loss, but. . . whatever shit we're in now, Taylor and I never would have even had a chance at life if it weren't for you."

"I was not ready for the apocalypse," Hood said. "I really do think you saved us."

Whiskey leaned his head back, taking in the sky. "I feel the same way, kid." He seemed to breathe easier. Even if his eyes still carried exhaustion. "Taylor, she's something else. She's the most amazing woman I've ever met."

"Yeah. She's pretty great." Hood smiled. "Not when you're seven and she's beating you over the head with a water gun, though."

Whiskey chuckled. "Oh, she's wanted to beat me over the head with somethin' a few times, I'm sure."

An insect buzzed in front of Hood's face and he batted it away. "So does that mean you always looked at Taylor as your sister? Damn, you *are* southern."

Whiskey threw his cat food can at Hood, who slapped it out of the air, making a Bruce Lee noise.

"You Goddamned asshole." Whiskey complained loudly. "I can't talk to you about nothin'."

"Man, that's so gross. What a sick bastard you are." Hood said, cackling.

Whiskey *hmphed* in annoyance.

The wind gusted and shook the trees into a soft coo of rustling leaves. After a brief reprieve, the owl resumed his hooting. Hood picked up a smooth, flat rock and tossed it from hand to hand.

"Kind of makes you think, doesn't it?"

"About what?"

235

"That maybe everything does happen for a reason."

Whiskey lay down on the grass with his arm behind his head.

"I don't much believe in that crap."

"Yeah, I don't think I do either." Hood assented.

"If this is all someone's design, it's a pretty fuckin' terrible one," Whiskey said, eyes closed.

"Yeah. Most of it, anyway." Hood said, putting his backpack down behind him, prodding it in the hopes it would transform into a pillow. He leaned his head back onto it, unsurprised to find it still lumpy and uncomfortable.

◆ ◆ ◆

Kerry tapped the bumper of the Sheriff's old truck with the heels of her shoes as she sat on the hood. It was on the other side of the broken bridge. The weather was sunny and beautiful.

"We're even, now," she said, sporting a grin of satisfaction. "You didn't think I'd be okay."

"I've missed you," Hood said.

"I don't want to leave," she said, now seeming wary of him.

"Where are you going?"

Kerry seemed to disappear; His mother and father were moving a coffee table in the middle of the cobblestone bridge that was simultaneously their living room. They looked at it, picked up either side and moved it again.

"Robbie, come here and give me a hand with this couch?" His father asked, staring at the table and scratching at his solar plexus.

"Dad, I want to talk to you." Hood paused. "About so many things."

"The new TV is coming in today. We want to rearrange the living room."

"I should've been there for you guys. It was my fault. I was scared to come home," Hood said.

His father suddenly held out a cell phone. "Tell your sister if she wants to talk, she should call me. I don't know how to work this damn thing."

His parents were gone. Kerry was standing in front of him. The wind across the bridge blew her hair in front of her face. He longed just to reach out and touch her, pull her into his arms. She smiled a brief warm smile at him, then looked down at his hand. She was holding his right hand open, drawing the blade of a knife across his palm.

"It's okay, my mother was a nurse," She said with calm reassurance.

"Ow, stop, that hurts," Hood implored. "Stop that, what are you doing?!"

Hood blinked awake, his eyes hazy. His cut right hand was pinned between his body and the forest floor. It throbbed in pain. He must've rolled onto it in his sleep. He heaved himself up into a sitting position, his other wounds aching as he moved.

Exhaustion had made the lumpy earth into a luxury bed. It was already well into morning. The sun was obscured by clouds but the day was bright. Hood stood up and stretched before tucking his Beretta into the back of his jeans.

He glanced over at Harper's Ferry. The picturesque town looked even more beautiful by day. The two brown railway bridges stretched nearly parallel across the navy-and-green northern river, which had to be the Potomac, Hood figured.

He rubbed his eyes, feeling the urge to relieve his swollen bladder.

Whiskey lay in the exact position he had fallen asleep in, snoring softly. Hood shuffled off northwards into the trees, his feet soundless on the soft ground, the woods motionless.

He'd reached down to unzip when he heard the unmistakable sound of a stream of liquid pelting against the dirt. Hood looked to his left, suddenly alert. Framed by boughs a good forty feet away, a young blond man was pissing. He wore regular clothes with a red kerchief tied around his forearm, and then a complete look of shock as his brown eyes locked with Hood's.

He let go of himself and scrambled for the rifle that hung on his shoulder. Without pausing to think, Hood reached back, whipped the Beretta into aim perfectly and fired one shot. It rang out into the woods. His heart sank knowing it would connect.

The young man fell backwards into the dirt with a thump.

Hood lowered the pistol, looking around.

Nothing else moved.

He dashed over to the soldier. He lay in the dirt in a patch of sunlight, neck covered in blood. The young man stared up at Hood with tears in his eyes, gurgling and choking.

Hood reached down and took the rifle. He felt the stinging in his own eyes. *He's just a kid. There are people he loves and a future he wished for. But he dies so you can go on.*

Hood couldn't turn away from the gaze of the dying young man. *Stop it. Stop thinking about it. You'll torture yourself. Just keep moving. It's the only thing you can do.*

The young man's manhood still hung out of his pants. Hood picked up a nearby branch and placed it over him, making him decent. *I'm so sorry kid. I am.* The young man wordlessly pointed to his own forehead. He was pleading for Hood to end the pain. He reached out with a bloody hand. Hood knelt down and held it as the young man closed his eyes. Hood raised the Beretta and fired.

I'm sorry you had to die. In a different world, you wouldn't have to. I am going to stop this war. I am going to give the world a chance to be a place where you and I could've met in peace. In that world, I would fight for you as if you were my family.

Whiskey crashed through the underbrush, rifle in hand. He looked around frantically even after he saw Hood, and lowered the rifle.

"Just a kid," Hood said, looking at Whiskey with bleary eyes.

"Get a hold of yourself." Whiskey said. "Whoever he was, he's not alone."

"He's one of the Sons. They're here."

"We have to leave *now*," Whiskey barked.

"Yeah."

The two of them ran at full speed back to the cliffs where they'd slept. The deep echoing boom of an explosion was followed by the sudden distant cracking of gunfire. From their high vantage point, the situation was clear.

The Crusade has begun. The Sons are making their move while they still have the element of surprise. Or so they hope. It was more than a scout or a raiding party. Hundreds of soldiers fired from the trees on the south bank of the river into the town as others forded the river below. Kaiser militants fired back from high windows and atop buildings. A single tank camouflaged in tree branches stood at the edge of the town, blasting into the trees on the other side of the river with reverberating booms.

"The Sons had the same idea I did." Whiskey cursed.

"Well, it's not working so well."

"Believe me, this is a lot less defended than the crossings up north."

"So we gotta get out of here."

Whiskey shook his head. "There's nowhere to go. This entire area is gonna be swarmed with Sons if this is where they're making their push."

An earthshaking boom caused the two of them to duck. Farther down the southern river fork, a huge plume of smoke rose from the bridge road that looped past the town. A section of it was completely destroyed, collapsed into the river below. The militants had blown the bridge so the Sons couldn't use it.

This was only going to get worse.

"To hell with it. Let's knife our way through. We can take the bike onto the railway bridge. The north one stays away from town." Hood felt a mixture of fear and recklessness surging within him.

"We'll get gunned down for sure."

"Not if we play both sides."

"What do you mean?"

"Get everything ready," Hood said, dashing back into the woods. He found the young soldier lying still in the sunlight, undisturbed. He pulled the red bandanna off his arm. *I don't know if it means anything, but I am going to do everything I can to make sure you didn't die for nothing.*

Hood dashed back through gnarled trees to Whiskey, who had

239

slung his pack onto his back. He tossed Hood's backpack at his feet. Hood tore the bandanna in half.

"This is ballsy shit right here." Whiskey looked up and rubbed his forehead. "They're gonna know we're not one of them."

"It doesn't have to totally convince them. It just has to give them a few seconds of doubt."

Hood wrapped one half of the bandanna around Whiskey's left forearm and the other around his own.

Whiskey sported a look of skepticism as he looked down at the red cloth. "This is going to get us killed."

"Well, if so, at least we'll die while still free."

"To hell with it. I'll drive. You shoot." Whiskey levered up the kickstand of the bike and hopped on.

"That's what I'm talkin' about. Let's roll the dice. We've got something more important to do than this." Hood said, checking the short magazine of the semi-automatic hunting rifle he'd taken from the young soldier.

Whiskey handed him his assault rifle, and Hood slung both of the guns over his shoulder. He strapped their packs to the back of the bike and hopped on. He gripped the Beretta tight in his right hand as he held onto Whiskey with his left, trying to physically force his nerves to stop firing wild. When adrenaline died down, only fear and doubt remained. Neither was useful in a gunfight.

If you don't take this shot, you'll never get another one. Focus on only the moment. Nothing else matters.

"Just don't miss," Whiskey said as they took off, rumbling down the hill and back towards the road.

Hood kept his eyes ahead, scanning between the trees. The bike bounded over the rough terrain, through open treeless gaps of patchy dead grass and back into the tree cover. They approached the clearing where they had left the Jeep. A row of Sons were combing the area.

"Be ready, 'cause I ain't stopping," Whiskey called over his shoulder.

The soldiers turned and raised their rifles to Whiskey and Hood as they approached, but didn't fire. A few of them lowered their guns. As they grew closer, Hood could see the apprehension on their faces. Whiskey slowed down slightly as if to stop as they approached the soldiers, only to open the throttle a few feet away. They flew between two Sons' soldiers into the clearing, where Whiskey steered the bike down the hill towards the road and the train tracks.

Hood could hear the Soldiers shouting at them. Then gunfire.

His heart clenched along with his gut, expecting the explosion of pain from a gunshot wound. None came.

He turned halfway in his seat and fired back with the Beretta. "Get us the fuck out of here!" He screamed.

"Hold on!" Whiskey shouted in return. He leaned the bike back to the west as they shot onto the tarmac of the road.

Hood turned to face forward just as Whiskey drove the bike off the edge of the short bridge crossing the train tracks. Hood's feet tingled as a feeling of weightlessness overtook him. Wooden crossbeams and glinting railroad tracks on a bed of dark stone ballast rose up to meet them as Hood braced for contact.

The bike slammed into the wooden beams, and Hood struggled for balance as Whiskey fought to regain control of the bike. The shocks absorbed the pressure, and Hood grabbed both Whiskey and the back fender to keep himself from being thrown off the bike.

Whiskey gunned the bike between the rails, bouncing them roughly as they rumbled over the wooden beams. The ride became smoother the faster they went. They crossed into the tunnel under the hill, cruising in complete darkness aside from the sunlit exit about five hundred feet away. Somehow Whiskey kept the bike steady, using the ambient light gleaming off the rails as a guide.

Hood reached up along Whiskey's arm and untied the red bandanna, making sure not to fall off the bike, before untying his own and letting the red rags float into the darkness of the tunnel.

"Act like we're running from the Sons!" Hood shouted.

"Isn't that what we're doing?" Whiskey shouted in return.

"You know what I mean!"

They burst forth from the dark tunnel onto the wood railway bridge across the north fork of the river, met by the glaring sunlight of the bright day and a deafening boom from the tank along with a continuing chorus of gunfire.

Hood pulled a rifle off his back and twisted to fire back into the empty tunnel.

"So far so good," Whiskey shouted. "They see us but they ain't firing!"

Hood felt his blood rush through his body along with a fresh burst of adrenalin. *Come on, just a bit further.* From his view backwards it looked as though they were about halfway across.

Whiskey cursed and a shot rang off the track.

"They ain't buyin' it, turn on em!" He screamed as he crouched low on the bike.

Hood turned to face forward. The railway was curving away from town, but across the river atop the buildings and out the high windows a few militants had turned their rifles towards them. Hood tuned everything out as the bike rumbled down the wood struts and tried to keep the rifle steady on a man standing atop a tall red-brick building. He pressed the stock firmly against his shoulder and squeezed the trigger. The shot cracked out of his rifle and the distant figure collapsed, the man's rifle falling off the building.

Holy shit. A surge of exultation ran through him. That was a fuckin' shot right there.

He sighted on another gunman peeking out a tall window and fired repeatedly at him. The man ducked back inside for cover. *It's a lot easier to pull the trigger when you can't see their faces, isn't it?* Hood banished the thoughts from his mind. He couldn't leave any room for doubt.

Hood unloaded suppressive fire towards the remaining gunmen while shots pelted off of the wood and ballast around them. *Just make it out of here. Make it past this town alive.*

A row of trees lining the peninsula gave them cover as the railway bridge merged back onto land. Whiskey slowed down, bumped the bike over the rails and onto the ground level platform beside the red wood train station and opened the throttle. The road and railway curved with the land, revealing a massive wall of upturned cars and sixteen-wheeled trucks across the road. Whiskey cursed and turned the bike up a grassy, tree covered hill. Beyond it was the town.

"Get ready; this might get ugly," Whiskey called over his shoulder, pulling his pistol out of its holster and gripping it along with the handlebars.

Hood pulled the automatic rifle off his back and put the hunting rifle in its place.

A deep shuddering explosion cut through the air and Hood ducked reflexively. They careened over the hill and sidewalk, then onto the main street that led through town. The tank at the bottom of the road was now a charred column of black smoke.

Gunfire screamed out the windows of the buildings.

Hood could see Sons of Liberty soldiers already entrenching themselves on the fringes of the town.

"Hood!" Whiskey's voice rang out as the bike lurched forward faster, moving west away from the battle. Hood spun around. Three Kaiser militants were scrambling away from a building when they saw Hood and Whiskey. They stopped and took aim at them.

Instinctively, Hood hip-fired towards them on full auto. They fired back wildly, but missed them as they sped by on the bike. Hood cut one of the three men down, and fired the clip empty at the other two, hitting one in the leg before the third dove behind a mailbox.

"Pay attention!" Whiskey screamed.

"I *am* fucking paying attention! There's hell all around us!" Hood snapped.

An arcing RPG blast drowned out his words as it sundered the side of a narrow gray building behind them. Hood glanced back at the flaming debris that floated out of the building with the wind.

Whiskey urged the bike onward down the small town road. He fired across his body at a group of militants that came charging around a southern street corner. The soldiers were taken completely aback, not expecting enemies this far inland from the river.

Whiskey then headed down the next side road north, between empty country homes. The road sloped away from town, the houses giving way to more trees. "We've got to get away from here and into the woods." he yelled, over the rushing wind. "Put distance be—"

Hood shouted out Whiskey's name.

One of the Kaiser's soldiers stood tall at the end of the road and had his chrome desert eagle raised directly at them.

The moment felt frozen. Within seconds, the man unloaded multiple shots at them and Hood's body clenched in a cold, despairing fear.

Whiskey gave a gutteral gasp and lost his hold on the handlebars as he fell forward. The man had hit his target. The front wheel jerked to one side.

Hood flew through the air, the world spinning end over end. The dirt-bike smashed onto the concrete, scraping loudly. Hood hit the ground on his back, then tumbled like a catapulted meatbag along the grass until he came to a rest. His chest felt locked in place with the wind knocked out of him, barely able to pull in the slightest breath of air. His vision was narrow and blurry, the world reeling around him.

Fear of his own vulnerability seized him, and his body raged to regain its bearings. Hood grasped for the hunting rifle that lay in the dirt beside him, clawing the strap and pulling it into his grip. He struggled to his knees, trying to regain his breath.

The dark-haired militant was some way away, his shining pistol raised to sight. Hood saw two mirror images of the man, his eyes struggled to focus. His whole body screamed in pain.

Pull yourself together. You can't die here.

Hood somehow raised the hunting rifle to his shoulder. He could barely keep the thing straight. The militant fired at him as he walked closer. Hood snapped the trigger repeatedly, the *crack-crack-crack-crack-crack* echoing through grassy lawn until the trigger locked, the rifle empty. The shots had no chance—purely suppressing fire to give him a chance to get himself right.

The man dashed behind a tree. Hood jumped to his feet, stumbling towards where his Beretta lay in the grass, five feet from the sidewalk. He fell down as he grabbed it.

The man had reloaded and now strafed out from behind the tree, firing at Hood as he lay prone. Hood whipped the pistol towards the man, his vision slowly clearing. He mustered all the willpower left in his body to hold his battered arm steady and fire the Beretta empty.

The man grabbed his chest, stumbling to one knee. The man's wild eyes grew wide as he stared at Hood across the grassy field. He raised his own pistol slowly, clumsily as he leaned forward.

Hood didn't move, frozen in place, out of bullets. *Fall down. Die. Just die, you bastard.*

The man fired the pistol twice, plumes of dirt erupting from the ground five feet in front of Hood. He struggled to lift his arm, taking better aim.

The air cracked again and the incoming shot pelted the dirt inches from his chest, just as the man slumped forward onto his face.

Hood exhaled and dropped his head back into the grass, looking up at the slowly creeping clouds in the bright sunny sky. His eyes wanted to close as the last vestiges of adrenaline faded from him. But he couldn't let them.

Whiskey!

He forced himself to his hands and knees. *Don't you fucking die here, because of these assholes. There's more for us to do. We have to save Taylor and you have to start a family and live and be happy and . . . you can't fucking die here.*

Hood lurched towards the street. The dirtbike lay on its side twenty feet down the quiet suburban road. Whiskey was face-down on the sidewalk, blood pooling around his head.

"No, no, no no no no no." Hood fell to his knees beside him. With a heave he rolled Whiskey over onto his back. His eyes were closed. Hood slapped him in the face repeatedly. "Wake up, asshole!"

Whiskey coughed violently, choking for a moment before turning his head and spitting out blood. A few of his teeth skittered on the sidewalk. He blinked and muttered something, his lips wet with blood.

"Talk to me buddy. Where'd he get you?"

Whiskey leaned his head forward, looking down at his body before dropping it back down onto the sidewalk, exhaling. He mumbled something incoherent. Hood pulled up Whiskey's shirt, searching for wounds. His black flak jacket was underneath, two slugs flattened against it. Whiskey struggled to speak, spitting out more blood first.

"I'm alive you idiot," he gasped. "Get off."

Hood fell back into a sitting position, hanging his head.

"You *fucker*." He exhaled, his body heavy with pain and exhaustion.

"I'm a-right." Whiskey groaned, patting the vest. "I feel like I been beaten with a baseball bat."

"If you died, I was gonna raise you from the dead and kill you again for dying on me."

Whiskey gave Hood a tired glance, a mad laugh bubbling out of him that turned into a coughing grimace as he grasped for his ribs. It wasn't pretty, since a number of his upper left teeth were missing.

"You look like a hillbilly," Hood said, slowly rising to his feet.

"Still look better than you." Whiskey gasped.

"Yeah, right. I look so good even that tree over there likes me." Hood cast an absurd smile at Whiskey as he slowly rose and stood up the dirtbike. He retrieved their backpacks, which had been thrown off it and into the street.

"I swear. . ." Whiskey grunted as he rolled over and climbed to his feet. "You say the dumbest shit."

Hood laughed, shaking his head. The high of making it out alive was a feeling he very well could be addicted to. The two of them had turned it into an art form. *The thrill is real. I'll take peace and quiet any day, though. Test your luck enough times. . .* "You sure you're not gonna

246

die?" He asked, mounting the dirt-bike and walking it backwards towards Whiskey. *If we can just make it through this, we can go somewhere far away from this war.*

Whiskey grimaced, leaning forward and still clutching his chest with the other hand.

"Not yet, kid." He heaved himself onto the back of the bike.

Chapter 19 – At The End of a Long Road

The once-great country stretched ahead of them endlessly, expansive in its emptiness. It served as a silent reminder of how huge and majestic the continent was, and that there were much less people now to inhabit it. *I wonder what all this would look like if we died off.* Hood imagined himself visiting the earth many years from now, empty, impossibly empty, cities and towns and open spaces all reclaimed by the earth. *It's weird how I think that would be beautiful. What's the world worth if there's no one to appreciate it? Nothing, I guess. Not that that matters. Worth will die out with us.*

Hood drove the dirtbike through the first light of dawn, despite the fact that Whiskey was practically falling asleep on his back. They pressed on through great overgrown farmlands, across long-untouched roads, abandoned towns and quiet woods. The only inhabitants were the few animals that staked their claims to the land, and the innumerable insects that buzzed above them.

This was deep in the Kaiser's territory.

Ian's territory.

It didn't quite feel real, though the fear and anticipation in Hood's gut told him it was. *There was a time growing up, when I thought that Ian could do great things one day.* Hood's short hair whipped against his head in the wind. *This isn't great, though, and it wasn't exactly what I had in mind.*

248

Great figures in history often did terrible things in the name of change.

If humanity survives enough to record this period, how will it be remembered? Will Ian be known as a great despot, a forgotten man, a hero? And will all the innocent people who have died be forgotten? As they usually are?

Hood bit his lip. *I won't let that happen.*

The long drive afforded him the luxury, or perhaps the cruelty, of such thinking. There was a strange mixture of relief that they had come so far, that they were so close to Taylor, and anxiety that they drove ever closer towards an impossible task. And Kerry. . . she was alive. Hood could live with that. Even if he found himself thinking about her more than he might have expected. *I know you might be alone out there, but I'm with you. If we pull this off and get Taylor free, I'll find you. I don't know how, but I will.*

There was a dark seed of doubt in Hood's mind he couldn't uproot. Ian had become ruthless and unwavering in his vision of a new country, a new sense of humanity. He had done horrible things in the name of curing the country of its bickering and rivalry. But despite it all, Ian was right about one thing: this world was the legacy of a human history built on war and hatred and oppression of others for the sake of one's own.

How many great tragedies can humanity repeat, swearing to learn from the mistakes of long-dead ancestors?

Maybe Ian's bloody war is ruthless, but what if it is the only future humanity has? What if he is the great revolutionary who changes the course of history? And you would kill him just to free Taylor if you had the chance. What if I am the one clinging to the dying world and he is the one to save us from it?

Hood gnawed on his tongue. It was impossible to know, and to guess the future was about as stupid as trying to roller-skate through the Serengeti.

You can't change the world through force. To hell with that. History is littered with dead kings who tried. I know you think you're trying to save us, Ian. But you're wrong. Even if you encompass the whole world under your banner, split up every family and spread them across the globe, people will forge new bonds, start new families, they will love and they will hate and they will make war and they will make peace because this is who we are. One day we'll die out and it will all have been worth it. The sprawling country was a blur, a still moment flying by as the bike pushed on down a dirt path which climbed up to a country road. *I don't know about you, Ian. But even if this is the end, and humanity amounts to nothing at all, I still wouldn't have traded my life for anything.*

The bike hummed lightly down the vast expanse of tree-lined, sun-baked two lane road. His life had veered off far from any expectations he or his parents might've had. *Most parents don't envision their sons and daughters fighting for their lives on a daily basis. He could still see them sitting around the kitchen table. Dad soaking up runny eggs with his toast, Mom flicking through the channels on the small flatscreen mounted on the wall in the corner. Mom, Dad, I'm sorry I didn't come home. I wish I had just one chance to talk to you two after the country fell apart. I want to know what you would have said. I really don't know if I'll ever be able to let that go. But I promise, I'm going to find Taylor. I will.*

Kids born into this world were in for a rude awakening. Somehow, Hood wanted that chance. It was a horrifying prospect, caring for a child in this world. But there was something enthralling about continuing the family line, pioneers on the ragged edge of a new world. *Thinking about this is a sure way to make yourself insane. I've got plenty more to be concerned about right now.*

A weather-beaten billboard on the side of the road featured a peeling advertisement spread for Greenridge University with a faded picture of a group of multicultural college students hanging out on a sunny terrace. The words STAY AWAKE, STAY ALIVE had been painted in broad strokes across the billboard in white. *Who is writing that? What does it mean?* Hood had seen it before, more than once. *It certainly had nothing to do with the Kaiser. Someone else had tagged places with those words. In dangerous places.*

This was not something Hood had the energy to puzzle out,

despite his piqued curiosity. His mind wandered to indulgent thoughts of food, of brownie sundaes with vanilla ice cream and double-stacked cheeseburgers with crispy fries. The images only made his stomach cry out in disapproval. *Oh man, what I wouldn't do for a cheeseburger. God damn were we spoiled with how good food was.*

They made it nearly to the foothills of the Appalachians before the bike crawled to a stop, the battery giving out. They were not far from the University, according to the map.

The two of them walked slowly through the thickening brush and cool, buggy air. It smelled like pollen, like the rampant growth of the wilderness. They smelled water, too, and heard the stream of a sharply winding river. The two of them both quickened their pace subconsciously at the first signs of it, approaching the tree-lined river bank with anticipation.

The blue-green waters moved at a modest pace, curving around with the bend of the river. A few rocks peeked out of the water, surrounded on either side by overhanging trees.

Whiskey pulled off his shirt and his flak jacket, revealing enormous purple bruises from the impact of the gunfire. Hood wondered how he could move or breathe without excruciating pain. He pulled his own clothes off, his shirt and hoodie getting stuck around his head before he yanked them free. Sharp pain shot through his side and shoulder at the motion.

Whiskey had already thrown himself into the river with a splash.

Hood pulled off his shoes and his pants and waded into the water, falling face-first into the body-chilling, enveloping sensation. He popped his head out of the water with a gasp.

"Oh shit, that's cold!" He exclaimed.

"Feels so damn good," Whiskey said, floating on his back.

It did have a numbing effect on Hood's injuries. The slice in his hand, the glancing wound in his side, the chunk taken out of his ear, and the sewn-up shoulder had all begun to mend, but the dull, throbbing pain was slow in subsiding. In the freezing cold water everything felt numb, gloriously numb.

I want to do this in peace. I want to live with family and friends and jump in rivers, farm and hunt our own food, live on our own in the country and be happy. I'd kill for that. Maybe existence is just the fight for the life you want. Maybe this is exactly the way the world was meant to be.

Hood pulled in a mouthful of river water and spouted it up into the air. He looked over at Whiskey, who continued to float on his back with his eyes closed.

"You think we can pull this off?"

Whiskey didn't open his eyes. "We'd better."

"If we do, we might be changing the course of history."

"You're thinking too much, kid."

"It's true, though. If we have to kill Ian to save her, this war between the Kaiser and the Crusader will be over. It will change everything."

"I don't plan on ending anyone's war. All we have to do is free Taylor. Either way, we ain't doin' it for history."

Hood smiled, and ran his fingers through his wet hair. *Maybe we should be.*

"I'm sure the Sons wouldn't mind if we ended it for them, though."

"To hell with the Sons."

Hood leaned back and poked his feet out of the water.

"I don't know. Maybe I'm wrong, but I think there might be something good about them."

Whiskey laughed, spraying out water that had washed over his face with an exhaling breath.

"I don't know how you can have been through all we've been through, and still think there's good anywhere."

Hood shrugged. "There's good people out there. I know it."

"They tend to have a short life expectancy."

"That's why they should work together."

Whiskey scrutinized him. "You sayin' we should join the Sons?"

Hood stared at the shimmering sun reflected in the river as it washed by him. "I don't know what I'm saying."

Whiskey grinned. "Yeah, I don't either."

They spent a few minutes in silence reveling in the river, listening to the chirping birds as they arced from tree to tree. Hood started to feel chilled, so he moved to the bank, picked up his backpack and clothes, and carried them across to the other side of the river. Whiskey followed suit. They sat in the sun, skipping rocks across the flowing water as the cool wind whipped downstream.

His appreciation of the beauty of the day gave way to anxiety. Hood felt wound up like a spring knowing that this was it. They were close to Ian's stronghold. He didn't know how they had made it this far, but the enormity of what lay ahead of them seemed to dwarf everything else.Maybe Whiskey had a plan. But Ian had an army.

All they had was a handful of bullets.

They put themselves together, gingerly replacing their clothes over their battered bodies and shouldering their packs before moving into the woods once more. Angular pillars of light between the trees carried the warmth of the sun to Hood's wet skin as he walked.

Ian did all of this to get to you. He kept Whiskey alive to get to you. He kept Taylor alive to get to you. He's waiting for you to come to him. He wants you to believe what he believes. He needs you to believe what he believes.

"Whiskey?"

"Mhmm."

"You know this place. But they know you too. How would you do this?"

Whiskey ducked underneath a low-hanging branch. "I know where he's got Taylor. There are underground classrooms they use as holding cells. Usually he keeps captives from the Sons or wastelanders there. All we have to do is wait for an opportunity to sneak in the south entrance, then make our way to the earth science building, where the captives are. Hopefully they'll all be too busy with the war to stop and ask questions. It's gonna get dicey when we try to free her, though. We're going to need a lot of luck."

Even if we do pull it off, where will we go? How long will Ian hunt us?

253

Hood remembered the man Donte, whom they'd found in the church. He'd said he was the only survivor. . .

"That's not going to work."

Whiskey looked over his shoulder at him. "Oh yeah? Why not?"

Hood shook his head. "Ever since Ian realized I was still alive, he's been trying to do something. He's trying to change me. This, all of this, he did in order to get to me. Taking Taylor away when he sacked Clearwater, telling the Sheriff where I could find him, meeting me in D.C., taking Kerry from the refugee camp, the trail of breadcrumbs from the slavers to you. . . he kept you alive for the sole purpose of finding me. He's *expecting* us. This whole time he's known what we were going to do before we did it. And that's because he knows we'll do anything to keep Taylor alive. He's doing this for a reason."

Whiskey stared at Hood, expressionless. "Why?"

"Because he's alone. Because he still sees me as a brother, no matter what he believes. I know there's nothing he wants more in the world than for me to fight this war alongside him. He thinks if I go through the same hell he did I'll come out the other side thinking what he thinks."

Whiskey turned his head, staring at the mossy bark of an oak. He ran the side of his pointer finger along his mouth before letting it drop into a balled fist. "So what do we do?"

Hood sneezed, rubbing his nose in annoyance. *God damn pollen everywhere.*

"The one thing he doesn't expect."

◆ ◆ ◆

The modern buildings of the University were full of weathered glass that reflected the sunlight. The campus sat quiet, nestled beneath the long, sloping tree-covered mountains of the Appalachians. The rolling foothills leading up to the college were striped with old college roads and ancient, emptied-out shops, diners and convenience stores.

Hood left his pack with Whiskey. He wasn't going to need it. His CD player had broken in the bike crash, but Whiskey had given him his. The squishy pads of the headphones were soft against his ears. Hood breathed in the warm mountain air as he strolled past the overgrown stone pillar that read *Greenridge University*.

The disc in the Walkman whirred to the next track as he walked up the empty, two-lane road with its mangled and gun-blasted speed limit sign. *When I come around. God, I love this song.*

Hood sang along to the old punk track that made him feel thirteen again, if just for a minute.

This is as good a day as any to die. The thought scared the shit out of him.

You're a resourceful bastard. Yeah, that'd be helpful, maybe, if one of those resources was a portable Panzer tank.

The road sloped up to the walled-in perimeter of the campus. Two men with rifles clearly had him in their sights. He held up his hands. *Please God, don't shoot me for no reason.*

The song continued as he walked at a relaxed pace to the gates. The lyrics seemed to fit the situation perfectly. *Funny how that happens so often,* Hood thought, taking a deep, easy breath. *All right, no dicking around. Moment of truth.*

Hood pulled off his headphones as he approached the gate.

"Who the fuck are you?" A gunman's melodious, annoyed voice came over the wall.

"I'm looking for Ian," Hood said calmly, keeping his hands up.

"Ian who?"

"Ian Lacland."

Laughter came back from several different voices atop the wall. "You've got about five seconds to tell me what you want with the Kaiser. My finger is getting tired of staying in place."

"I'm his brother. I've been looking for him."

There was a pause, and the murmur of low voices.

"What's your name?"

"Rob Huntington."

"Open your hoodie."

Hood zipped it open.

"Both sides. And lift up your shirt. And your pant legs. And turn out your pockets."

Hood obliged, taking the time to show he was unarmed. "Happy?"

The reinforced metal gate slid open to show three militants standing with their rifles raised and pointed at Hood.

"It's been a long, long trip to get here," Hood said, making eye contact with one of the soldiers. "Getting shot at this point would really suck."

"The Kaiser's expecting you." The melodious-voiced man said, with a hint of surprise and confusion about the entire scenario. Letting strangers in of their own free will was clearly not a common occurrence.

One of the other soldiers was staring at Hood's CD player in skepticism. Hood took it off, offering it to the man.

"Here, take it. I won't need it anymore."

The man stared at it, then looked back at Hood, rifle still raised.

"Fine, suit yourself." Hood shrugged.

Two militants took him through the checkpoint and into the open central square of the campus. A huge stone fountain stood in the center, dry. Massive tents filled much of the open space between buildings, while other areas were filled with buses, trucks and cars parked in an organized fashion.

The place was well lived in, but also meticulously kept. No garbage littered the area. It felt like a military base. The smell of manure wafted to Hood's nostrils.

A short administrative building and surrounding fenced area had been converted to a stables. It was much as Whiskey had described.

Except there was hardly anyone around. *They're all off fighting Ian's war with the Sons.* Hood breathed more easily. *For once, just a little bit of luck. We have a chance.*

256

The two soldiers flanked Hood, one on either side of him. They walked him towards a huge central campus building. Hood kept his eyes up, looking for the building Whiskey had described. *It's tall and faces west, with sheer walls of plexi-glass.*

Hood stopped.

"This is the wrong place. He told me he was meeting me at another building."

The soldiers looked annoyed.

"We know where he is. I don't care what you heard." The man with the gruffer voice said, from behind his thick beard.

"He told me specifically he was going to meet me at that building, right there." Hood pointed up to the plexi-glass building with his left hand. The soldiers turned to look at it, the blinding sun glaring bright off the windows.

Hood snatched the holstered pistol of the man in front of him. He whipped it behind his back and fired twice at the soldier standing behind him, then forward, firing into the heart of the bearded soldier in front of him. The man stared at him in wide-eyed shock and rage. Both men slumped to the ground.

Now's your chance, Whiskey. They're going to be awfully fucking busy with me.

Hood grabbed the other man's pistol in his left hand and dashed towards the Central Campus building, pulling open a heavy glass door. He heard distant shots behind him.

To the left four soldiers with cigarettes hanging form their mouths had risen from a table covered in playing cards, their game disturbed by the commotion. Their eyes grew wide at the sight of Hood. Clearly the last thing they expected was an outsider running free.

Hood raised both weapons. *Crack-crack-crack-crack-crack-crack-crack-crack.* Hood unloaded as the soldiers scrambled for their weapons, diving away from the table in vain.

The last casings clinked against the cement floor, worn smooth from countless footsteps. One soldier was groaning but they all lay still. Outside an alarm sounded, and he could hear distant voices yelling. Hood grabbed two more semi-auto pistols from the fallen soldiers and tucked them into the back of his pants.

It was easy to imagine Tommy, Billy, Lucky and Whiskey sitting around a table playing cards, staving off boredom like those soldiers. *You don't know who these guys were. They could've been good men or evil men or something in between. But they were in your way. Is that all that matters anymore?*

Hood threw himself towards the short open staircase to the upper level of the lobby. *I never wanted this. But I'm the only one Ian would let close. I have to stop this. Not just for Taylor, not just for Whiskey or for the friends and family I've lost. Because this war needs to end. I loved you like a brother my whole life, Ian. But I'm not afraid to kill you. Not anymore.*

The lobby extended down a long corridor, with open doors to dark empty ballrooms on either side. A shop, emptied of merchandise, featured a mannequin with a paper cigarette taped to its mouth. It proudly wore a Greenridge University sweatshirt, a water gun around its neck and a baseball cap that read *Mountaineer Militia.*

He's gotta be upstairs somewhere.

Hood ran towards the stairwell with the pistols in his hands. He kicked the door open and stepped inside.

From atop the stairs, a soldier wearing a camo cadet cap and flak jacket locked eyes with Hood. They both raised their weapons, the stairwell exploding with the echo of gunfire. The side of Hood's left shoulder exploded in pain, still not fully healed from the fight in the Metro. The soldier's head snapped back as blood sprayed onto the wall. He slumped to the floor.

"Fuuuuck!" Hood screamed. The empty pistol clattered to the floor. He pressed his right hand to his left shoulder. His fingers came back red when he pulled away. The shot had only clipped the side of it. Hood clenched his hand slowly into a fist. The entire arm's worth of nerves was on fire. He crouched down on one knee, picking up the pistol he hadn't realized he dropped. He tried to raise it to sight. The pain was immense.

Hood breathed in and out rapidly. *You can't stop. You have to keep moving.*

He stood up and pulled one of the pistols out of the back of his pants and cocked it painfully. He pushed himself forward, one foot after another, charging up the staircase with the right pistol raised around each corner.

He pulled open the heavy door atop the staircase and hopped back away from the doorway. A soldier on one knee fired two blasts from a shotgun.

Hood went careening backwards, tumbling down the staircase, desperately clutching onto his pistols. The world spun end over end as the pain of each step smacked into his bones. He landed sprawled out on his back on the landing, his body aching everywhere. A grenade thumped into his chest and landed in his armpit.

Oh shit.

In one motion he dropped his pistol and tossed the grenade down the lower level of the staircase, covering his head as the deafening boom shook the building. His ears echoed with a high-pitched whine. Dazed, he picked up the pistol again and put it to sight atop the staircase. Slowly his vision steadied. His chest rose and fell quickly.

He's jittery. He fired too quickly and he tossed the grenade without cooking it enough. Hood lay there on his back, staring down the sight. *Don't make a sound. He's going to sneak a glance.*

The man's head popped out for a second around the doorway. It was all Hood needed.

Crack. The shot echoed, the hot casing landing on Hood's stomach. He brushed it off clumsily with his left hand, keeping the pistol raised, waiting for more. No one came.

He struggled to his feet. His head spun and swam. The back of his skull felt as if it had been split in two. He reached back and touched it with his left hand, but there was no blood.

Slowly he pulled himself up each step, keeping the pistol to sight. The closer he felt to death, the less he cared about the people he killed to survive. *We're just animals.*

Hood swung the pistol around to either side of the hallway before entering. It was dark, save for some light that emanated from an open doorway at the east end of the hallway. A placard on the wall read *Mountainview Terrace* with an arrow pointing east, and *Rooms 303-320* with an arrow pointing west.

Nothing Ian liked better than a good view. Hood urged himself down the hall. He could hear the distant clatter of boots as more soldiers came to find him. *Nowhere else to go.*

Hood looked over his shoulder more than once. The hallway remained still for now, lit only by the ambient light surging from the doorway ahead of him.

Hood forced himself into a run to the double doors. He closed them quietly behind him, twisting the lock shut with a light *click*. Hood winced at the sight of a short staircase leading to yet another level.

Hood moved deliberately up each step, not making a sound. *Don't hesitate.*

Light enveloped the entire room, illuminating tables and chairs and couches along the walls. The entire west-facing wall was made of glass, with an open double door out to a balcony.

"You always were late to everything." Ian's voice came from the east side of the room.

Hood spun around to face him. Simultaneous shots rang out. Hood's right hand blossomed with pain as he dropped the pistol. He stared down at it, shaking uncontrollably. His pinky had been blown clean off at the first knuckle, and was now pouring out blood. He clutched it in his left hand. He felt weak, enervated except for the burning nerves all over his body.

He looked up at Ian, who lowered his silver revolver.

"Hi, Rob." He said with a dark, almost sentimental smile. "Some timing. I almost couldn't wait any longer."

Hood stared at him, his heart racing. *You aren't the man I grew up with.*

"With all but a handful of my men deployed, this was still pretty reckless, even by your standards," Ian said.

"Fuck you." Hood said, breathing heavily. "Murderer. Family killer. Where is the man I was proud to call my brother? How can you live with how much death you've brought to this country?"

Ian shook his head. "If it wasn't me, it would just be someone else. At least I'm fighting for a future." Ian looked down at the table beside him, covered in maps that were anchored by a single bottle of scotch and highball glasses. "Everyone else is fighting for themselves."

"You're not fighting for a future. You can fool everyone else, but I know you." Soldiers began to pound on the locked double doors at the bottom of the stairs. "You've spent your whole life searching for something to hold on to. You're just fighting to prove your existence is *worth* something. You're fighting for your own glory."

Ian said nothing, staring at him.

"Kaiser. What a fucking stupid name," Hood said with a smirk.

"How many people did you kill to get here?" Ian jibed. "For what? To 'save' Taylor? Did it ever occur to you that she wasn't free only because *you* were chasing her?" Ian shook his head. "Do you really think I'd kill or imprison my sister for no reason?"

Hood snorted. "You massacred everyone I cared about at Clearwater. You took Taylor captive in some insane hope I'd sink down to your level. I've seen firsthand the slavers who work for you. You're the Goddamned devil."

Ian looked away, as if searching for some new method of communication.

"You're smarter than this, Rob. You've just been living on raw survival for too long. Defending your little outlaw country town, fighting and stealing so you can plug your ears and pretend the world isn't doomed—that's the very way of living that got us here. Every damn person kept their head down and ignored the state of the world as we slowly tore each other apart. You know it's true."

Hood wanted to bind up his pinky but didn't even have the capacity to tear his own shirt in the weakened state he was in. Blood dripped out of the stump of his finger. He clenched his teeth hard, the pain in his gums distracting him from the pain everywhere else. He took in a deep breath.

"You're right." Hood said, nodding. "Believe me, killing to survive—it's something I've fought for a long time. But no matter how great a war you fight, you can't change human nature. We will hate and love and fight and make peace and die and live on. You say we have to kill the very idea of family? You're wrong. That's not possible. People will always forge bonds of family. Like we did. Even though we weren't blood. Every good person worth fighting for, every person who wants peace. They are family."

Ian sighed, looking forlorn. "I really thought you might get it." He ran his hand through his short blond hair, working his mouth. "You, out of everyone, I thought would understand. I don't *like* having to kill and manipulate and spend my life fighting a war against human nature. But this shattered civilization is a rare opportunity to really change the course of history. How many more chances will humanity get to change before we wipe ourselves out? America was a great country, but we hated ourselves. Political parties, racial hatred, religious division. It was a matter of time before we tore ourselves apart. As long people see each other as others, humanity will die. Maybe not this generation, or the next, or ten generations from now, but we will destroy ourselves. I know the chances are slim I can change the course of history. A lot has to go right. But I know I can build a new country that is truly unified, where loyalty is not to your blood but to everyone who stands beside you. Even if it takes our lives and the lives of millions more of our generation, isn't it worth it?"

Hood locked eyes with Ian. "Even if you win your war, build your new civilization, nothing will change."

The words felt strangely familiar, and Hood had a strong sense of deja vu. *Why does it feel like I've done this before?*

"Everything will change. It has already started. Anyone smart enough to see the need to unify will join, and all those who can't will

262

die. We have to force the hand of natural selection. People believe the world is me versus you, us versus them. But it's not. It's humanity versus time, and we're losing badly because of our own weakness. Animals can drive themselves to extinction fighting for their bloodline. But we are something greater than animals. Rise above that primal instinct. Become a part of something great, Rob."

Hood smiled. "I already am." He reached back and grabbed the last pistol he had tucked into the back of his pants, ignoring the searing pain. *Save Taylor. Save her and run, Whiskey. Love each other and be free of all this.*

Images of Kerry flooded his mind. Sitting in the truck on the bridge, looking nervous. Talking to him in the cellar of Leonard's bar. Smiling at him outside D.C. as the wind blew the hair in her face.

I know you're doing well out there. Hood smiled. *You're a lot better at survival than I ever was.*

He squeezed the grip of the pistol, ignoring the burning pain in his hand. *Do this, and people you love can live on. People you don't know can live on. Whether it's for one more hour or for the rest of time, it's worth it.*

"Don't do it Rob. You're not thinking clearly."

Hood's expression relaxed, and he met Ian's worried gaze.

"Yeah. For once, I am."

In one motion he whipped the pistol in front of him and fired, just as Ian raised his revolver and fired back.

Everything felt numb for a second. Hood fell to one knee, then onto his back. Pain spread through his chest like a bolt of lightning. Hood craned his neck to look up.

Ian clutched at his chest. He tore off his blue shirt, the sleek Kevlar vest beneath sporting a compressed bullet square over his heart. He coughed, propping himself up on his knees. He gasped for breath, the wind fully knocked out of him. Slowly he rose to his feet.

"Jesus Christ, that was some shot." He took a swig of scotch from the highball on the table and walked methodically towards Hood.

"Why did you have to make it like this. . ." Ian's voice carrying a heavy weight. "Why are you forcing me to do this alone?"

Hood struggled to breathe. His voice creaked when he tried to speak. *God damn it.* Hood reached for his own chest gingerly. He didn't want to look down.

"Well. I have a war to go win. As I'm sure you saw, the Sons over-committed their troops to the southern bridges, as I hoped. Now I'm taking my full force and blitzing straight to Boston. I'll tear the heart out of their crusade while they think they're out winning it."

With each breath Hood took, more pain surged through his chest. He hoisted himself to his feet, slowly. *This can't be it.* Cold fear seized him.

"I really wanted you to be a part of this." Ian said, staring icily at Hood.

"If I still had my pinky, you'd be dead." Hood said, punctuating the words with a cough.

Ian grabbed his arm and dragged him over to the railing beside the staircase. He walked back to a nearby table, produced a thick zip-tie and bound Hood's right hand to the railing.

"Goodbye, Rob. I'll give you your time to make your peace. I guess this is the way things had to be."

Ian turned and walked down the staircase, unlocking the doors and opening them.

"Sir, is everything okay?" A soldier barked.

"Yes. Is everyone mobilized?"

"It's only us remaining. The other divisions are at Paw Paw awaiting your arrival."

"Then let's not keep them waiting any longer." Ian said calmly. "There's nothing left for us here."

Only the sound of their dissipating footsteps filled the room. Hood turned his head, looking out the east-facing wall of glass, which showed the great, sunny valley below the campus. It was full of overgrown fields, sun-baked, two-lane roads and distant tree-lines.

Well, at least it's a beautiful view. Hood bowed his head. *I don't want to die. I don't want it to be like this.* He looked down. He'd been shot in

264

the far left of his pectoral. *An inch more to the left and he would've missed.*

But he hadn't, and the wound produced an unrelenting pain that wracked his body and wanted to seize his mind whole. *No.*

Hood's heart began to pump wildly, the familiar rush of adrenaline taking him.

No, I won't let it end like this. I won't just lie here and die slowly.

On a nearby table sat a modest sized river stone. It held down papers that fluttered in the wind from the open balcony doors. Hood inched his legs toward the table, gritting his teeth. He propped his left leg up on the seat of a chair, the ziptie clawing at his contorted wrist. With a heave, he threw his foot up onto the table and pulled down the stone. It fell next to him.

He pulled the rock close to him using his heel, every breath excruciating. He eyed the palm that had been cut. He hadn't had anything to rebandage it with after the swim in the river, and it was swollen, infected, and radiated pain. *Well, maybe that will make this easier.*

Hood clasped the stone tightly, gathering up the nerve to do what he had to: get the hell out of the zip-tie that trapped him.

With all his strength, he smashed the rock into his right hand. Lightning shot up his arm and he roared, not even registering that the noise came from his own throat. He felt the adrenaline surging through him once more.

He swung the rock at his hand with a wild, unabated anger, somehow disconnecting himself from his pain. *I won't let you do this. I won't leave Taylor and Whiskey to a life of being hunted. I refuse to die while you bring only more death to the world.* His entire body cried out at him to stop, but again and again he swung away at his hand until he felt the bones crack.

He screamed at the top of his lungs, yanking at the hand with all his strength. The blood slicked his hand as it squeezed out of the zip-tie and sent him falling backwards to the floor.

His breath hitched and for a second he just lay there, looking up at the white ceiling. *I'm free.* Hood's mind exulted.

Get up. Get up and do something.

Laboriously, he pulled himself onto all fours and stood up, stumbling towards the open balcony. He crossed the threshold, greeted by cool mountain air. Below, Ian climbed into the driver's seat of a truck, the soldiers with him filing in. Hood looked down. A sniper rifle sat propped against a chair on the balcony wall. Hood looked down at his destroyed right hand. *No fucking way I can shoot that.*

He felt panic grip him. *You can't let him get away.* A supply box sat beside the rifle. Hood fell to one knee and pulled it open with his left hand. Extra rounds and three grenades sat inside. Hood's blood raced.

The truck started up, slowly moving towards the east exit of the campus. Hood didn't think twice. He placed a grenade in his right hand and pulled the pin, which clinked as it hit the floor. *This is the last thing you have to do, so give it everything you've got.*

Hood leaned back, gripping the grenade, the broken bones grinding in his hand. He swung with all his weight, hurling the grenade high into the air towards the eastern exit. He collapsed against the wall of the balcony, staring at the grenade as it arced through the blue sky. Ian's truck was nearing the exit.

Chills rushed through Hood's body. *Come on.*

His mind was empty as he watched it fly. *Come on!*

The grenade hit the concrete and bounced to a stop, right in front of the truck. The tires squealed as Ian slammed on the brakes. But the truck went skidding and swerving right over the grenade.

A beautiful, towering burst of fire and metal exploded into the air. He slumped down, back against the wall, exhaling softly. The rush of victory was tinged with regret. *All I ever wanted was to live in peace.* Hood managed a weak smile.

Clearly I'm pretty bad at it.

His eyes closed of their own accord.

♦ ♦ ♦

"Hey!" Came a familiar gruff voice. "Wake up."

Whiskey?

"Hood, come on!"

A stinging in his cheek pulled Hood back into reality. *Did you just slap me?* The blurry world slowly came into focus. He was still sitting on the balcony. He remembered everything suddenly. I killed him. *I hope you can forgive me, Mom and Dad. I've killed so many people. I never wanted any of this.* Whiskey and Taylor sat crouched in front of him. Taylor's eyes were filled with tears, her hand over mouth. Her heart shaped face looked more gaunt than he remembered, her hair bound back and her clothes in sore need of wash. The sight of her face, here, now, made his heart soar. *Is this real? Am I alive?* Whiskey looked unscathed, relatively speaking. His face was creased with concern.

"Don't cry, Tay." Hood said with a labored breath. "We're free."

She sobbed, hugging him fiercely.

"Come on, kid. We're gettin' out of here." Whiskey hoisted him up and hung him over his shoulder. He smelled of sweat and gunpowder. The world flipped upside down, the blood rushing to his head. His chest screamed with every step.

Hood grunted in pain. "Easy, you fucker. Eveything hurts." He wheezed.

Whiskey hustled down a fire escape. Hood's body started to feel numb and tingly. He reached out for Taylor with his left hand. She took it, following behind him.

"It's good to see you again sis." Hood said quietly. "I didn't think. . ."

"Shh, don't talk, you idiot!"

"I had to kill him, Tay. I didn't want to." Hood said, his head swimming. She nodded back at him, kissing his hand.

He was pretty damned sure he was going to die.

Just a little more time. I want just a few more days. A few more days to be free with my family. Is that too much to ask?

267

Whiskey carried him off the campus and into the foothills towards the Appalachians not far from the campus. Hood couldn't shake a deep feeling of regret that he would be leaving them on their own.

"Put me down, big guy." Hood whispered.

Carefully, Whiskey set him down on his feet on the wet grass. Hood hung his arm around Whiskey's shoulder, motioning for them to walk towards the wooded mountainside. He shambled forward, each step a labor.

"I don't think a hot iron is gonna cut it this time," Hood said, coughing.

Whiskey let out a choked laugh. He was crying silently. "Just hang in there, kid."

Hood felt as though he was floating, as if his consciousness swam in and out of his body. He looked up at the swaying branches and thick trunks of the oaks where the forest began.

"I'm scared, Whiskey."

Whiskey's grip on Hood's shoulder tightened. "I'm always scared. You're gonna be alright."

God, or whatever, and all the people who died, if you can hear me . . . I never wanted to kill anyone. I'm sorry for that.

"Robbie. Please, stay with me. I won't let you go," Taylor said, her teary gaze meeting his. He smiled at her.

"I'm glad you're okay, sis." Hood's breath caught.

The three of them moved slowly to the first tree they saw, a tall yew with great enveloping branches that hung low. Hood nodded at it, dropping down to recline against a thick cord of its trunk. He winced.

"Lift up your shirt. We have to patch you up." Taylor reached for his Hoodie. Hood put his hand on hers, shaking his head slowly. He patted the grass beside him, motioning for her to sit. Taylor looked up to Whiskey, searching for support. Whiskey cast her a loving, yet strangely forlorn glance. The two of them sat down beside him.

There's so much more I want to do. I'm not ready for this.

His body tensed, fighting instinctively to survive. His mind raced back through the memories of his life: lying in his backyard looking up at the sky as a young man. Sledding down steep hills with Ian and Taylor while Dad watched over them. Billy and Lucky getting so drunk they reenacted a Street Fighter match on the lawn. The feeling of adventure he got the first time playing a RPG early Easter morning before church. The awkward, passionate first time having sex with his high school girlfriend. He saw Kerry, her head lying on his chest as they slept, columns of light coming into the room through open windows. *I loved you. I hope you know that. If we had met in a time where we didn't have to fight to survive every day. . .* His eyes welled up. *Why the fuck did this have to happen to me?*

He wanted to hold on to the memories, find a golden moment that somehow represented his entire life. *Stop. Just let it all go. You're with your family again. Are you going to die reminiscing about the past?*

Whiskey and Taylor looked at each other, then out at the university and the countryside, eyes red. *I brought them back together. I fought and killed and I don't know if it was right or wrong, but I don't care. It was all worth it.*

He felt a weight lift off him, and breathed more slowly now. He remembered sitting in the passenger seat as he and Whiskey drove down the countryside. *He never did get my jokes.* A smile crept on Hood's face.

He leaned over towards Whiskey. "He tried to destroy the ring." Hood said it just above a whisper.

Whiskey's brow furrowed. "What?"

"The joke. How did the Hobbit ruin the boxing match? He tried to destroy the ring. Remember?" He managed a smile.

Whiskey breathed in a shuddering breath, bowing his head.

"God damn it, kid."

"Worth the wait, wasn't it?" Hood whispered, still smiling.

"I won't lose you again," Whiskey said, tears rolling down his face.

Taylor stood up quickly, walking a few paces and wheeling around to face Hood.

"Get the fuck up. I wont *let* you die. If I have to carry you myself, I will!" She shouted, her eyes wet with tears.

"Where you gonna carry me? There's nothing you can do, sis." Hood looked up to meet her gaze of desperation and love. "But I'm glad you haven't lost your fire."

"Rob. . ."

"It's okay, Tay. I love you. I love you both. Don't be weighed down like I was."

Whiskey stood up, enveloping Taylor in his arms. The vision of seeing them hold each other even just one more time brought the sting of tears to his eyes.

We did it, Whiskey.

The two of them came to sit by Hood once more.

He looked out over the empty campus, the sprawling countryside rimmed with trees, the beautiful, blue sky with the radiant sun trying to burst through a thick band of clouds. The wind blew strong, the mountain air smelling of pine. The sound of thousands of leaves swishing against each other was a fitting dirge. Mosquitoes began to buzz around his head.

"It's still beautiful," Hood said quietly.

"What is?" Whiskey asked, looking over at him.

"Everything." Hood glanced at him, his vision narrowing, then back at the open expanse. He breathed the cool air into his lungs, the pain starting to fade. He wanted to hold on to the moment forever; it was so exquisite, so simple. He felt a heavy sleep pulling at his eyes, and his head dropped back against the trunk of the yew.

I'll see you again someday.

Chapter 20 – The Lion and The Legacy

Whiskey grunted, hoisting himself up onto the mossy rock shelf. He pulled himself to his feet, arching his sore back. He wiped his brow with the back of his wrist, knowing it was an exercise in futility.

He turned around, getting down on one knee and holding out his hand.

Taylor got a running start up the patchy hill, bounded nimbly off the rock face in one step and grabbed onto his hand. She walked up the wall as he pulled her. At the top, she stood up, wiping her hands off on her jeans.

The two of them turned to face the scene below, the setting sun casting its glow upon the valley from west of them.

"Well, that's a view," Taylor said, sighing.

Whiskey chuckled. "Yeah."

In the distant valley below, what had once been a city lay in ruins, the jagged corpses of sheared buildings resting among mountainous rubble and upheaved earth. A raised highway lay collapsed among the quiet suburbs nearby, huge beams of metal sticking out of the tarmac like bent whiskers.

"Do you think we'll ever rebuild back to where we were?" Taylor asked, taking a sip of water from a bottle, the sound of the water sloshing as she pulled it away.

"Eventually, yeah." Whiskey said. "For all that's worth."

Taylor wasted no time in moving ahead, following along the crest of the rock wall, hopping down to meet the worn rut of a trail that was besieged by encroaching flora.

Whiskey followed her, easing himself down onto the trail. A hanging canopy of maple hung over the west side of the path, the east a sloping grassy hill with a view down into the valley. Taylor was outpacing him badly. The air seemed warmer and heavier than normal. He pulled a bandanna out of his pocket and wiped his forehead. *I bet you'd have some smart ass thing to say, wouldn't you, Hood?*

He kept his eyes on Taylor's fit figure as she moved easily through the brush. He followed behind, feeling sluggish. *I should'a gone with him. I let him do it. He gave himself for us.*

Whiskey ran his hand over his shaggy, overgrown hair. He clenched his jaw, looking at the broken city. *He knew what he was doin'. He knew he'd die doin' it.*

He bowed his head, closing his eyes. *How many people's lives did he save? How many people will never even know what he did?*

He raised his head suddenly, inhaling through his nose. It sent calm waves through his chest. *I'll know. We will. We'll never forget you, kid.*

Taylor had doubled back and was standing still some feet away, waiting.

He glanced away.

"You okay?"

"Fine," he said. "Just need a breather."

She moved closer, the tall grass swishing against her legs. "Hey. Look at me."

He hesitated.

Her face was calm, but determined. *Damn, is she beautiful.*

"Speak, dummy."

"I just. . ." Whiskey bit off his words. *You are some piece of work, needin' her for support. This is all sideways. She lost her brother. You should be there for her.*

"I just can't believe he's gone. I keep runnin' through it in my mind. There must have been something I could've done, something . . ." His eyes welled up. "It just ain't right."

Taylor strode over to him, reaching up to give him a quick kiss. Her lips were soft on his.

"I miss him too." She said it with a smile, though her expression indicated regret. "But I know what he wants. He wants us to be free, to live on, and above all, to be happy."

Whiskey nodded slowly. *It should'a been me. In the back of my mind, I knew what he was doin', but I kept thinking, whatever it takes. Whatever it takes to get her back. But the kid. . .* Whiskey dug his fingernails into his palms. *He deserved something better than this.*

"Would you like me to get you some soup for you to cry into?" Taylor said, sporting an absurd frown.

Whiskey laughed loudly, wiping his face with his right hand.

"That sounds like something he would say."

She gave him an are-you-kidding look.

"Uh, yeah. We are fuckin' family, you doofus." She turned and walked down the path.

Whiskey took the balmy, grassy air into his lungs and laughed before following behind her. The waning light reached through the branches of the trees and illuminated the swirling motes of flora in the air. His mind wandered back to a conversation he'd had with his mother when he was a child. He'd had a dream that she had died and he was inconsolable. *Someday, I will die, she said. But we live on in those we love.*

Whiskey strode forward on the path, his body feeling re-energized. *I'll never let it weigh me down again, kid. I promise.*

The blood seemed to course through his body. He wanted to run, though he had no reason to. *I know what you'd want. You'd want me to keep her safe. I will, as long as I live she'll be safe. She's a hell of a girl.*

"First priority, we need some more food," Taylor said over her shoulder. "God, what I wouldn't do for a mountain of loaded French fries."

"Take it easy, now." Whiskey said. "Talkin' like that will drive us up the creek."

"I think I'd jump around naked on a trampoline covered in fire ants for it."

"Well, maybe if the Sons of Liberty are half as great as they say they are you won't have to," Whiskey said, brushing a strand of spider-web off his face.

"You think going to the Sons is a good idea?" Taylor said, hopping over a stream that cut through the path.

"Your brother seemed to think there was somethin' there." Whiskey's boots splashed in the gurgling stream.

"Well, the way I see it, they owe us a debt of gratitude."

"Heh, yeah." Whiskey wriggled his nose, the pollen making it tingle. "Doubt they'll believe it."

They pushed on down the trail as it wove and climbed through rocky terrain and open fields and thick swaths of trees. Whiskey pulled out the journal Hood had taken from the dead man way back when. *He always seemed to take comfort in this thing.*

He opened it to a random entry.

There are good days, and there are bad days. Most days are bad days. Today is a good day.

Melanie showed up in my room in the morning. I would say I must've charmed her with my wiles, but she and I both know I have none. She just seemed to think I deserved her love. Maybe it was the Ronald Reagan joke I made. Maybe she was tired of me making a fool of myself around her. Regardless, I am smitten.

On top of that, we had beef today. Real beef. God, it tasted good. Danny and Kim are doing well, too. They're illustrating their usefulness in a way that doesn't involve a rifle. That's the kind of thing to make a surrogate papa proud.

Cherry on the whipped cream, I'm not on patrol today. Divine intervention--just to make sure everything was at its peak level of awesome for me. I'm finishing off that rubbing alcohol they call vodka, and going to play some poker with my extra ration cards. With a day like this, there's no way I can lose.

Days like this, I gotta remember. Days like this are what it's all about. I wish I could remember to be as easy about it all as I am now. I'm happy, someday I won't be, doesn't matter. I'm alive, someday I won't be, doesn't matter. Everything just is the way it is. And that's a good thing.

Whiskey closed the journal, tracing the faux leather cover with his fingertips. He pulled his backpack around his torso and replaced the journal inside. *Everything is the way it is.*

They moved on easily through the quiet trail, Whiskey feeling a determination he hadn't in quite a long time. *There's plenty enough for us to undertake yet.* Whiskey felt a sense of peace, taking in the beauty of the wild expanse as they passed through it. The path wound down into the valley and over another ridge to the north. Taylor had crested it, staring out through the treetops to the Sons of Liberty camp below.

"Well, we found them," Taylor said, hands on her hips as she stared down at the scene with a mix of triumph and trepidation on her face.

"We found 'em," Whiskey echoed as he exhaled, gazing down at the tiny soldiers milling about between the tents and lounging about in groups. A white flag with a red lion on its hind legs flew on a makeshift flagpole over the Sons' camp.

"Come on. They'll want to know who killed the Kaiser and won their war for them." Taylor started moving once again down the trail.

They'll never really know who he was. Whiskey smiled. *But that's all right. We do.*

Note from the Author:

Thank you for reading the book, I hope you enjoyed it. If you want to help me out, write me an Amazon review of what you think! For all those looking for more, stay tuned for:

Whiskey – Book 2 of the American Rebirth Series

CPSIA information can be obtained
at www.ICGtesting.com
Printed in the USA
FSOW01n2031010916
24524FS